BENDING the
BLACKSMITH'S
Heart

Other Books By Lorin Grace

American Homespun Series
Waking Lucy
Remembering Anna
Reforming Elizabeth
Healing Sarah

Artists & Billionaires
Mending Fences
Mending Christmas
Mending Walls
Mending Images
Mending Words
Mending Hearts

Hastings Security
Not the Bodyguard's Baby
Not the Bodyguard's Widow
Not the Bodyguard's Boss
Not the Bodyguard's Princess
Not the Bodyguard's Bride

Misadventures in Love
Miss Guided
Miss Oriented

Spellbound in Hawthorne
(with Maria Hoagland)
Taste of Memory
Sprinkle of Snow
Hint of Charm
Dash of Destiny
Stir of Wind
Essence of Gravity

Bradford Brides
Rescuing the Sheriff's Heart
Bending the Blacksmith's Heart
Converting the Preacher's Heart
Healing the Doctor's Heart

Stand Alone Titles
A Little Clean Fun
Love in the Valley

BRADFORD BRIDE No. TWO
BENDING the BLACKSMITH'S Heart

Lorin Grace

CURRANT
CREEK PRESS

Bending the Blacksmith's Heart © 2022 by Lorin Grace

Cover design © 2022 by LJP Creative Cover photos: iStock
Formatting by LJP Creative
Edits by Eschler Editing
Published by Currant Creek Press

Utah, United States

This is a work of fiction. The characters, incidents, and dialogue are products of the author's imagination and not meant to be construed as real.

ISBN: 978-1-970148-20-6

Printed in the United States of America

First edition 2022

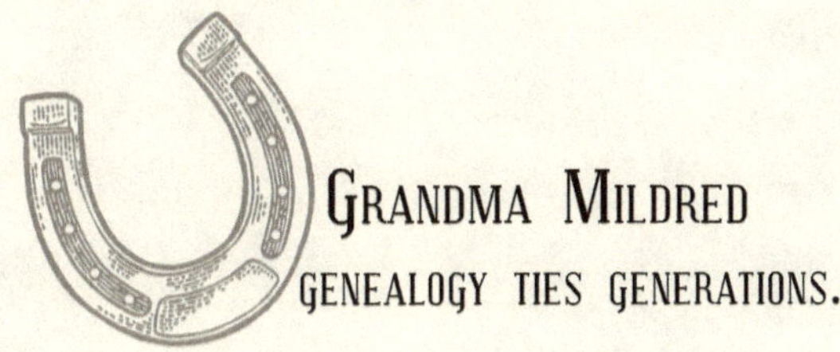
GRANDMA MILDRED
GENEALOGY TIES GENERATIONS.

1

orty-two.

In preparing for each of the forty-one funerals he'd offi-ciated since becoming an ordained minister, Ebenezer had always wondered how death felt. What would a man's last thoughts be?

Now, the missing puzzle pieces came together in his mind, revealing the part of the picture he'd missed. The clues he'd left behind were not enough. It would take a miracle.

"Ama—" He struggled to push the words past his lips.

"Too late to pray, Reverend. You're going to hell with the rest of us now." The observation came from the parishio-ner sitting at the table, waiting for Ebenezer to take his last breath.

Ebenezer's last words had not been the ending to a prayer but to the name that had caused his demise. A paper flut-tered to the floor. The telegram. If only he had not shown everyone her message.

A wave of pain convulsed through Ebenezer.

Death by poison. How many of the forty-two had died this way? Five? Six?

Amanda.

Would she suffer as he did? There was no way to warn her.

Please let there be guardian angels. She did not deserve his fate.

The wedding gift. If she could figure everything out in time…Ebenezer sighed. If only she were poor and not so naïve.

He was no better than those who were going to kill him. He had proposed the marriage for her father's money. Could she not see that he'd used her? Of course not. He'd planned it too well. He'd wanted her money.

Now, they needed her money.

Unable to speak, he sent one last plea to God for Amanda's safety.

His murderer laughed.

Ebenezer's eyes dimmed. The last image he saw was of his supposed friend smiling down at him.

awn had yet to break over the eastern sky. Gunter's forge burned bright. In mid-June, the Texas day was too hot to work much past noon. The predawn hours were the perfect time to finish the silver accents Reverend Coolidge had ordered on the green, leather-bound box for his new bride. He'd completed the project last week, but late yesterday afternoon, the reverend had appeared with the box and asked for a sturdier lock, along with silver filigree. The box was now heavier than when Gunter had finished crafting the gift two weeks ago. The reverend insisted the contents were safer inside the box. Because Gunter needed to hurry to complete the work before driving the reverend into Austin to pick up his bride for their wedding this afternoon, he'd overlooked the odd request to redesign the box.

As Gunter walked outside and around his blacksmith shop, a rooster crowed in the distance. No sounds of people met his ears yet. He rarely worked with precious metals and preferred to keep what little ore he had hidden, along with valuable commissions his customers brought him. Sure no one was around he entered the smithy and closed the door. With ease, he lifted his father's old, rusty anvil off the hogshead barrel and removed the false top. The barrel swung open on silent hinges, revealing the custom safe hidden in plain sight. A minute later, the anvil was back in place and the burlap bag the reverend had brought sat on his worktable.

Gunter pulled out the tarnished spoon the reverend had given him to melt down for the embellishment. The utensil was not pure silver, as the man claimed, but plated silver over nickel. He couldn't melt the spoon down as planned—or could he? Would the two metals separate or blend? Gunter tapped the spoon against the palm of his hand. He needed to ask someone with more experience. If only his father were still here. He'd been a silversmith in Germany before coming to America to fulfill his dream of owning land.

Not wanting to ruin the spoon, Gunter put it back in the bag and worked on adding a stronger lock to the box. After breakfast, he'd ask the reverend if he wanted to pay to use some of the silver from Gunter's supply.

Gunter opened the box, wishing the reverend had left it empty. Taking care of people's personal items wasn't always a good idea. Inside was a worn Bible with an envelope tucked inside. He wrapped the Bible in a length of flannel and put it on the highest shelf.

As he soldered the new lock in place, a shadow fell across his worktable. Gunter looked up to see who needed him so early in the morning.

"Morning, Deputy," Gunter said with a guarded expression. "Can I help you?"

"Dunno. You talk to Reverend Coolidge yesterday?" The deputy slurred his words more than usual. He must have been up late at the saloon on the other side of the creek.

"He came to see me." Gunter set down his tools.

"What did he talk about?"

It wasn't Gunter's place to tell the reverend's business to others. "Why don't you ask him?"

"Can't." The deputy spit a wad of chewing tobacco on the dirt floor. "He's gone and died in his sleep."

"The reverend is dead?" Impossible. The reverend was healthy and not even thirty. Mutter would say the premature death was because the Americans didn't eat enough sauerkraut—the same declaration she'd made when the assistant banker died in his sleep last month.

"Yup. Mr. Fife found him this morning. Now, what did the reverend talk about?"

"Picking up his bride." Everyone in town knew Ebenezer had hired Gunter and the freighting wagon to pick up his Boston socialite bride-to-be.

"What else? Mr. Fife said he left the parsonage with a heavy sack."

Gunter pointed at the box. "He asked me to finish some work on a wedding gift."

"Lemme see that thing." The deputy grabbed the leather-covered iron steel box off the table to inspect it. "Odd sort of wedding gift. I'll take it."

"An empty box?"

"He's dead and doesn't need it now."

"Reverend Coolidge paid for the box as a wedding gift. I should give it to his Miss Ashford before I send her back to Boston."

"She needs to come here."

"Why?"

"That's none of your business, blacksmith. You just pick her up and bring her to the church."

"For the funeral?"

"Already diggin' the grave. Too hot to wait, and the ground is soft from the rain. We will bury the reverend before she arrives."

"Can't you wait?"

"Mr. Fife says it is better this way. She don't need to see him dead."

"A few hours won't matter." Gunter felt Miss Ashford might find solace in a funeral. Grappling with a beloved's death wasn't an easy thing.

"Look here, we stay out of the German church's going-ons, and you best keep out of our church's affairs. He paid you to bring her here and nothing more."

"I should tell her he is dead." She'd traveled hundreds of miles and deserved to be told as soon as possible.

The deputy dropped the box and stepped closer, eyes narrowed. "Blacksmith, it would be a shame if you was careless and let this place or your mother's boardinghouse burn to the ground. You is paid to bring Miss Ashford to town. Nothing else."

The scars across Gunter's back stretched as his muscles tightened. The deputy's threat was as close to an admission that the fire that had killed his wife was not an accident.

"Do you hear me? Not one word. Bring. Her. Here."

"I hear you. I don't agree."

The deputy was a bully of the worst sort. Standing up to him could mean a night in jail or worse. As a father, he couldn't risk it.

"Don't matter if you agree, German swine. All that matters is you do what I say."

Defying the deputy wasn't worth the risk. Someone would tell the woman the sad truth as soon as she arrived. "I won't say a word."

"Good."

Gunter forced his fists and shoulders to relax.

The deputy kicked the box on his way out. "Go ahead and give this to her. Ain't no use to us."

Gunter waited until the deputy disappeared around the corner, then retrieved the box. Despite the abuse, there was only a slight cut on the leather lid. If Gunter decorated the box as the reverend asked, the cut would be hidden. Completing the reverend's last request was the least he could do. Maybe the bride would have something to remember the reverend by when she returned to Boston. Gunter lifted the anvil again and removed a small bar of silver from the safe.

⬥

Through the train's window, Texas appeared to never end. Amanda checked her watch again. In less than a half hour, she would see her betrothed for the first time in eighteen months. By nightfall, she would be Mrs. Coolidge, wife of Reverend Ebenezer Coolidge. Or perhaps tomorrow night at the latest.

She and her traveling companions had experienced five days' worth of delays since leaving Boston. She longed for a proper bath, not washing from a pitcher. Hopefully, there would be time to wash and dress before the ceremony. Train travel was ever so much dirtier than she expected. Even in first-class, keeping her white graduation dress clean as she added the yards of lace she'd crocheted to the flounces for her wedding was a chore that often required the assistance of her two companions—the two sewing and Amanda keeping the rest of the gown wrapped in sheeting, the women switching tasks every so often.

Her college friend Emily had departed their little party in Dallas, sure she would arrive days late for her teaching job and lose it, and Mrs. Smythe's son-in-law had retrieved her from the station four stops back. Now, without a chaperone, Amanda rode alone for the remaining thirty miles.

Though Mrs. Smythe had offered to accompany Amanda to the final destination and stand with her for her wedding, it would have added another day to the woman's journey, and

Amanda didn't have the heart to deny her former governess the comfort of her daughter's welcome, nor subject the sixty-year-old to a wagon ride to Amanda's final destination. If Eb was correct, the dusty fifteen miles would take two hours. Amanda wished he could bring a carriage, but her trunks were too heavy.

The train slowed. One more stop. A queasiness that had nothing to do with the rocking of the coach filled her. There was nothing to worry about. Ebenezer was her match. Didn't their single kiss after his proposal prove that?

The conductor flung the door open. "Austin!"

Amanda gathered her travel bag with the completed wedding dress and everything else she needed for the ceremony, then followed the other passengers off the train. All around her, people greeted loved ones or rushed off to destinations unknown. The crowd thinned. No Ebenezer.

A porter approached. "Ma'am, where are your things?"

Amanda pointed at her two monogrammed trunks, a graduation gift from her mother. "I am waiting for my fiancé to arrive."

"I'll move them around front."

Amanda followed the porter and her trunks to the front of the station. He put the smaller trunk on top of the large one. Amanda watched in horror as the smaller trunk toppled onto the dirt roadway, landing in a pile of horse dung.

"Excuse me, my trunk is covered with—"

"That thing was so heavy you're lucky I didn't break it." The rude man touched his head in a salute and retreated around the building.

Amanda turned, searching for Ebenezer or someone to complain to. On the steps leading into the station, a man she assumed was the stationmaster stood looking at her trunks and shaking his head. "Sorry about that, miss. I'll fetch something to clean it off."

As Amanda waited for the man to return, she searched every passing wagon. Still no Ebenezer.

The man returned with an old flour sack. "This should do. Where are your people?"

"I don't know. Reverend Coolidge was supposed to meet me."

The man's brow furrowed. "I don't know him, ma'am."

"He has a congregation in Greenleaf."

"And he told you to get off here?"

Amanda nodded.

"It would have been better to get off one town back. Last night's rain flooded the road again. Would you like to come in and wait?"

"No, I'll stay out here."

"Suit yourself, miss." He handed Amanda the cloth and returned to the station.

Amanda walked from one end of the building to the other, stretching her legs.

A wagon piled high with boxes and barrels stopped in front of her, and a man jumped down from the seat. He wore a shirt with no vest or coat—not surprising because of the heat. His shoulders were as broad as half of Texas, the cloth of his shirt doing little to conceal his muscled arms. He bounded up the steps, ducking as he entered the building. Realizing she'd been staring, Amanda turned back to look at the street.

"That's her."

Amanda turned at the sound of the stationmaster's voice. He was pointing at her.

The tall man removed his hat. "Miss Ashford? I'm to drive you out to Grünlauf."

She took a step back from the bear of a man and the building. Ebenezer would have never sent this giant for her. The man stepped forward again, his hand extended. As Amanda took another step away, the heel of her boot found air. Unable to stop herself, she pitched backward.

unter lunged forward, wrapping an arm around Miss Ashford's waist and pulling her into him. She slammed into his chest. Neither of them moved. Regardless of the circumstances that brought them to this point, she should not be in his arms. Moving his hands to her elbows to be certain her feet were both on the boardwalk, he stepped back. "Careful, miss."

She craned her neck to look up at him from under the brim of her hat, her face pink. "Thank you, Mr.—?"

"Braunig."

She looked down before stepping to the side and dusting the contact with him off her dress. "Mr. Braunig, you said my fiancé sent you?"

"Reverend Coolidge asked me to fetch you to Grünlauf."

She looked around as if hoping for another answer or the reverend. Gunter wished he had the right to tell her the truth.

The stationmaster stepped forward. "I'd trust Mr. Braunig with my daughter if I had one. I don't say that about many of the freight drivers that pass through here. He'll get you to Grünlauf safely."

Miss Ashford pursed her lips and squinted her eyes.

Gunter longed to put the woman on the next train north, sending her home, where she and her fine clothing belonged.

Holding up the old flour sack, she pointed to the trunks. "Those are mine. The small one needs to be cleaned off. It landed in ..."

Gunter bounded down the boardwalk stairs and inspected the trunk. Though undamaged, dung covered most of the side. "These are your only things?"

"I have this too." She picked up a carpetbag from the boardwalk.

From Ebenezer's description of her, Gunter expected twice the amount of luggage. He lifted the larger trunk into the back of his wagon. Before cleaning the smaller trunk, he checked the ground for other horse leavings. Most of the dung slid away as he upended the trunk. Miss Ashford approached with the sack, intent on wiping off the remains, but Gunter took it from her, careful not to touch her fingers. He'd already touched her far too much for his comfort.

"Thank you. I could have cleaned my trunk."

"No point in risking your dress." Satisfied the trunk was as clean as possible, Gunter added it to the back of the wagon and studied the load, which wasn't balanced as well as he liked. Leaning over the side of the wagon, he pulled out two crates meant for Grünlauf Mercantile and set them on the boardwalk, then moved several items around, clearing the space to position the heavy trunk nearer the center of the wagon. Then he added the crates to the back.

Gunter grabbed the carpetbag and placed it behind the wagon bench. "Let's get moving."

Miss Ashford hurried down the stairs to the freight wagon. At five feet tall, her head was even with the seat. "Do you have a step?"

"No. Use the wagon wheel, and I'll help you."

She gripped the side of the wagon as he directed. At least she wasn't wearing one of those huge bustles. As Gunter gripped her waist and lifted her the rest of the way, a small gasp escaped her.

Gunter checked the horses before climbing onto his seat. "Do you own a parasol?"

She looked behind her. "In my trunk. I should have thought about the sun. My hat will suffice."

The hat didn't have as wide a brim as most women wore around town, but it shaded her face enough that she shouldn't burn. Gunter released the brake and signaled his team. This morning, he'd taken the longer route to avoid the muddier road. Wisdom dictated he do the same on the return trip. As he approached the crossroads for his usual route, he debated. With the added weight of her trunk, the chances of becoming mired in mud on the direct road were too great.

Beside him, Miss Ashford seemed to take in everything the town offered. She blushed and looked down at her hands when she noticed the row of brothels they would have avoided had they taken the shorter route. Ebenezer had been correct on that point; her upbringing had sheltered her from the rougher parts of life. The town thinned as they traveled northwest, giving way to farms and the occasional ranch.

"What are these trees called?" Miss Ashford pointed to one of the many crooked trees dotting the landscape.

"Mesquite."

"I was expecting them to be greener and with larger leaves. They don't have leaves at all, do they?"

"Nope." The greenery was closer to pine needles than leaves.

"Are the trees the same in Greenleaf?"

"Grünlauf," Gunter emphasized in his German accent.

"You mean Greenleaf?"

Gunter shook his head. Another American who didn't understand the German name. Most Texans couldn't pronounce the name correctly. "*Nein*, the name is German. *Grün* for green and lauf is for *Wasserlauf*, or what you would call a waterway. It has nothing to do with trees."

"Oh. I thought Eb was misspelling the name. Those must have been accents, not ink dots. He isn't particularly good at spelling."

"I can't say I am either, ma'am." Discussing his own failure at spelling would be better than any conversation involving the late pastor.

"I always won our spelling bees in school, but don't ask me about arithmetic. I am simply not good at math. Are there any other types of trees in Grünlauf?"

"Spanish oak."

"Any others?"

"The Volmer's have a peach orchard."

"I always pictured trees being like the ones in New England, with huge leaves and pretty colors in the fall. Do the trees change colors in the fall?"

"Not like in Germany. Each September, Mutter is sad because we don't have the beautiful colors. Then she remembers we also do not have the snow and is happy."

"Eb said there wasn't any snow last year. I can't imagine Christmas without snow."

"Our first year in America, I argued that St. Nikolaus could not come since it was not winter. Vater told me if I didn't believe, he would put out his boot and eat all the candy St. Nikolaus left and I would have none."

"Put out your boot?"

"St. Nikolaus comes on December sixth and leaves presents for all the good German boys and girls."

"Only the German children?"

"Ja. The kids who go to the English church have to wait until Christmas." One of the few advantages the German school children had was that they received gifts twice in December.

"So, you must go to the German church. Eb wrote that your minister was nice but difficult to understand."

"Reverend Ellerbrock speaks German much of the time, as do most of the older Germans."

Miss Ashford nodded. "Eb said he asked the German reverend to perform our wedding."

Any topic but this.

"Eb said he wanted to get married as soon as I arrived. I added the last of the lace to my dress last night. I scandalized my mother, planning to wear my college graduation dress as my wedding dress. But if I am going to be a minister's wife, I need to economize, and no woman needs two white dresses. They are impractical to wear. I suppose I will use it to make baptismal dresses for my babies. Everyone agrees that is the most practical thing to do. Although my friend Emily is going to dye her graduation dress blue if she doesn't get married this year. She is a schoolteacher and won't be allowed to court anyone."

Perhaps if he acted disinterested, she would stop talking. There was time to turn back to Austin, have her purchase a ticket home, and find her a hotel for the night. He'd be late enough he could claim she never arrived. But the stationmaster had seen them leave and knew him. If anyone asked, his lie would be discovered. Jasper's threat hung heavily on his mind. Although Gunter couldn't see the point of bringing her to Grünlauf, he'd best do what he'd been paid to do. "Is that so?"

"It is the rules. I am ever so glad I am getting married instead of teaching. I am not that good at it. Eb says he still wants me to teach Sunday School, but that is different from having to teach reading, writing, and arithmetic every day. They made us go teach a lesson in a school as part of my classes at Bradford College. It was so uncomfortable. Emily loved it. To each their own, right?"

"Um-hm."

"Am I talking too much? When I am nervous, I always do. I shouldn't be, even if I am getting married today. I haven't seen Eb—he doesn't like it when I call him that, but Ebenezer sounds so stuffy—for 519 days. That is such a long time. I put a dime in a jar every day, so now I have $51.90 saved for us to start our new life. It isn't much, but it will be a start. Tonight I am adding another dime, so it will be fifty-two dollars even. I should have saved a quarter a day."

Gunter never had a chance to answer her question. She talked too much. Of course, he couldn't answer truthfully or tell her that her wedding was not to be.

⟫◆⟪

The wagon crested a low hill. Below them lay a small town divided by an even smaller river. Amanda at once understood the name Grünlauf. Broadleaf trees grew near the banks of the waterway that snaked through the area. Two steeples stood over the town, one on the far side of the river and the other nearby. The church on the far side resembled the white steepled churches in New England. The other was stouter and had a shorter steeple.

"Which one is Ebenezer's church? I mean, not his church; it's God's. The one he is over?"

"The white one." Again, the driver answered in clipped words. He was the oddest man. One minute he seemed warm and friendly, the next he was distant. If only Eb had come. She was much too aware of this large German, just as she had been of Catherine and Clara's friend at last fall's social—the last social event she attended. It was difficult to be faithful to

Eb if her heart raced around other men. It had to be because Mr. Braunig had saved her from falling off the boardwalk. He could be married. Maybe it was the Texas heat or wedding jitters. She refocused on the town and her imminent nuptials.

The road passed through the heart of the town. Her mother's lessons on first impressions rang through her mind, and she dusted off her dress. "Is there any place I can stop and clean up?"

Mr. Braunig glanced her way. "My instructions are to bring you straight to the church."

"It's bad luck for the bride to see the groom before the wedding. I can't see Eb like this."

The driver didn't respond. Children watched them pass from the safety of their porches and yards. A woman stopped gathering her laundry to stare. Amanda shifted in her seat. They passed a building that looked to be a store, but the words above the door were not in English. The horses' hooves echoed on the wooden bridge as they crossed over the stream. The first building she saw had blue lettering that pronounced it "The Mercantile," as if a similar store didn't exist by a German name only a few hundred yards away. Amanda looked over her shoulder to the other side of the bridge. Like Boston, Grünlauf was divided by neighborhood and culture. Eb had never written about that aspect of the town.

When the driver slowed to a stop in front of the painted white church, a young boy ducked inside the building. They were waiting for her. Mr. Braunig hopped down and circled the wagon. No one exited the church.

"I need to unload the wagon. I'll return with your trunks." He offered his hand to assist her down.

"Thank you, Mr. Braunig." Her eyes focused on the painted church door. Why didn't Eb greet her?

As she neared the door, she heard murmuring through the open windows. As she entered, a violin began playing

Mendelssohn's wedding march. Amanda squinted to make out the figures at the front of the shadowed room. None of them resembled Ebenezer. Had he changed so much? No, no one of the right height stood there. Heads swiveled to face her. A few of the women looked as if they had been crying. Amanda never understood crying at weddings.

She took a step forward. "Where is Ebenezer?"

No one moved.

Another step. Was he hiding? "Where is Reverend Coolidge?"

Faces turned away from her. The violinist's bow slipped, the stanza ending with a screech.

Halfway up the aisle, she paused and turned a slow circle, searching every face. "Where is my fiancé?"

A gray-haired woman stood. She spoke to the men in the front as she exited her pew. "I told y'all you were fools." The woman walked toward Amanda. "The good reverend is gone, dear."

"Gone? Gone where?"

Two of the men standing at the front of the room hurried up the aisle.

The woman reached for Amanda's hand. "To get his reward."

"He's dead?" Nothing in the surrounding scene made sense. Why play a wedding march if Eb was dead? Amanda backed up until she ran into a pew. "When?"

"We just buried him," answered one man.

"Buried?" A sudden buzzing filled her ears, and she grasped the pew back to stay upright. She would not faint like some belle in a dime novel.

The woman stepped closer, shielding her from the men. "We told them to wait to hold the funeral. We also told them that their asinine notion to have you marry the assistant pastor when you arrived was as sap-headed as they are."

A man's hand clamped on the old lady's shoulder. "Keep your nose out of this."

"Don't you tell me what to do. I'm a member of this congregation, same as you. That deputy badge doesn't give you any authority in this church." She pushed his hand off her shoulder. "You can't expect a woman to come in here and marry a stranger because her intended is dead. You got to give her time."

Ebenezer was dead.

Voices argued around her. Amanda didn't focus on them.

A whiny male voice cut through the fog forming in her brain. "But she's gotta marry someone. It may as well be me."

"No." Amanda managed a firmness she didn't know she possessed. She would never marry the owner of that voice.

Everyone near her started yelling. The old woman stuck her thumb and forefinger in her mouth and whistled a high sharp note, and silence filled the room. The woman looked heavenward. "Lord, forgive me for whistling in your house."

Several people dropped their gazes to the floor.

"I think it's best if you all leave now. Like I told you, there won't be a wedding today."

"But she needs to—" said the man with the high, whiny voice. His sentence cut off under the woman's glare.

"What she needs is some air and to see her fiancé's grave. Everyone go home and leave her alone." The woman linked her arm through Amanda's and dragged her outside.

Behind them, the man whined again. "She said her highest aspiration was to be a preacher's wife. She has to marry me."

The woman stopped. "Mr. Fife, you are not an ordained minister, and this is not the dark ages. She doesn't have to marry anyone. Now, all of you get on about your day. You too, Deputy. You have no authority here."

The woman nudged Amanda along a path to the side of the church. A newly covered grave with a wooden cross lay next to a tree.

"Is that Eb?" Amanda hated how her voice shook.

"That is his grave."

Amanda let go of the woman and stumbled to the dirt mound. A paper tacked to the cross fluttered in the warm breeze.

Reverend Ebenezer John Coolidge
December 9, 1854 – June 19, 1879

Her knees buckled, and she fell to the ground, kneeling at the foot of his grave. How could this be? All the planning, all the classes, everything she'd done to be a good minister's wife—gone. A million thoughts froze in her mind like frost on a windowpane in December, then evaporated under the Texas sun, leaving her empty.

4

Mrs. Roberts came to the churchyard gate as Gunter stopped his wagon. "Did you bring her here?"

"Yes, ma'am."

"You should have told her."

"The deputy was clear it wasn't my place." Poor defense. The widow was correct. He should have stopped Miss Ashford and all her plans for the future.

"Did you know they were going to marry her to Mr. Fife?"

"What?" Gunter reprocessed her words. He'd learned English when he was ten. The words worked together, but the outrageousness of the idea stunned him.

Mrs. Roberts tilted her head and narrowed her eyes. "I see you didn't. Glad to know you weren't party to it. I always thought you had more sense than most men."

"They tried to marry her off?"

"Yup. Is your ma's boardinghouse full?"

"No." It hadn't been full since last fall.

"Best take her there until she can get back to Boston. I'd take her in, but my stepson shouldn't be near her. And he doesn't respect my rules." Neither of them suggested the hotel, knowing it wasn't a respectable place for a single woman.

Interesting. The widow didn't trust the deputy either, at least as far as a pretty woman went. "I'll take her to Mutter's."

"You know you shouldn't have brought her here."

"Didn't have much of a choice, ma'am."

Mrs. Robert's eyes narrowed. "We always have choices. It's the consequences that are the problem."

"Yes, ma'am."

"I'll see if she's ready to leave." Mrs. Roberts crossed the cemetery and knelt next to Miss Ashford.

Gunter looked at the American church and shook his head. They hadn't postponed the funeral for her, and then they'd tried to force her to marry Mr. Fife. Who'd thought of such a thing? Despite his conversation with the deputy, he'd hoped to be on time for the funeral. Reverend Coolidge would have been furious at the thought of forcing her to marry Fife. The sooner he could get the lady back to Boston, the better. She didn't belong in Grünlauf. As he watched the widow comfort the girl, he regretted not telling her the truth. It would have been better to drive her back to Austin and claim she'd never showed up.

The sun commenced its descent over the western hills, and a breeze blew into the hollow. Finally, the two women stood. Mrs. Roberts wrapped an arm around Miss Ashford's shoulders and brought her slowly to the edge of the cemetery. Gunter hopped out and walked around to help her into the wagon.

Miss Ashford glared at him through red-rimmed eyes. "You knew he was dead?"

"Ja."

"Why didn't you tell me?"

"It wasn't my place."

"Why not?"

"I'm German."

She scrunched her eyes. "Can you vote?"

"What?"

"Vote in an election?"

"Ja."

"Have you voted?"

Of course, but Samuel J. Tilden hadn't won the presidential election. This time he remembered to use the English word. "Yes."

"Then you are an American, Mr. Braunig, which must mean you are a liar and a coward." She stepped on the wheel spoke and tried to pull herself into the high wagon.

Mrs. Roberts frowned. "Help her up."

Gunter did as he was bid, earning himself a glare from Miss Ashford.

The widow reached up and took the younger woman's hand. "Don't worry, dear. Mrs. Braunig runs the best boardinghouse for miles."

"Thank you for—" Miss Ashford waved her hand in the church's direction.

"The pain does end, dear. My housekeeper is cleaning the parsonage now. Is there anything you want?"

"If he kept the letters I sent..." Her voice cracked and was replaced by a sob.

Gunter wished he could tell her he understood, even if he disagreed with the widow about the pain ending. Pain left scars.

Mrs. Roberts stepped back. "Take care of her. And tell your mother to serve extra strudel, not sauerkraut."

Gunter nodded and touched the brim of his hat before commanding his horses to move.

By the time they reached Mutter's boardinghouse, her sobs quieted. Perhaps it was better that she was told the sad news in Grünlauf; at least here, she would have his mother's care instead of being left alone in some hotel.

Gunter stopped in the side yard.

His mother exited the kitchen door, wiping her hands on her apron. "Vat is this?"

"Mutter, this is Miss Ashford." Enough gossip passed through the boardinghouse dining room that Mother should know who the woman was.

"Minister's bride?" She said the words in German.

Gunter nodded.

"Velcome, Miss Ashford. Come in."

Miss Ashford accepted Gunter's assistance and followed his mother into the boardinghouse kitchen.

"Papa! *Ich habe Oma beim Strudelmachen geholfen.*" His daughter Greta sat on a stool at the worktable, a bit of misformed dough in front of her.

Gunter dusted a bit of flour off his daughter's nose and set her on the floor. "In English. Grandma's new guest doesn't speak German."

"I helped Grandma make strudel." Her English words came out slower.

"For supper, ja?"

Greta nodded. "Who is the pretty lady?"

"This is Miss Ashford. Miss Ashford, my mother, Mrs. Braunig, and my daughter, Greta."

"How long will you stay with us?" asked his mother.

"Only as long as it takes to return home," said Miss Ashford.

Mrs. Braunig pointed to Gunter. "Take her things to the yellow room."

"Miss Ashford, will you need both trunks in your room?"

Miss Ashford rubbed her temple. "I'm not sure. If I am leaving tomorrow, I'll only need my bag."

"We'll head to Austin in the morning. I'll store your trunks in the washroom. If you need anything, you should have some privacy to open them." Gunter nodded to the door of the kitchen. The trunks were heavy enough he didn't want to haul them upstairs and back down in the same twenty-four-hour period.

His mother handed Miss Ashford a key. "Greta, will you show her to the yellow room?"

"With the flowers?"

"Ja."

"Thank you." Miss Ashford politely nodded before following his skipping daughter out of the room.

Mutter spoke softly in German. "Is it true? The American reverend is dead?"

"They had the funeral today."

"Why did you bring her here?"

"Mrs. Roberts suggested she would be better off in your care."

"Not here to the boardinghouse—to town."

"The deputy didn't give me much of a choice."

"I suppose you are going to tell me again that we should move."

"I do not like living this way, but I cannot risk more lives by fighting. Something I don't understand…they tried to get her to marry Mr. Fife. I should have stayed at the church. I didn't realize…I thought if I returned with her trunks after they told her…"

"No." Mutter opened the door of the huge cast-iron stove and checked the dinner.

"Schnitzel with noodles?"

"Of course. Did they really try to marry her to someone else?"

"Yes, and they held the funeral before she arrived."

A German expletive that would have earned him a spanking as a child crossed his mother's lips. "Mrs. Roberts is right. You get her to Austin first thing."

"I plan to."

"Good thing Greta helped make strudel today. That girl will need something sweet. Go get her trunks."

Gunter stowed both trunks in the washroom and took the carpetbag upstairs. The door to the yellow room stood open.

"...and this is another drawer." Greta's voice carried into the hallway.

Gunter tapped on the doorframe.

"Come in." Miss Ashford turned from the dresser.

Gunter pushed the door open and set the bag just inside. "Come, Greta, it is time to go home."

"But we made strudel."

"Perhaps Oma will give you some to take home."

His daughter crossed her arms. "*Ich möchte bleiben.*"

"Greta."

"I want to stay."

"Thank you for remembering to speak in English. It is still time to go home. Hurry and see if Oma has any strudel for you."

Greta flew out of the room.

Gunter searched for something to say. "I am sorry for my daughter. She is—"

"Precious."

"I was going to say precocious."

The corner of Miss Ashford's mouth lifted in a half smile.

"We'll leave early for Austin, and you can catch a northbound train."

"Yes, that would be best." She spoke in the oddly distracted way of one who'd received a great shock—a feeling he knew all too well. What would be best was if loved ones surrounded her.

"Mutter will have dinner ready soon."

She may have nodded a response, he couldn't be sure. Gunter closed the door, leaving her to her grief.

Greta was still in the kitchen, talking with Mutter in German.

"Will she be all right?" Mutter asked.

"Eventually. I'll be here at about seven in the morning. There is a northbound train at ten. That should give us plenty of time to get to the station."

"A voman traveling alone? That is not good."

"She arrived here alone."

"She must have had a traveling companion."

"Miss Ashford mentioned something about a friend she traveled as far as Dallas with and a chaperone, although I am not sure where she is."

"She could go to Dallas and find her friend."

Gunter shook his head. "Nein. The friend traveled west from Dallas to a job at a school."

"It isn't wise for a woman to travel so far alone."

"This isn't the old country. Miss Ashford comes from money. She can purchase passage in the best cars and be well looked after."

"Are you sure she has money?"

"Reverend Coolidge spoke of her wealthy father. He'd even received a dowry. You saw her trunks. Miss Ashford has money." Oddly, she wasn't uppity about it. She'd been kind to his daughter. Other women would have chased her from the room.

"All the more reason she can't travel alone."

"She is not our responsibility."

"She is God's child. And what are we worth if not to help our brothers and sisters?"

Gunter would not argue his mother's logic, if only not to start a fight. If God cared for His children, would He allow men to harm each other? Would He have allowed Pauline and little Hans to die while their murderers went unpunished? Maybe God cared more about wealthy society women than He did poor German immigrants.

5

Plunging her hatpin into her mattress did nothing to alleviate the emotions bubbling inside her and threatening to overflow like a boiling pot of porridge. Neither had crying at Ebenezer's grave. Why hadn't Mr. Braunig told her at the train station instead of letting her carry on about being a minister's wife? And what right did Eb have to die, anyway? Twenty-four-year-old men didn't just die. No one had mentioned how he died. Was he shot? Men were always being shot in the dime novels, but those were outlaws and sheriffs and such, not preachers. Someone would have said if the reverend had been murdered, wouldn't they?

Probably illness. Eb had written about some of the things people died from down here, like cholera.

Whatever the cause, it wasn't fair. This was not in her plan. For two years, she had worked toward this—marrying and becoming a preacher's wife.

The first lecture she'd attended at Bradford College centered on stories of missionaries, including Ann Hasseltine Judson and Harriet Atwood Newe—the first female foreign missionaries from the original Bradford Academy. The professor had concluded with Lucy Goodale Thurston, who'd married a stranger in order to live her life in missionary service in Hawaii. From that moment on, Amanda had wanted to be a missionary too.

Unfortunately, mission work required being married to somebody with the same dream. Since there were not as many missionaries being sent abroad, the next best thing was to be a minister's wife. She could run charities, clothing drives, teach Sunday school, and so on.

Her roommate, Emily, was a scholarship student who worked hard to stretch her resources. She showed Amanda how, as a preacher's wife, she might save money and economize.

Amanda yanked the hatpin from the mattress, inspecting the mattress for damage. She should change for dinner. She hadn't eaten since her hurried breakfast that morning, but the thought of eating with strangers overruled any desire for food.

She had no business in Texas and should return to her parents' home. It was the only logical thing to do, even if she didn't want to be there. At least the house would be empty until Father, Mother, and Charles returned from Europe in the fall. No one would berate her for her stupidity or point out they'd been correct in their assumptions that marrying a minister was folly.

Tears resurfaced and the numbness that started when she walked out of the church grew until it filled every corner of her being.

Amanda curled up on her side and pulled the unfamiliar pillow close. She was in a strange town and alone, her fear threatening to overcome her. She was afraid of what her father would say when she returned to Boston, afraid Mother would arrange her future. Her parents always planned for her, and she'd be married off to a Boston mogul. Her sole job would be to look pretty at parties, host teas for other women exactly like her, and volunteer at some place "charitable" every Thursday afternoon. She was afraid she would live the meaningless life she wanted to avoid.

"Oh, Eb, why did you have to die? I may not have loved you passionately, but I was passionate about what we both loved. And we were great friends. I am so confused."

Talking to the dead would not help. She tried to pray, but her questions were the same ones she'd cast into the universe to Eb.

⊱◆⊰

Greta slid under the single sheet, ready for Gunter to tuck her in. "Who is the lady that came to Oma's?"

"Miss Ashford. She came to Grünlauf to marry the American preacher."

"But he died."

"How did you know he was dead?"

"All the people who visited Oma today talked about it. Oma says it's because the preacher didn't eat sauerkraut. But I think she only wants me to eat all of mine." Greta made a face and stuck out her tongue.

Gunter couldn't help but laugh.

"Is the reverend in heaven with Mama?"

"Yes, I believe so."

"Is the lady very sad?"

"I'm sure she is."

"Then why weren't you nice to her? Oma said you did wrong."

Gunter was filled with embarrassment, unsure of how his daughter had heard the argument. "I was not mean to her. I just should have done something more for her. And Oma was upset because I didn't. I didn't mean to not be nice to her. But I made the wrong choice."

"So grown-ups make bad choices too?"

"Yes, *Liebling*, we do."

"Do you need to say 'I'm sorry'?"

Gunter nodded.

"Miss Ashford needs a husband. And you need a wife. Miss Ashford smells pretty, not like Fräulein Volmer. She smells like vinegar. You should marry Miss Ashford, not Fräulein Volmer."

"Ah, Liebling, that is not how marriage works. Miss Ashford will need to grieve before she wants to marry anyone else."

"What does *grieve* mean?"

"It means she needs to spend some time being sad first."

Greta reached up and touched her father's cheek. "Are you finished with your sadness?"

"Sometimes I am still very sad. And I miss your mother and brother every day."

"I miss Mama too. But some days it's hard to remember her. And all I can remember about Hans is him crying a lot."

"Babies cry a lot. You howled as loud as the coyotes."

Greta giggled. "Oh, Papa, I did not. Babies can't be as loud as coyotes."

"You need to sleep now, Liebling. I need to take you over to Oma's early tomorrow morning so I can take Miss Ashford to Austin so she can catch the train home."

"She should stay here. It's much nicer than Boston."

"How do you know? You were born here."

"Because Frau Temming says that this is ever so much nicer than Berlin and Berlin and Boston sound the same."

"You spend much too much time listening to Oma and her friends."

"No, I don't. Oma always sends me from the room."

Gunter shook his head. He wasn't sure what to do with his little eavesdropper. "Good night, little one."

He picked up the lantern and left the room.

"Papa?" Greta yawned. "I still think you should ask Miss Ashford to stay. She smells like flowers."

"Good night." Gunter retired to his room. Greta was right. Miss Ashford smelled like lavender mixed with something else he didn't know, probably some very expensive perfume. She smelled a great deal better than Fräulein Volmer, whom Gunter had no intention of ever marrying. He didn't like how she treated his daughter.

Despite her grief, Miss Ashford had been kind to Greta. However, kindness and smelling like flowers were not good enough reasons to ask her to stay in a place she didn't belong.

6

Amanda struggled to open her eyes. Someone had pounded on her door. The knocking came again, but this time the door opened and a woman entered holding a lantern. "Vake up. You have less than an hour until you leave for the train."

Amanda pushed the hair out of her face and sat up, the white blanket falling away. Not a blanket—her wedding dress. It had been in the travel bag carefully folded so she could wear it. She still wore her traveling clothes.

Mrs. Braunig stepped farther into the room, setting the lantern on the dressing table next to a cloth-covered tray.

It seemed the tray had been there an exceedingly long time. She'd meant to eat and inquire about a bath but was sure neither had occurred.

Mrs. Braunig lifted the corner of the cloth covering the tray. "Did you eat anything last night?"

"I don't think so. I was looking for something to change into, and my wedding dress was on top—" Amanda swallowed the lump forming in her throat. She held up the white dress.

"Oh, zat is beautiful."

"I made the lace myself."

Mrs. Braunig rubbed the lace between her fingers. "*Sehr gut*. Do you make it to sell?"

"No." Amanda clutched the dress to her bosom, then relaxed her arms and studied one of the lace flounces. "I never thought of selling my work."

"Make good money."

Mother would be more scandalized at her daughter selling homemade lace than she was when Amanda announced she was marrying a poor preacher. "I should pack it away."

"You need a bath. Hurry, it is ready." The woman grabbed Amanda's carpetbag. "Bring your dress and bag down the stairs."

Amanda followed Mrs. Braunig to the washroom off the kitchen where steam rose from a large clawfoot tub near the back wall of the room. Against one wall sat Amanda's trunks.

"I'll knock in fifteen minutes. Hurry." The door shut with a click as the woman left. Amanda untied the ribbon holding the trunk keys from her neck and opened the smaller trunk. She desperately needed to clean her clothes, but her traveling dress would have to do for a few days more. For the first time since leaving Boston, she wished she'd followed her mother's advice and brought the third trunk of clothes. Hurriedly, she pulled her last fresh combination out of the section for her underclothes. Once those were soiled, she'd have to return to her old-fashioned drawers and underbodice. Too bad she had not bathed and washed her foundation garments last night. There was no time to clean her clothes or wash her hair. Wet hair would only attract dust from the road and soot from the train, so she brushed her hair and piled it on her head before slipping into the bath.

The water was the perfect temperature, and Mrs. Braunig had added a bit of dried lavender. Amanda washed her face and leaned back to soak for the few moments she could. There would not be another bath until she returned to Boston.

A knock sounded at the door.

"Almost done!" Amanda scrubbed the last of the dirt away. The wedding dress was returned to the smaller trunk. All the clothes in her carpetbag were in desperate need of washing. At least Mother and Father were in Europe and wouldn't see or smell her upon her return.

Dressed and as refreshed as possible, Amanda entered the kitchen.

Mrs. Braunig pointed at the plate on the table. "Eat. You do not want to faint on the train."

The apple-filled pastry melted on Amanda's tongue.

"Strudel makes a good breakfast, ja?"

"Delicious."

"Eat the egg too. I made you a basket of food."

The back door opened, and Mr. Braunig entered with his daughter, whose left braid was thicker than the other, her dress slightly rumpled.

"Good morning. I'll load your trunks. Finish eating." He lifted the smaller one with ease and walked out the door.

Greta spoke in German to her grandmother. Mrs. Braunig cut a small piece of strudel and put it on a plate.

"Danke."

"English in front of the nice lady."

"Thank you."

Amanda finished her breakfast and opened her handbag. "What do I owe you?"

"Nothing," answered Mr. Braunig as he carried the second trunk out of the kitchen.

Amanda appealed to Mrs. Braunig. "I stayed the night and ate. Surely I owe you something."

"Nein. You are like the man by the wayside. This is our time to be a Good Samaritan."

Amanda's heart warmed. She'd not received such kindness in her life. She blinked back tears. "Thank you so much."

Someone knocked on the front door of the boardinghouse, and Mrs. Braunig disappeared into the hallway.

"Papa says you are going on a train. I've never been on one. Do they go fast?"

"Faster than the fastest horses."

"Someday I will go on a train."

"Where will you go?"

"I don't know. Oma tells stories of Bavaria. I want to go there."

"Then you will sail on a ship."

Greta frowned. "Boats make Oma sick."

Mrs. Braunig returned with Mrs. Roberts. The widow carried a hatbox. "There you are, dear. I am so glad I caught you before you left. There were some things I thought you should have. Letters you wrote. A photograph of you. His watch. Do you know his family?"

"I met his mother and father once. They live near Springfield, Massachusetts."

"There are letters for them and some important-looking papers. I'll make sure his clothing goes to the poor. Mr. Fife wanted the theological books and the new Bible. You don't mind that he keeps those, do you?"

"No. I have no need for them." Amanda wasn't sure she wanted anything of Eb's.

Mrs. Roberts set the box on the table. "It's sad that one's worldly possessions take up so little space."

Mr. Braunig reentered the room. "We should be going now."

"Thank you for your kindness." Amanda picked up the hatbox. Mr. Braunig beat her to the carpetbag. She followed him out to the wagon, where he placed both items in the back before helping her up. Not only was he tall, he also seemed incredibly strong.

Greta came outside with the older women. "Can I please come?"

"Not today, Liebling."

Amanda waved at the little girl, and she waved back. Greta was the brightest part of Texas.

⸺◆⸺

Gunter checked his father's pocket watch. They would need to hurry to catch the train to Dallas. Mrs. Roberts's hatbox reminded him of another box he needed to give Miss Ashford. Instead of taking the road that led to Austin, he turned down a side street and stopped at the smithy.

"Why are we stopping? Do you need something fixed?"

"I'm the blacksmith. This is my shop."

"I thought you made deliveries."

"I do both."

Gunter unlocked the building and closed the door behind him. As quickly as he could, he removed the green leather box still wrapped in its burlap bag from the hidden safe and returned the old anvil to its place.

Miss Ashford watched as he added the bag to the space under his seat. Fortunately, she didn't ask him any questions. He didn't want to explain when there could be someone nearby. She clutched the seat as he started the wagon in motion.

Unlike yesterday, today's ride was silent.

Two miles out of town, Gunter spoke. "In that bag is a gift Reverend Coolidge commissioned for you. I thought I should save it for you."

"Why didn't you give it to me earlier?"

"I wasn't sure how to give it to you. Yesterday was not the time. Also, there are those in town who shouldn't know you have it." He couldn't explain well what he didn't fully understand, and sharing his suspicions that the minister's death was not natural would not help her. It was best she left Texas ignorant of any foul doings.

Miss Ashford gave him a questioning look. "Why shouldn't people know I have a gift?"

Gunter had said too much already. "There are thieves among us."

"Oh."

Gunter leaned down and pulled the burlap bag from under his seat and gave it to her. "Reverend Coolidge gave me the spoon to melt down to make some decorations on the box."

"It is heavy. What is in it?"

Gunter pulled the key tied to a green ribbon from his pocket and handed it to her. "There is a letter and an old Bible inside. It is best if you open the box later, when there is not so much dust."

She added the key to the ribbon she wore around her neck with the trunk keys. "I should try to put this in my trunk before we get to the station. I can't carry the hatbox and my carpetbag."

Gunter checked the time again. She was right. It would be best to add it to her trunks, away from prying eyes.

"Do you have room for it?"

"I can make room."

He stopped in the shade of a live oak. With his help, she climbed over the seat, opened the smaller trunk, and took out a snowy white dress. She set the box inside its burlap bag in its place and replaced the dress. The trunk wouldn't close. She sat on the top of the trunk and still the latch wouldn't quite meet. Tears welled up in her eyes. "Come on, you stupid thing. Close!"

Standing, she opened the lid and moved the dress around with no better result. She kicked the trunk, and her shoulders shook.

Gunter jumped over the seat to join her.

Tears streamed down her cheeks. "It won't close."

He needed to pass her in the narrow confines of the wagon. He gripped her elbows so he could sidestep. At his touch, she crumpled and fell into him, Gunter pulled her into his chest and let her cry.

So small. Holding her while standing in the wagon bed wasn't exactly inappropriate since it wasn't the most private place in the world, even if the deserted road made it feel that way. Gunter turned them both so he could step away and help with the trunk. "Is there anything breakable inside?"

She stood frozen for a second, then shook her head. "My coin jar. It is safely wrapped."

Not wanting to go through her things, Gunter tried the same trick she had and sat on the lid. The trunk closed, and he turned the key in the lock. By the time he stood up, she'd climbed back over the wagon bench.

He joined her and held out the ribbon and keys. It took a moment for her to look up from the handkerchief she held over her face.

"Sorry. I shouldn't have …your wife would think …I didn't mean …"

He said the only thing he could to calm her nerves. "I'm a widower."

She stopped dabbing at her eyes and responded, "I didn't realize. Still, I shouldn't have."

Gunter signaled his horses, and they continued to Austin. What could he say to help? It was better she found comfort and safety somewhere else. He wouldn't take advantage of her, but someone on the train might. He'd pondered all night as to who could travel with her. There were some in the German community he trusted, but none would be open to leaving home for more than two or three days. Mrs. Roberts might, but that would mean Jasper would know.

As surely as a dark-green sky warned of a tornado, the events around Miss Ashford's arrival told of impending doom. Gunter had yet to put together all the pieces to the trouble in Grünlauf, but he'd learned the sheriff's deputy was not to be trusted. Better to get Miss Ashford out of Texas as fast as possible. In her current state, she might not believe him if he told her there were far worse things than losing a fiancé before the wedding.

7

ustin looked much the same as it had yesterday afternoon. Men on horseback negotiated streets crowded with conveyances of all sorts. Shouts and yells for others to make way or move sounded from all sides. Today, the sights and sounds were duller, as if no trace of joy remained. Mr. Braunig's wagon slowed as the traffic thickened. Men whistled at her as they passed, the same way dock workers did. Amanda did her best to ignore them. At last, they arrived at the station.

"Can you see to getting your tickets? I should stay with the horses and your trunks." His request was completely reasonable.

If she was going to make the trip back to Boston on her own, she could surely buy her own tickets. Except she never had before. Her brother had purchased her tickets to Texas and had even been kind enough to exchange Emily's seat so they could ride together. New experiences. Buying a ticket couldn't be that hard. "Yes."

"Mutter says you'll be safer if you book first class."

"Of course." Ashfords always booked first class.

Mr. Braunig descended from the wagon and came around to help her down. His hands about her waist reminded her of how large and strong he was. If she had laced her corset tighter, his fingers might have even met. It was an odd thought, and she chased it from her mind as her feet touched the ground. "Thank you. I'll be back in a moment."

The line at the ticket counter was short. Amanda listened intently to those ahead of her as they ordered their tickets. When it was her turn, she stepped to the window and said with all the confidence of a Bradford College graduate, "One first-class ticket to Boston, please."

"Boston? Massachusetts?"

Was there another one? "Yes, sir."

The man nodded and turned away, rifling through several papers and muttering. Clutching three of the papers, he turned back to the window. "Your passage will come to $116, miss."

Amanda had counted her money that morning—$53.40. She had fifty cents, but she'd added the last dime to the coin jar, although there was no reason to. There had been enough for a ticket and meals if she supplemented with the ten dollars in dimes she'd removed from the jar that morning. "One-hundred and sixteen? Emily said it only cost fifty to get to Dallas from Boston."

"That would be the cost of the immigrant class ticket, not first class. Do ya want the first-class ticket?"

Even if she used the $42 left in the jar, she was still short of the fare, "Is there another sort of ticket? What types of tickets do you have?"

"There is first class, which has sleeping berths—no doubt the type of travel you are used to. Second class has padded seats on most of the line but no sleeping accommodations. And the immigrant cars—they have wooden seats and are usually crowded."

Someone behind her yelled for her to hurry.

The ticket master shook his head. "Are you going or not? The northbound leaves in twenty minutes."

"How much for a second-class ticket?"

"Seventy-eight. Are you going to buy it or not?"

Amanda pinched her lips. "Not at the moment."

She hurried out of the station, her face burning. Without looking at anyone, she walked as fast as she could to the wagon.

"Did you get your ticket?"

"No, I need my jar of dimes."

"Don't you have enough money?"

"Not for a first-class ticket. But with my dimes, I can purchase a second-class fare."

Mr. Braunig frowned. "A single woman shouldn't travel second class alone."

Her spine stiffened. Who was he to tell her what she should and shouldn't do? "I don't see how it is any of your concern."

"As Reverend Coolidge's friend, I must insist that you think of your safety."

"Then you should have thought of that yesterday when we stood here." The answer was waspish, she knew, but the man deserved a bit of a sting. She walked around to the back of the wagon. "If you will please help me up. I need to get my jar of coins."

Mr. Braunig did as she asked. Discreetly, Amanda took the key from around her neck and slipped it into the lock of the smaller trunk, her breath catching at the sight of the white dress. Not now. She blinked back the tears and grabbed the jar from its nest of clothes, the dimes clinking against the glass, the same sound they'd made every night. These were Eb's coins. She wasn't supposed to spend them on herself. But he wasn't here. The jar slipped from her fingers, the glass shattering as the jar connected with the metal-edged trunk rim. Dimes and glass sprayed all over the interior of her trunk and wagon floor.

"No!" She reached for the dimes before they could disappear into the folds of her gowns. As her hand closed over the coins, a stinging pain shot up her arm, and she dropped the money. Red stained her wedding dress. Helpless, she stood over her trunk. She should move the dress. She reached out to do so, but a hand around her wrist stopped her.

"My dress!" Amanda strained against the force.

"Miss Ashford, your hand." Mr. Braunig turned her palm up as gently as if she were a small child. Three large shards of glass had pierced her hand. Mr. Braunig pinched the first between his thumb and forefinger and pulled it free.

Amanda gasped. Mr. Braunig didn't pause as he removed the rest of the glass from her hand. Then he pulled a blue square of cloth from his pocket and wrapped it around her hand.

Without thanking him, she turned back to the trunk. "I need to hurry. He said the train leaves soon."

Again, his firm grip stopped her hands. "Why do you need these coins when you have all that money in the bank?"

"What money?" *Father* had money in the bank. She didn't have anything that wasn't in her purse. Father had been clear on that score. Once she got married, there wasn't another penny.

Mr. Braunig straightened. "Sorry, I spoke out of turn."

"Tell me."

He shifted, and the wagon rocked. "We should get your trunk closed."

Amanda looked around to see that people were staring. Mr. Braunig was correct. Mother would be fanning herself so fast. "But my train."

"They called for the all-aboard. There isn't time to get a ticket." He didn't need to explain further.

Amanda sank onto the larger trunk and watched Mr. Braunig close her smaller one. Then she let him help her over the wagon seat.

The sounds of the wagon and men on horseback and shopkeepers yelling covered the sounds of her heart crying out as they left Austin the way they had come.

Some women cried loudly so the entire world knew. Miss Ashford tried to hide her tears. Gunter wasn't sure which he preferred. In some ways, sitting next to her with her stiff back and occasional sniffle was more uncomfortable than when a woman screamed and yelled and raged. His wife had done that often enough. He'd give all the money in Grünlauf bank for Pauline to rage at him once more. If only Miss Ashford would yell at the world. He again reminded himself that she wasn't his responsibility.

Yet he felt responsible.

Five miles out of Austin, she broke the silence. "What did you mean about the money?"

Gunter cleared his throat. "Reverend Coolidge received a large bank deposit from your father."

"How do you know this?"

He thought for a moment. "Everyone knows." At least, everyone talked about it. "There was a special Wells Fargo courier who came through a couple weeks back."

She turned to face him, eyes wide.

"When the reverend commissioned the box, he was upset that it was so small because the marriage gift you were bringing would be so big."

"How much money?" Her voice was rough—from the crying or the heat he couldn't be sure.

"I don't know. There are many rumors about that." Gunter wondered if the money had anything to do with the reverend ordering a new lock on the box, but unless the Bible was hollowed out, there was no money in the box now. And the worn Bible was not worth securing in a box.

"The money is at the bank?"

"I assume so." Reverend Coolidge didn't have any extra money to pay his bill yesterday.

"Then I can withdraw it on Monday and go home." The slightest smile changed the despair on her face to hope.

"I would have told you earlier. I just assumed you had money."

Her laugh had a sharp edge to it. "Everyone assumes I have money because I am an Ashford. My father is one of the wealthiest men in Boston. My brother will be too. My father said the money he handed me at the train station in Boston was the last money I would ever receive. I am somewhat surprised he sent money to Eb. So very proper of him."

Gunter wasn't sure how to respond. He hadn't realized that people in America followed the custom.

"I can't imagine it is much. Father was extremely displeased when I chose to marry a minister, and he threatened to marry me off with no dowry. At the very least, it should be enough to pay for a first-class ticket and your mother for two more nights. Do you suppose she'll have room for me?"

"She wasn't expecting anyone new." Few visitors came to Grünlauf. Or, more specifically, few came to the German side of town. It was better that way.

With Greta close behind, Mutter came out of the kitchen door as Gunter pulled the wagon to a stop. "Did you miss the train?"

It would be faster to explain the situation in his native tongue. Still, it was considered rude. "Do you mind if I explain to her in German?"

A weak smile formed on Miss Ashford's lips. "Fewer questions for me. Will you help me down?"

Gunter hopped down from the wagon. Cradling her injured hand, Miss Ashford didn't attempt to climb out by herself this time.

"You are hurt," Greta said observantly.

"Yes, I cut myself." Miss Ashford nodded and walked in the direction of the outhouse.

"Miss Ashford said I could explain in German," Gunter said as he launched into an explanation of the morning.

"She must stay here longer?"

"She cannot go to the bank until Monday. If she hurries, she can make the afternoon train to Dallas."

"I don't like her traveling alone."

"She is not our responsibility," Gunter repeated the words he'd told himself a thousand times.

"Yet God has put her here with us. I wish I had the money to loan her."

"We both have mortgages to pay."

"I know, son. I can still wish."

Miss Ashford returned. "Mrs. Braunig, I find I need to extend my stay. The sign next to the front door says $2.50 a week. I will be here until Monday at the very least. Would you like me to pay now?"

"Ve vill...how do you say it? Settle up vhen you leave. You must save your money to go home," Mutter replied in English.

"But—"

"Help me with work. I give you a discount." Mutter gestured to Miss Ashford's bandaged hand. "Come. I vill bandage your hand. Then I vash blood out of your pretty dress." Halfway to the house, Mutter turned around. "Put the trunks in the washroom."

"Greta, fetch me the broom." Gunter needed to get the glass out of the wagon before his daughter cut herself too.

Greta returned in a flash with the small broom she used when helping her Oma clean.

"Did Miss Ashford come back so you can marry her?"

"No. She wasn't able to leave today, so she came back to stay in a safe place."

"You are wrong."

"Greta," Gunter stopped sweeping, "I know you hear Oma and the other ladies say I should get married again. And someday I will—when I find the right woman."

"Miss Ashford is beautiful."

"Yes, she is."

"I want a pretty mama."

"I want a kind mama for you."

"Is she mean?"

Gunter thought through his interactions with Miss Ashford. There had been some frustrated and well-deserved words berating him. However, they were not malicious. "I don't think so, but we have only known each other a day."

"Then she should stay longer."

"She needs to go home."

Greta spread her arms. "This is home."

Gunter finished sweeping. There was no way to convince a four-year-old that her logic was wrong. This wasn't Miss Ashford's home.

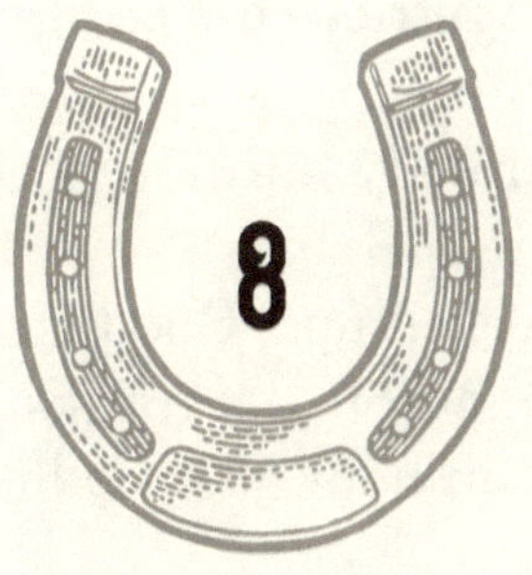

8

Somewhere, a rooster crowed. Amanda rolled over. The sun had yet to rise enough to lighten her room through the lace curtains. Unlike yesterday, she felt somewhat refreshed—probably because she hadn't cried herself to sleep. Apparently, there was a bright side to crying during the day: she could sleep at night. Hopefully, she wouldn't need to repeat the performance today.

Unable to ignore the day, Amanda rose and washed the best she could with one hand. Mrs. Braunig had been insistent that she didn't get her hand wet for three days or more. Last evening, all she was allowed to do was to read to Greta from a worn book of nursery rhymes. Mrs. Braunig said that it was important that Greta hear them in a real American accent. While she read, Mrs. Braunig cleaned all the blood out of the white gown.

Sunday. Church. The thoughts froze Amanda in place. She could not step foot in the church where Eb once served, not after having been nearly forced to marry. But she had not missed a service since starting Bradford.

Today would be the first in over four years. She could read the Bible in Eb's box and feign a headache. Instead of dressing, Amanda wrapped a shawl around her shoulders and hurried down to retrieve the box from the trunks before anyone else was about.

Lamplight was already burning in the kitchen. "*Guten Morgen.*"

Amanda's head jerked up. "Good morning, Mrs. Braunig. I just need something from my trunks."

"I serve breakfast an hour later on Sunday before church service."

Amanda smiled, not willing to admit she had no intention of going. She held up her key and stepped into the washroom to retrieve the box from her trunk. Her bustle and best dress peeked out from the folds of protective tissue. She could at least dress up for the Sabbath. Amanda gathered the clothing too.

Back in her room, she set the box on the bed.

It was an odd wedding gift. She traced her finger over the delicate, flowery, silver vines adorning the box. The key turned easily in the lock. Inside was the old Bible Eb had used at the seminary. During almost every discussion they'd had, he'd pulled it out of his shoulder bag and pointed out a verse relating to his comment. Even during his proposal, he had stopped to share a passage. In between Genesis and Exodus was a sealed envelope with her name on it.

Amanda broke the wax seal.

June 18, 1879

Amanda,

If you are reading this, I was not able to remove this letter from the box before our wedding night. I fear I have fallen victim to a fanciful imagination these

last few weeks. Twice I have had the most unusual
dreams. Please go home as fast as you can. Something is terribly wrong. I do not wish you to know
what I suspect, as you will be in danger too.
I pray I am wrong. Tell your father he was right. Money had more reason for my choices than sense.
I am deeply sorry. Hurry home, my friend.

Ebenezer

PS. Burn this letter immediately. Take the Bible to
the Texas Rangers and give it to George Washington. I met him and trust him. ONLY the Rangers.

She dropped the letter as if it were on fire already. Eb
was the most practical of men. No one ever accused him of
being imaginative. The handwriting was his; she'd recognize
it anyplace. She had dozens of letters to compare it to.

No longer wishing to be alone for the first time since
leaving Boston, Amanda put on her bustle. Mrs. Smythe had
declared even the collapsible Langtry bustle most uncomfortable for the train ride. All three of them had worn more
functional skirts that lacked trains. From the few people
she'd seen on the street, it was a style most women in Grünlauf preferred. Sunday would likely be different.

Over the last several months, Amanda had perfected
the art of dressing without a maid or roommate's help, her
front-buttoning corset making all the difference. Doing her
hair by herself was another matter. She'd needed to wash
it days ago. Without a curling iron or having rolled it in
rags overnight, she found it quite unmanageable. The bun
she concocted was definitely not high fashion, but her hat
should hide it.

She slipped the letter into the front of the corset. She would drop it in the stove at first chance. The Bible was another matter. She locked it back in the green box and returned it to her trunk in the washroom.

Even with her early start, she was not the first one to breakfast. An old man sat at one end of the table, his gray mustache neatly trimmed. "Guten Morgen, Fräulein."

The phrase was easy enough to decipher. "Good morning, sir."

"No German?"

"Only English and some French."

"*Französisch.*" The man looked as though he had bitten a lemon as he said the word, which sounded like it must have something to do with France. "English is good."

Mrs. Braunig came in from the kitchen with a platter of sliced bread. "Ah, Herr Schellenberger, you have met Miss Ashford. She doesn't speak German, so practice your English, please. Herr Schellenberger is the butcher. He saves the best cuts for the boardinghouse."

"I vill try." Herr Schellenberger frowned.

Before he could say anything else, the two elderly sisters Amanda had seen the night before entered the room.

"Good morning, Miss Ashford, we love your dress." The two spoke in unison. Both wore gingham dresses, one pink, the other blue. Their gray hair was pulled back in identical braided buns.

It took a moment for Amanda to respond. "Thank you. Yours are lovely too."

"Miss Ashford, these are the Kerksiek sisters." This time the boardinghouse owner didn't add any further information.

Neither the women nor Mrs. Braunig wore bustles. Amanda hoped she wasn't overdressed, but changing now would only make her look silly. "What time is church?"

"The English church meets at ten." Only the sister in pink

spoke this time, dispelling the gloomy feeling their last statement brought about.

"I don't wish to go to the church where—" Amanda found she couldn't utter his name.

"Of course not. The German church meets at nine thirty," answered the other sister. Her warm smile felt like a grandmother's hug.

"Come with us." Again, they spoke at the same time. Amanda wondered if they might be twins. She'd known a set at Bradford. While they'd looked the same, their personalities had been quite different, and they'd never spoken in unison.

Breakfast consisted of leftover bread, strudel, and boiled eggs, something that wouldn't have been too difficult for Mrs. Braunig to put together. From the sign by the door in German and English, Amanda knew the only other meal that day would be a late luncheon instead of the normal supper.

Strudel was quickly becoming Amanda's favorite food. She cleared the plates, hoping to have a moment alone. The stove was cool to the touch. Burning the letter would have to wait. She didn't need to reopen it to read the peculiar message. The least surprising thing was that he'd called her friend. Eb was never one for romance. If he had ended it with a term of endearment, she would have doubted its authenticity.

The German church wasn't much different from the one she had been inside during her first few moments in town. It had one large room with wooden benches spaced evenly and a small riser for the stage. One window was transparent glass, while the other contained a stained-glass scene of Jesus with sheep.

Not wanting to disturb the Braunigs, Amanda sat next to the sisters in the second to the last pew. As the placement put her directly behind Mr. Braunig's wide shoulders, she could not see the preacher who, like everyone else, spoke in German.

An organ of questionable age sat in the front right corner of the room. When the opening notes filled the room, relief filled Amanda. Finally, something she recognized—Martin Luther's classic "A Mighty Fortress Is Our God"—a small comfort to a woman who felt so lost.

⋘◆⋙

Greta turned around on the bench and stared at the woman behind her. Gunter had been trying to ignore Miss Ashford's presence—difficult to do when she was the only one not singing *"Ein feste Burg ist unser Gott"* in German. Her sweet soprano voice carried the English words in perfect harmony with the rest of the congregation. Greta was not the only person to turn around during the hymn.

Miss Ashford didn't need her voice to set her apart from the rest of his friends. She wasn't the only woman who sported a bustle, but the fabric of her dress was much finer than any other lady's. It wasn't fabric one ordered out of the Montgomery Ward & Co. catalog at fifteen cents a yard or even one of the three-dollar women's suits he'd purchased for his mother last Christmas. Still, the dress wasn't as extravagant as some of the dresses he'd seen in the windows of the fashionable boutiques in Austin. After seeing her wedding dress, he was sure she could have dressed to the height of fashion if she wanted to. Maybe she really did want to fit in as a preacher's wife in Texas.

He speculated on her reason for coming to the German church, likely the same reason he didn't want to go to church after his wife had died. Still, she didn't belong. The sooner she left Grünlauf, the better.

As if reading his mind, the minister chose to deliver his remarks based on the text of Luke chapter 10, the parable of the good Samaritan. Guilt filled him for helping her under duress. Still, Gunter had fulfilled his duty. He could have left her in Dripping Springs to find her way home or at the church, for the English speakers to care for. Hadn't he done enough?

After all, the good Samaritan left the injured man in good hands. Beside him, Mutter straightened in her seat. No doubt she would find more ways to help the unfortunate woman sitting behind them.

Finally, the closing hymn was announced. The English translation must not have been as popular among Americans as Miss Ashford's voice was barely a whisper for the first verse and she didn't attempt to sing the others.

As the closing prayer was offered, dread filled Gunter. The worst part of church was yet to come. The visiting. In recent months, he'd made a game of seeing how many of the unmarried women he could avoid. They'd given him a wide berth the year after Pauline passed. Then, as if by invisible consent, they'd declared open season on him.

He waited for the pew to clear out. Three of the more curious gossips waited to meet Miss Ashford. She would learn that the German church wasn't all that different from the English church. He nodded at his friend Peter, who'd been absent the last several weeks as he courted a woman in Fredericksburg. Gunter hoped he would stay long enough for a conversation.

Greta tapped on his pant leg and reached her arms up, a silent request to be carried. Gunter swung his daughter up into his arms. Greta was growing so big there wouldn't be many of these moments left. Mutter led the way out of the pew. Miss Ashford managed to extract herself from the one behind them at the same time.

He overheard her thanking the Kerksiek sisters for sitting with her.

Reverend Ellerbrock approached from the front of the church. "Guten Morgen, Fräulein," he continued in German. "I had not heard we have a new congregant."

"Good morning, Reverend. I'm afraid I didn't understand a thing after 'Good morning.'"

"You are not German?" The reverend switched to heavily accented English.

"No, but your sermon on the Good Samaritan was lovely. I could tell from the others' faces, and I did find the reference in my Bible." Miss Ashford held up a small New Testament.

Since his mother had already exited the building, Gunter felt it his duty to make introductions. "Reverend Ellerbrock, this is Miss Ashford of Boston. She is visiting for a few days."

"My condolences on your intended's passing. I did not recognize you from Reverend Coolidge's photograph. You are much more beautiful in person."

Miss Ashford smiled tentatively and bowed her head.

"Reverend Coolidge asked me to perform the wedding. I am ever so sorry I could not. I trust you arrived in time for the funeral?"

"No." She covered her mouth with a gloved hand.

Reverend Ellerbrock turned to Gunter, a brow raised in question.

"*Später*." Gunter answered in one word. "Later." Now was not the time or the place to rehash the odd goings-on of Friday.

"If there is anything I can do…I did enjoy discussing theology with him."

"Thank you for allowing me to attend your church." Miss Ashford turned to leave.

"You are always welcome here."

Greta snuggled her head into Gunter's shoulder as he watched Miss Ashford exit the building.

Reverend Ellerbrock continued in his native tongue. "How did she miss the funeral?"

"They deliberately held it without her. Then they expected her to marry Mr. Fife the second she stepped foot in the church."

"I will never understand the American ways."

"Judging from Miss Ashford's reaction, I don't think she does either."

"Will she be with you long?"

"She is staying at Mother's boardinghouse. If all goes well, she should be on the train by tomorrow and back to Boston."

"That is good."

Precisely Gunter's thought.

The church was now empty, with the exception of Fräulein Schultz, who sidled up to Gunter. "Papa says we will eat at three. Mama wonders if your little girl will be coming too."

Gunter had forgotten about the dinner invitation he had not been able to wiggle out of. "Greta often takes a nap with her grandmother on Sunday afternoons."

Greta shifted in his arms as she pretended to sleep. Her dislike of Fräulein Schultz was the main reason Gunter avoided the woman. If he remarried, it would be to someone his daughter adored.

"What of your visitor?" Fräulein Schultz inclined her head toward the doorway. Gunter wasn't sure if it was curiosity or jealousy that spurred her question.

"Miss Ashford is boarding at my mother's."

"She could stay in the American hotel."

Gunter couldn't help frowning. The hotel on the other side of the river sat next to the brothel. He'd heard there wasn't much difference between the two buildings—not a place Gunter would send any woman, single or married, for that matter. "Mrs. Roberts suggested Miss Ashford would be more comfortable on this side of the river."

Fräulein Schultz narrowed her eyes. "She went to Austin with you yesterday."

"I am hired to be her driver." He'd only stretched the truth a bit. Reverend Coolidge had hired him; Miss Ashford had not offered to pay him. But considering the current state of her funds, he would not have taken pay anyway.

"She is very pretty, don't you think?"

It was the sort of a question that could get a man in trouble. Gunter shifted Greta in his arms. "I will see you at three, Fräulein."

If Gunter thought he had gotten away with having to deal with only one flirting Fräulein, he was sadly mistaken. Fräulein Volmer waited near the bottom of the steps. "I broke my mother's measuring cup this morning. Can you fix it?"

"I do not work on the Lord's day."

Fräulein Volmer reddened. "I didn't mean today, of course."

"I am sure your father can drop it by the smithy when he picks up the ladle you broke last week."

"Of course, Mr. Braunig." Fräulein Volmer had yet to move on to open invitations.

The churchyard had emptied too. Peter was nowhere in sight. There was a chance Kurt and his wife had asked Peter to dinner. After Gunter took Greta to the boardinghouse, he'd go see. Voices of the congregation of the English church singing "A Mighty Fortress Is Our God" carried from across the river. On Sunday, at least, the German and English sides of the town agreed.

9

"Oma says you have a visitor in the parlor." Greta stood in the doorway, hands politely clasped behind her back.

Amanda looked up from the hatbox, saved by the four-year-old. She had been getting up the nerve to go through Eb's things. "Do you know who it is?"

"No. He's not German. But I've seen him before."

Greta turned and hopped down the stairs. Amanda followed at a more sedate pace. To her surprise, there was not one but two men sitting in the parlor. They both rose from their seats as she entered.

The shorter man was the one who had been her supposed groom on Friday. The second wore some sort of badge indicating he was a peacekeeper. He'd also been at the church on Friday. If she were home in Boston, she would've had the butler throw them both out on their ears.

"Gentlemen, what a surprise." Amanda took a seat as far from them as possible.

The men looked at each other before retaking their seats. The shorter man spoke first. "Imagine my surprise when I discovered you were still in Grünlauf."

"Since we have not even been properly introduced, I imagine absolutely nothing about you. Now, if—" Amanda's attempt to end the conversation before it started was thwarted when the lawman stood.

"Pardon my friend's poor manners. I am Deputy Sheriff Jasper Roberts. And this is Mr. Fife."

"Am I in some sort of trouble?" Amanda held her hand to her heart, a move she had been taught rather than felt. The letter was still there. Eb hadn't mentioned the sheriff. Could she trust him? It would save time to not have to find some Ranger named after the first United States president.

"No, ma'am. We were only concerned because we heard you were still in town but did not come to church services today."

"I was unaware of any laws in Texas mandating church attendance. We did away with those types of laws in Massachusetts years ago." Amanda did her best to act like her friends.

"There is no law," said the deputy. "We were only concerned about your welfare."

"As you can see, I am quite well."

Mr. Fife cleared his throat. "I am wondering if you have reconsidered my offer of matrimony."

"I received no offer. I was, however, the victim of a wild assumption. How dare you think that because my fiancé was dead I would marry someone else?"

"Ebenezer often said you were only marrying him because you wanted to marry a preacher. I don't see how it makes any difference who it is if that is why you were marrying him."

Was that what Eb honestly believed? Amanda had wanted to marry a preacher, but she was particularly taken with Eb and thought he had been with her as well. "Pardon me. My understanding is you are not an ordained minister. So even if my purpose in marrying Reverend Coolidge was to become a preacher's wife, you do not fit the bill."

"Nevertheless, my offer remains open. With Reverend Coolidge gone, it is only a matter of time before I am appointed to his position."

"Texas can be very dangerous for a woman alone." A chill ran down Amanda's spine at the deputy's words. Was he threatening her?

Amanda stood. "I see we have nothing further to discuss."

It took the men a moment to rise to their feet.

"Good day, gentlemen." Amanda marched out of the room with her chin held high.

She made it to her room before she let any emotion out by screaming into her pillow. The nerve of those men! Why on earth would she marry Mr. Fife with his screechy voice? She had not known him for five minutes. He was one of those simpering, cowering men, the ones always giving their will to others, the type of chump Father would delight in her marrying as long as he was of the correct Boston set because a man like that would always bow and give way to her father.

And the deputy—something about him scared her. Not that he was powerful. More of the feeling she had around Emily's cousin Barbara, who retaliated and lorded over others. She would not tell him about Eb's note or show him the Bible.

Still full of fury, she removed the lid from the hatbox. As Mrs. Roberts said, it did not contain much. On top was the framed photo she sent Eb last Christmas. Below it, wrapped in a bit of twine, were the letters she had sent. Amanda had no reason to read them again. She had agonized over every word, trying to balance being a supportive fiancée with wanting to add some romance as her classmates did. She understood it was natural that those who were engaged should exchange some little notes of love. A lock of her hair tied in a pink ribbon peeked out from one of the letters.

Amanda had hoped he would make some sort of keepsake of it and it would've been on his person rather than tucked in the pages of a letter she sent over a year ago. She'd tried to write a properly romantic letter with her dorm mates' help. There was little to go on as Bradford's 2,500-volume library didn't stock poetry books by Byron or Keats. Poets who were reported to write stanza upon stanza of romantic things were not among the assigned readings. Obviously, she'd failed in her attempts at romance.

There were also several letters from Ebenezer's mother. Unlike hers, they were well worn, evidence of being read many times. Amanda turned over the packet. What was more interesting about his mother's letters? Perhaps Ebenezer didn't need to reread Amanda's letters because he carried the words in his heart.

She picked up a folded piece of paper and read it.

Dear mother,
I'm afraid I have made the most terrible of mistakes.
I should never have agreed to marry Miss Ashford.

Amanda dropped the letter back into the box and slammed the lid to hide it from her eyes. Questions she could never ask filled her mind. And after all this? Did Ebenezer not care for her at all?

He did. She knew he did. Perhaps, like her, he only had prewedding jitters. They were perfectly natural. And it didn't matter. She tucked the paper away, determined not to read the half-written letter since it was not addressed to her. She wasn't going to do anything to mar her memory of Ebenezer. After all, it was all she had left.

She missed Eb. He'd been a good friend, and she was looking forward to their relationship growing. The last eighteen months had been filled with many letters talking about their hopes and dreams for the church, the same as most of their conversations in the few weeks between when they met and when he proposed days before leaving for Texas. Amanda had chosen him carefully from among the prospective ministers at the nearby seminary. Ebenezer, while not handsome, was pleasant enough to look at. He had a strong orator's voice, necessary for any minister. Smaller voices were much more suited to clerical or even missionary work, where they talked with people one-on-one. Best of all, Ebenezer desired to go to the frontier rather than stay in an established town. There were many people on the frontier in need of help.

A popular topic of conversation at Bradford had been "What does love feel like?" Several of the engaged girls often compared their feelings with those written about in various novels. Some were sure they could not live without their soul mates; others, like Amanda, were more practical. One girl seemed more excited about her fiancé's place in New York society than she did about him. Amanda would be hard put to be excited about a man with an overbite and a prominent Adam's apple even if there were a quarter of a million reasons in the bank. A woman in the class above Amanda caused a great scandal when she eloped with the butcher's son. She claimed she simply couldn't live without him.

Amanda had lived without Ebenezer for eighteen months, yet, through their letters, they'd become of one mind in many things they discussed, and built a strong friendship. Eb said that a good marriage was built on a good friendship. For months, Amanda had been saying she loved Eb because it sounded weird to say she only liked him when all her friends who were engaged so often talked of love.

She wiped her tears. She must have loved him. Otherwise, why was she crying so much? But crying wasn't helping anything. Papa would tell her she needed to plan her life. It was how he ran everything—with a plan.

10

The bank was one of the few buildings built of brick on the American side of the river. Thick black bars protected the windows. If not for the sign, the building could be mistaken for the jail across the street. Amanda pushed open the door. Unlike the bank in Boston, no marble floors or expensive, heavy wooden furniture greeted her. Instead, an exquisite rug in reds and greens and blues covered the floor. Well-crafted, pale wood desks and counters gleamed under the light of brass lamps.

A single teller stood behind the barred counter. Amanda approached him, her steps firmer than she felt inside. She'd never withdrawn money from the bank before. Never had to, though she'd watched her father do it often enough.

"Excuse me, I would like to withdraw $200 from my account." Amanda was sure there was at least that much. A Wells Fargo special would not deliver a small amount of money. The balding man behind the counter peered over his glasses. "And you are?"

"Amanda Ashford."

"Do you have your account book?"

"I only arrived on Friday. I am here to pick it up and make a small withdrawal."

The man stepped away from the counter to a large cabinet filled with drawers. "Ashford, you say?"

"Yes, Amanda Ashford."

"I have no record of an account in your name."

"But you must. My father sent the funds two weeks ago."

"Your father is?"

"Mr. Quincy Charles Ashford II."

The man paused and turned, taking off his glasses. He studied Amanda from the top of her head to whatever he could see over the counter and back to her face. "I will need you to talk to the vice president. If you will have a seat, someone will be with you directly."

In a few moments, a man in a dark suit came out of one of three offices along the far wall. Amanda thought she'd seen him before. It must've been at the church. Yes, he had been one of the people waiting for her to marry Mr. Fife.

"Miss Ashford, if you will come with me."

Amanda followed him through the door marked M. Denton Vice President in gold lettering.

"May I give you my condolences for the premature death of your betrothed? I am Mr. Denton, vice president of the Grünlauf Bank. How can I help you?"

Not needing to introduce herself, Amanda sat in the chair in front of the desk. "I would like to withdraw $200 from the money my father deposited."

"That is quite impossible." Mr. Denton sat down behind the desk.

"Did my father not make a deposit in your bank?"

"Yes, quite a sizable one, but the money is not yours."

"Then whose is it?"

Mr. Denton opened a drawer and pulled out a black leather case. He opened it and withdrew several papers. "According to these papers, the money belongs to your husband."

"Reverend Coolidge is dead. I have no husband. Therefore, the money must be mine."

"These documents are quite clear, miss. The money is to be given to your husband after you have lived together as husband and wife for one month and not before."

"But I have no husband. I don't want all the money, just $200 so I may return home. Then you can return the rest of the funds to my father as he no doubt requested."

"Miss Ashford, I am not authorized to give you any of these funds, not even two bits."

Amanda held out her hand. "May I see those papers?"

Mr. Denton lifted his nose. "I doubt you would understand them."

"On the contrary, I am familiar with my father's contracts. He often had me look over them for errors." *Often* was stretching the truth. Last summer when Father's secretary had been sick for two weeks, Father brought everything home so Amanda could check for misspelled words—her father's one weakness.

"I meant you *might* not understand them."

"I am a graduate of Bradford College. I assure you I understand a basic contract."

"One of those little women's colleges they have in the East? No doubt good enough to turn out teachers and wives for ministers."

Condescending man! That may be the primary purpose of Bradford, but it also offered advanced classes in a variety of subjects. Amanda made a point of looking around the room. "I don't see your diploma. From which school did you graduate?"

Mr. Denton's face turned red, and he thrust the papers toward her. "Very well. Read for yourself. I cannot give you any money."

"Thank you." Amanda turned slightly away from the man to see the papers in better light. The majority of the document had been typewritten and was quite easy to read. Surprisingly, Ebenezer was not listed anywhere. Whenever the contract referred to him, he was listed as "the husband of Amanda Christine Ashford." The transfer of the money was to be completed thirty-two days after her nuptials. One stipulation struck her as odd: if she left her husband before 32 days, the entire amount would return to her father's possession. Obviously, Father felt she would not remain in Texas. And on the last page she found Father's signature and a handwritten note.

Mr. Coolidge,

There will be no further funds nor gifts or loans made to you for any reason as per our discussion the day after you engaged yourself to my daughter. I have granted you half of what would've been her normal dowry, which is more than she deserves. I haven't succeeded these past eighteen months to convince my daughter of the foolishness of such a match. You'll find she is headstrong. And you deserve what you get.

Quincy Charles Ashford II

P.S. In case of my demise, my son has also been informed that he is to never send funds to his sister, her spouse, or their posterity.

Father had been angrier than she knew about her refusal to marry a member of Boston or New York society. Still, half her dowry was more than she'd expected. She took a deep breath before looking up. "These papers are clear. I see why you cannot give me the funds. I find it odd that Reverend Coolidge is not mentioned by name."

Mr. Denton raised his brow. "Apparently, you understood those better than I thought you did. As you can see, I can only give the money to your husband after you have been married for thirty-two days."

"But I have no desire to wed now that my fiancé is dead. Surely you can extend me a loan of $200 so I may return to Boston."

"Our bank is not in the habit of loaning women of questionable character money for any reason."

Amanda pinched her leg through her dress to remind herself to keep calm. "In what way is my character questionable?"

"If your character was solid, your father would've deemed to give you some money."

"My father is upset because I chose to marry a poor minister rather than one of his society connections. Would Reverend Coolidge choose a bride whose reputation did not match his own?"

"Some ministers have married beneath them. How am I to know what Reverend Coolidge's motives were?"

If only it was acceptable to slap the man! Amanda fought for a calmness she did not feel. "Then what am I to do?"

"There are ways a woman can make money in Grünlauf." He counted off on his fingers. "Take in laundry, work at the stores if there's an opening. Work at the saloon. They always need fresh women. Or, in your case, marry someone."

Amanda pursed her lips. She suspected the last two options were much the same. Either way, she'd be selling herself. If her father knew Ebenezer was dead, he would, of course, want her to return to Boston with all haste. As Father was in Europe or on a ship headed there, reaching him was nearly impossible. Mr. Dewey, his secretary, should be authorized to extend funds in an emergency. "If I receive a communication from my father or his man of business authorizing a $200 withdrawal, will you order it?"

"I suppose we will have to."

"Where is the closest telegraph office?"

"They have one at the general store and post office."

"Thank you, Mr. Denton. I shall return." If a teacup had been balanced on her head, not a drop would have spilled as she crossed the carpeted room.

The soft chuckle of the bank's vice president followed her to the door.

<hr>

Clang. Clang.

Mutter claimed to work out her frustrations when making bread. Gunter poured out his on the anvil. He couldn't list the number of times he'd imagined his hammer hitting something other than the iron he formed. Seeing Mr. Fife and Jasper leave the boardinghouse yesterday afternoon set him on edge. They'd been to see Miss Ashford. Gunter understood why Mr. Fife might have called, but Jasper? If he was investigating Reverend Coolidge's death, Miss Ashford was the only person in town who couldn't have done it.

Clang. Clang.

He thought a sheriff's job was to keep the peace, not create problems. Yet, whenever the deputy was in town, things happened.

Clang.

More brawls at the bar.

Clang.

More lewd women on the street.

Clang.

More slurs against the German community.

Clang.

And more funerals.

Gunter paused. He'd never thought about Jasper and funerals before. Setting his hammer down, he reviewed the deaths of the last two years. Some of them were because of cholera, and there was the boy who was bitten by a snake. Several women died in childbirth, as well as the young and the aged. But the others, the healthy, the strong—had Jasper been in town for Pauline's funeral? Of course, the deputy hadn't attended as there had been only Germans at the service held for Gunter's wife and young son. He had been there afterward because Gunter asked him to investigate, suspecting arson. The fire had started outside the house, not in the kitchen, as first assumed.

Last Friday morning, Jasper had made some comments about fire and burning things down. Mutter always said Gunter's suspicion that the deputy knew who set his house on fire was grief talking. But what if it wasn't? This was a dangerous path, but Gunter's mind couldn't help following that path. The sheriff rarely came north of Dripping Springs. And from what Gunter had heard, people liked him enough. Gunter had only met him once. He was older than most lawmen he'd met. Grünlauf was Jasper's jurisdiction. It even had a jail, although Gunter couldn't remember anyone being held in it for longer than one night.

But who would kill a reverend? Even those not superstitious would shy away from murdering a man of the cloth. Gunter couldn't recall ever seeing Reverend Coolidge with the deputy. Of course, Gunter avoided the other side of town whenever possible. Thankfully, the river provided a natural barrier between the Germans and Americans. There were some Mexican families in the area, but they lived farther out. Gunter saw them even less.

In all his pondering, the iron had cooled too much. Gunter thrust the piece back onto the hot coals. He needed to stop seeing villains at every turn. After all, the sheriff was a good man; his deputy must be as well.

As for Miss Ashford, with a little bit of luck, she would be on the afternoon train to Dallas. Perhaps he should make her a horseshoe to hang above her door. If anyone needed luck, it was Miss Ashford.

⎯⎯◆⎯⎯

Gunter checked the time on the shelf clock. It was well past when Miss Ashford should've returned from the bank. The combination of heat from the sun and the forge seemed worse than usual. He longed to remove his shirt, plunge it deep in water, and put it back on as he so often did to cool himself. With his luck, Miss Ashford would appear as he undressed. He was determined to wait another half hour before looking for her. After all, she was not his responsibility.

He'd given her directions to find the smithy when he stopped by the boardinghouse at breakfast. Of course, he'd never known a woman who could follow a map or directions. Best go find her. She was probably wandering the streets of Grünlauf, looking for the livery.

Gunter removed his heavy leather apron and gloves and stepped out the door and into Miss Ashford, nearly knocking her off her feet. He reached out to steady her.

"Oh!" She placed her gloved hands on his arm. He was as aware of them as he was a heated coal.

Gunter stepped back out of her reach. "I expected you sooner."

"I was coming to find you." Miss Ashford fanned herself in the shade of the building. "I'm afraid withdrawing money was more difficult than I anticipated. I have sent a telegram to my father's secretary, asking for the funds to be released to me."

"Isn't it your money?"

"Apparently not." Miss Ashworth frowned but didn't offer any more information, which was unusual. From their earlier conversations, he had come to believe she told all she knew. This time, she held back.

Sweat ran down his forehead. Gunter turned his back to her and wiped his face the best he could with his bandanna, aware that Miss Ashford stared at him. He turned to face her, but as soon as their eyes met, she looked away. "When do you expect to hear from him?"

"I hope this evening. But more likely sometime tomorrow. I'm afraid I will not be able to leave until Wednesday. Will that inconvenience you too much?"

Being rid of her would not inconvenience him in the least. "I am sure I can arrange things."

"I apologize again for being such a burden." She stared at the fire in the forge. "Would you mind if I burned a paper in there?"

"Why?"

She pinched her lips. "Eb asked me to."

"It is just a paper?"

"A letter."

Gunter wondered if it was the letter from the box. "You may."

As Miss Ashford turned her back to him and fished the paper from the front of her dress, Gunter diverted his gaze to the collection of horseshoes hanging on the wall.

Miss Ashford advanced on the forge.

"Stop. I'll put it in. I don't want you to burn yourself or singe your dress." She wore a fancy one today with a bustle and short train.

She held the paper close to her. "You won't read it?"

"You can watch me and make sure it burns."

She extended the paper toward him. It shook like a leaf in a summer breeze. Gunter didn't try to analyze why she might be scared. It wasn't his place. He touched the paper to a hot coal, and it flamed up. In seconds, the yellow flames had consumed the note.

Miss Ashford watched until there was nothing but a few black ashes. "I'm going to return to the boardinghouse and see if I can help your mother in some way."

Her comment surprised him. He did not expect someone of her station to help around the boardinghouse. Probably all she was good for was dusting fine china, and there was none of that at the boardinghouse. "Will you tell Mother I'm working through the midday meal, but I will join her tonight?"

"Of course. Anything else?"

"No." *Go. Go far from here.* Gunter wasn't sure why he wished her away. Perhaps it was because she represented more danger than he had been in since the night his wife died. Among her most dangerous charms was that when she smiled, a man could forget everything else in his world. Too bad she wasn't German. Gunter shook his head. The last person in the world he needed to think about was a Boston socialite who'd just lost her fiancé.

11

The gap-toothed boy standing on the boardinghouse porch held out his hand expectantly. Reluctantly, Amanda removed a precious dime from its hiding place in her pocket and gave it to him. Funny. A week ago, a dime seemed like no money at all. The boy smiled and ran off in the direction of the river.

Amanda returned to the privacy of her room. Her father's secretary had taken far longer than she anticipated in answering. Three days of sitting and going through her things. At least now she could go home. Amanda sat down at the dressing table and opened the telegram.

Cannot reach Mr. Ashford STOP
No authorization STOP
Mr. Dewey

That was it? No explanation. Not even a hundred dollars?

The urge to scream in a very unladylike way filled Amanda. She picked up the pillow from the bed and yelled into the feathers. She'd worried the few words she'd sent had been too cryptic. Even then, the telegram had used fifteen of her precious dollars, one for each word she'd written. Perhaps Mr. Dewey hadn't understood the gravity of the situation.

Amanda took a fresh piece of paper from her trunk, writing and crossing out words, conscious that each word ate away at her savings.

> Preacher dead need return ticket STOP
> Release $100 dowry STOP
> Miss Ashford

It wasn't much different from last time, only she asked for less money, closer to the $116 price of the ticket, which would give her enough for meals, delays, and to pay the Braunigs.

She counted her money again. After another reading, she scribbled out "preacher" and replaced the word with "fiancé." Maybe Mr. Dewey hadn't understood that she'd never married.

She debated about putting on her nicer suit for the errand rather than a work dress. Unlike Monday, when she'd gone to the bank, there was no one to impress. She pinned her most serviceable straw hat in place and checked her appearance in the mirror. Two freckles had appeared on the end of her nose. They were not nearly as repulsive as Mother claimed, so there was no point in taking extra money to see if the mercantile carried a cream to remove them.

Greta played on the front porch. "Good afternoon, Miss Ashford. Where are you going?"

The rhymes they'd been practicing must be working. Greta's diction had improved over last week. "I am off to the mercantile and telegraph office."

"May I come?"

"Only if your grandmother agrees."

The child ran around the house only to return a moment later, shoulders slouched. "Oma says it is too far for me to go before I take a nap. Can you wait until later?"

"I am sorry, no. But perhaps we can go for a walk along the river when you wake up."

Greta perked up at the suggestion and waved at Amanda as she left.

No one stood in line at the telegraph office. Amanda sent her message, hoping the answer wouldn't take as long. There were two new dime novels in the mercantile. Amanda longed to purchase one. It would help the time pass ever so much quicker if she could read it away. But she restrained herself. After all, she had books of her own she could read, even if it was for the second or third time.

On her way to the bridge, she passed the bank as Mr. Denton exited. "Good day, Miss Ashford. Have you news?"

"Not yet. He is trying to reach my father in Europe."

"Very well. Let me know as soon as you hear anything." His self-satisfied smile irked her for a reason she couldn't place.

Amanda nodded and continued on her way. At the bridge, she looked back. Mr. Denton walked into the jail. Was there a problem at the bank? Was her money safe? Amanda shook her head. Eb's letter was making her imagine things that were not there.

⊰◈⊱

A cowboy who kept his face covered with a bandana appeared in the smithy's doorway. After getting Gunter's attention, he dropped a paper on the ground and left. It was another offer to buy the land Gunter's father had left him at far less than what it was worth.

Gunter hadn't been out to his land in days. After the fire, he'd moved back to his parents' house across from the boardinghouse, and the land sat waiting for him to make a decision. He'd sold all the cattle that year rather than rebuild, and the barn stood neglected and empty—a testament to the fact that his dream of raising anything other than Greta had died two years ago—not his dream. His father's dream. Vater wanted to become a cattleman, but a heart attack on Greta's second birthday had cut his father's plans short.

For three years, Gunter had divided his time between the smithy and the ranch, but the fire ended it all. Though he had no desire to keep the land, it galled him that someone wanted to buy him out for less than half its worth. Mutter and Vater had worked hard with the boardinghouse and smithy to purchase the land. Gunter dropped the offer in the forge. Mutter didn't want him to sell, so, regardless of the offer, the land would sit for another season.

Herr Volmer came for the repaired ladle and dropped off the damaged measuring cup. Neither of them mentioned Volmer's eligible daughter. Not expecting more customers, Gunter closed up shop. It was still early, so he stopped by the livery and collected his quarter horse, Riese. He thought the German word for giant fit the dark horse.

Making sure the animal had water, Gunter set off for the property that spread into the hills. Here and there, the fence had either been blown down or cut down. Although for what reason, Gunter wasn't sure, as there were no tracks. Near the west end of the property, where the land sloped into a dale, the fence was down again. Tracks from wagon wheels rutted the ground.

Someone was crossing his property. Gunter considered following the trail, but the chances of whoever had been driving through the area being more than one person was too great. Wisdom dictated he come back with reinforcements. If they found something, he'd contact the sheriff.

Maybe this time he would find something to convince Mutter to sell.

12

Condolences STOP
Mr. Dewey

One word? That was all her father's secretary could send in another early-morning telegram? Obviously, he understood her situation. The answer had come with remarkable speed, showing up before breakfast the next morning. Had Mr. Dewey even tried to contact her father in Europe?

Amanda faced the fear she'd been trying not to feel all week. However was she supposed to earn enough money to return home? Yesterday's telegram had taken more money than she'd counted on, putting a second-class ticket out of her reach. Then there was the boardinghouse bill. Mr. Braunig would balk at her taking an immigrant-class ticket to Boston, yet she had no other choice.

Amanda paced between her trunks. Maybe she could sell some of her dresses. She didn't need the white silk one. In Boston, it might fetch ten dollars or more in a resale shop. There was no point in taking much of what she'd brought back to Boston. She definitely would not be needing the serviceable dresses Emily helped her choose at her parents' house—dresses her mother considered hardly good enough for the staff. Then there were the linens. It was unimaginable to think of using them when they had been meant for her new home with Eb. No man in her parents' circle would want them in the house, with the possible exception of the lace doilies. Several of her coeds had gifted her with them, and she had the ones she'd made. Given the size of the homes in Grünlauf, she had more than enough for two or three houses.

Below, the bell rang for breakfast. Not wanting to be the last in the dining room, Amanda wrapped her still-braided hair into a bun. Serviceable clothing was ever so much easier to put on and walk in. Amanda wondered who exactly it was that created fashion. The straight skirts and bustles hindered movement so. At least it was possible to run in the dresses her mother wore at her age, as long as there was nothing on either side to catch the hoops.

Amanda rounded the corner into the dining room to see three empty seats. The other two would be for Mrs. Braunig and Greta if the little girl was here. Amanda was last again.

Herr Schellenberger raised his bushy eyebrows at her entrance but said nothing before saying what she assumed was a prayer in German. This time, no one reminded him that there was an English speaker in their midst. A quiet conversation started between the sisters on the other side of the table, again in German. Amanda ate her egg and toast in silence. Perhaps there was a boardinghouse on the other side of the river. Not that it mattered. She would sell her things and leave tomorrow as planned.

"Vat news do you have?" asked Mrs. Braunig the moment Amanda took a large bite of egg.

Amanda chewed so she could answer. "Not what I was hoping for. However, I think I could sell most of my things and raise the money that way."

Across the table, the sisters stopped talking. They looked at Amanda and shook their heads in unison. They whispered together. Amanda had no idea what they said, but she imagined the translation was along the lines of "Poor lost girl. She is so stupid."

Mrs. Braunig frowned. "I do not know of such things. Perhaps Mrs. Roberts could help you."

Amanda nodded her acknowledgment. The rest of the boarders finished their meals and scattered, leaving Herr Schellenberger, Greta, and Mrs. Braunig at the table with Amanda. Herr Schellenberger said something to Mrs. Braunig, all the while looking at Amanda. The only word she caught was *Fräulein*, confirming her suspicions that the conversation was about her. Herr Schellenberger left by way of the front door. Greta spoke in German to her grandmother. At Mrs. Braunig's nod, Greta turned to Amanda.

"Papa didn't eat breakfast this morning. Will you help me take it to him?"

"Of course."

As Amanda and Greta cleared the dishes and took them into the kitchen, Mrs. Braunig filled a basket with food. "This should be enough for my Gunter until suppertime."

Greta took the basket, but it threatened to drag on the floor. Amanda held out her hand. "Do you mind if I help you carry it?"

"Yes, please." Greta attempted to lift the basket higher. Amanda made a show of needing her help the same way Mrs. Smythe had when Amanda was little. The little girl giggled.

The morning was warmer than yesterday's yet not as unpleasant as she expected after her sleepless night. Greta led Amanda through an alley to a street parallel to the river. At the livery, Greta turned again. Behind the large barn, the land opened up to a field. The peculiar adobe building Gunter stopped at on Saturday morning to retrieve her box stood at the side of the field, guarded by two large trees, exactly as Gunter had described in his directions yesterday morning.

"That is Papa's forge." Greta pointed, pride evident in her voice. She let go of Amanda's hand and ran ahead. Not knowing if it was safe for the child to run into the blacksmith's domain, Amanda hurried as fast as she could.

"Papa!" Greta stood in the open double doors of the forge. As she was taught, she did not venture in.

Gunter set down his work and scooped up his daughter. Greta patted his cheek and pointed to Miss Ashford. "We brought you food."

"Thank you, Liebling." He set Greta down and retrieved the basket from Miss Ashford. "Thank you too. You saved my mother a trip out here. I'm afraid I started before sunrise."

"Do you often work so early in the morning?" asked Amanda.

"Yes, especially in the summer." Gunter led the way out of the forge and around the side of the building where a bench sat under a huge oak tree. "I assume you two ladies have already eaten?"

"Yes, Papa, Grandmother let me eat in the dining room with all the people. Herr Schellenberger said an extra-long prayer. He said he hoped that the English lady would go away."

Miss Ashford blushed and turned her head away. Gunter surmised Herr Schellenberger must have prayed in German and Miss Ashford had not been privy to every word.

Gunter dug around in the basket for a moment before addressing her. "Do you have any news today, Miss Ashford?"

"I received another telegram this morning. My father's secretary cannot authorize the release of the money from the bank. However, I am hoping to sell most of the things I don't need and raise enough money for a second-class ticket."

"I thought you had enough money for a second-class ticket." Gunter ate a boiled egg in one bite.

"I did before I sent the telegrams to Boston. And I still need to pay your mother. I've been staying there for a week, so don't tell me I owe nothing. I can read the sign. I also must owe you a bit for taking me to Austin and back."

"I will not charge you. It is the least I can do."

Amanda's cheeks burst into flame. Gunter guessed she wasn't used to being on the receiving end of charity.

"Thank you. You are sure I cannot pay?"

With his mouth full, he didn't answer immediately. "Yes, what day do you expect to leave?"

"Tomorrow, if I can find someone to purchase my things."

"What are you selling?"

"My dresses, linens, books." She'd save her pearl earrings and other jewelry for last.

"You'll have a tough time selling your fancy things here. In Austin too. Many people come to Texas to make a new life here. You are not the only woman with fine dresses to sell." Immigrants from Europe, people from the West looking for a fresh start, Northerners looking for land and opportunities. They all brought dreams with them. Some dreams were sold for wagons and horses, others for tools, and saddest of all was when they were sold for food. Secondhand goods, even of the highest quality, wouldn't fetch much.

"I thought you wanted me to leave."

"I do. Just don't think you'll be leaving here tomorrow." He continued to eat under the woman's glare.

"Well, I won't know unless I try. Might the general store purchase some of my things?"

"Maybe." Gunter watched his daughter follow a bug on the ground. Her braids were uneven. Mutter hadn't fixed them yet. Two years and he still hadn't mastered making braids each morning. If it were not for his mother feeding them, they would live off potatoes and porridge.

"Is there any other place?"

"What?"

"Another place to sell my things."

"Not in town." It wasn't his fault the honest answer was discouraging. "Sorry. I was watching Greta."

"She is adorable."

Greta continued to follow the bug's progress.

The silent moment—the shared wonder of watching a child—held a comfort to it that Gunter hadn't felt since his wife died.

"I should get back to work. The day will only get warmer. Will you walk Greta back for me?" Gunter looked at the empty basket. "And this too?"

Miss Ashford took the empty basket and held her hand out to Greta. "Can you help me find my way back?"

Greta hopped over to his knee. "Can we walk by the river?"

"Only if you keep Miss Ashford from falling in and stay far from the bank."

"I won't let her fall in, Papa." Greta grabbed Miss Ashford's free hand. "Let's see if we can find a *Frosch*, er, a frog."

Miss Ashford went off with a smile on her face and laughter in the air.

Gunter watched until they were out of sight, unsure of what he was seeing. A Boston socialite going to see frogs with a little German-American girl. Miss Ashford would have been a perfect preacher's wife. When Reverend Coolidge had spoken of her, Gunter doubted a woman would give up living in luxury to come to Texas. He'd only been ten when they'd emigrated, but he remembered traveling through Dresden and seeing castles. Mutter had told his sister stories of princesses and knights. Miss Ashford belonged among them, not the cowboys of Texas.

13

The bell of the mercantile rang overhead as it closed behind her. Amanda fumed. Eight dollars. That's all the shopkeeper had offered her for the entire contents of her trunk, sight unseen, plus another two dollars for the white dress she carried. It cost over ten times that much to make. The stingy proprietor informed her the fabric, fine stitching, beading, and lace on her clothes were simply not in demand in Grünlauf, Texas.

All the help-wanted postings on the wall next to the telegraph post office were for men. Ranchers, farmers, cowboys—nothing she understood or was capable of doing. Amanda asked the mercantile proprietor if he knew of a job and was met by laughter. He suggested the saloon. The lewd comment that followed confirmed her worst fears about the establishment. Amanda would sell all her clothes but never herself.

She wandered down the boardwalk. The diner next door wasn't even in need of a dishwasher. Boot- and hat-making were not skills she possessed. The school was closed for the summer and already had a permanent teacher. During her first year at Bradford, she'd taken a class that included spending several days at a nearby public school observing the teacher and ultimately taking over the class for one afternoon. Teaching was not the profession for her. Although she could deal with children one-on-one or in small groups, an entire classroom full terrified her. Besides, teaching meant she'd have to commit a year to living in Texas, which ran counter to her goal of going home.

Reaching the end of the boardwalk, Amanda turned back the way she came and saw Mrs. Roberts exit the bakery—a place Amanda hadn't sought work because her baking skills were negligible at best.

The widow smiled broadly. "Good morning, Miss Ashford. I am surprised to still see you here."

"Good morning, Mrs. Roberts. It seems that leaving Grünlauf is a bit more difficult than I expected."

"I just purchased a loaf of Mrs. Higgins's finest bread and was overcome by the urge to buy four of her eclairs a la creme. She only makes them on Fridays. If you are not expected anywhere, would you like to come and share them?"

Amanda sensed the invitation had little to do with food and was more of an offer to be a listening ear. She readily agreed and accompanied the widow to her white-framed house on the street immediately behind Main Street.

"Come in. We are alone. My stepson is off doing whatever he thinks the deputy should do and not raiding my larder."

"So, Deputy Roberts is not your son?" Amanda paused at the entrance to the kitchen.

Mrs. Roberts put her loaf of bread in her bread box and set the eclairs on a plate. "I have some nice lemonade—or would you prefer tea?"

Memories of iced lemonade on her mother's veranda tingled on Amanda's tongue. "I would love some lemonade."

"I'm afraid I don't have any ice. Oh, how I loved ice in my drinks in the summer—one thing I miss most about living in the North. They have those newfangled ice machines in Austin. Jasper says he's going to bring me some and never does. Sometimes Gunter brings some out to the mercantile, but that stingy proprietor sells it at triple the price." Mrs. Roberts filled two glasses and set them on the table. "I should go to Austin and purchase some myself. Have a seat."

Amanda sat, dozens of questions swirling in her mind.

"And, no, Jasper is my late husband's son by his first wife. Jasper was already a grown man of twenty-five when we married. A war widow, I was Mr. Roberts's third wife. Mr. Roberts and I had no children."

"Where did you live in the North?"

Mrs. Roberts sipped her lemonade. "I was born in Philadelphia. When I was nine, we moved to Texas. A year later, Father was among those killed at the Alamo. Mother received his land grant from the army and eventually remarried."

"You still miss ice after all those years?"

"Mama sent me back to Philadelphia to live with my grandparents and go to school. I married in the fall after my graduation. Mama always wanted me to come back to Texas. But then the war broke out…" Mrs. Roberts stopped to take a bite of her eclair. "After the war, I returned to take care of my mother. Mama died and Mr. Roberts proposed in the same week. Since he was willing to let me keep the money from my mama's land… I married him. Then he left me last year."

Amanda filtered which of the questions she could ask politely. "Do you have family around here?"

"All my family is buried somewhere. My babies are back in Philly, one husband is near Gettysburg. I don't like cold winters, so I figure I may as well stay here near Mr. Robert's grave. Although I've been rethinking that some lately."

"Why?"

"Two reasons. One, I'm tired of Jasper coming round as if he owns my place. He has perfectly good lodgings at the jailhouse. Two, there are far too many new graves in the cemetery. Your reverend isn't the only one to have died an untimely death."

"Eb mentioned that cholera took several lives last fall."

"That it did." Mrs. Roberts finished her eclair. "We expect something like that every couple of years. But the doctors are getting better at fixing up folks, so we should have fewer deaths, not more."

Amanda contemplated the widow's meaning. Hadn't Gunter said something like that about Eb's death? If it had been an unnatural death, someone would have noticed.

"So, why are you still in town?" Mrs. Roberts brought Amanda out of her thoughts.

Amanda related a condensed version of her attempt to purchase a ticket to leave.

"Gunter is right. No one around here needs your fancy things. You'd get a better price in Austin but still not enough for a first-class ticket. I'd fear for you riding the train alone in second class."

"Mr. Braunig says the same thing. I don't see I have an option but to travel second class."

"You could wire your father's secretary again."

"My father traveled to Europe with my mother and older brother. Even if Mr. Dewey manages to reach my father with a message, I don't know that my father would send money. He was so terribly angry that I wouldn't marry the sons of his friends. He considers it a waste that I would choose to be a minister's wife."

"Did he not approve of Reverend Coolidge?"

"Father believed Ebenezer only wanted my money. Father believes all religious leaders only want money to build up their churches."

"Some do. And some don't. And what did your mother think?"

"Mother was concerned that I was marrying into poverty. I told her it didn't matter. Ebenezer was so exceedingly kind. Definitely my favorite out of all the men attending the seminary."

Mrs. Roberts's brow furrowed. "So, did you decide to become a minister's wife before you met Reverend Coolidge?"

"I really wanted to be a missionary. Bradford has a tradition of sending so many missionaries to Africa and China and all over the world. The problem is that not as many men are willing to go on foreign missions. When Eb told me he was to come to Texas…" Amanda let her voice trail off. No one had ever asked her which came first, being a minister's wife or Eb. "We got along very well. And I enjoyed his kiss."

"He only kissed you once?"

Amanda knew she was blushing. "That's all that would be proper for a minister's wife."

"So, when you return to Boston, do you intend to find another minister to marry?"

"Perhaps. I know Ebenezer had friends who were in want of wives." Her parents would do their best to keep her as far away from them as possible.

"Not one of your father's society friends?"

"I haven't met one I like enough. And I would find it terribly boring to sit around all day as Mother does—meeting with friends and gossiping and perhaps once or twice a month doing something in the name of charity." Amanda made a face.

Mrs. Roberts laughed. "I understand. My grandmother was much the same way, as was my first husband. If you want to really live, I suggest you stay in Texas. There is always adventure here."

14

horse, two buggies, and a wagon stood in front of the boardinghouse. Gunter entered through the kitchen entrance to find his mother standing over her worktable chopping vegetables. Gunter wasn't expecting such a crowd on a Saturday afternoon.

Mutter moved the dinner to platters in the kitchen. "*Guten Abend*. You're back later than I expected. Dinner will be on in a few minutes. Go clean yourself up."

"I can take Greta home to eat. It looks like you have many more boarders."

"Boarders? No. Callers."

Greta flew in, allowing the screen door to slam behind her. "Papa! Everyone wants to marry Miss Ashford."

His mother dropped the vegetables into a pot of boiling water. "Ja, it seems so. And what did I tell you about listening to other people's conversations, little one?"

"I was playing outside like you said."

"Under the parlor window?"

"No, up in the tree, so I could see better."

Despite Gunter's own curiosity, he felt it was better to rein in his daughter. "It isn't good to spy on people."

"I wasn't spying. I'm not a soldier. Only soldiers spy. I was just looking."

Mutter coughed.

Gunter looked at the floor to keep from laughing. "Looking through the window to see what is going on is the same as spying. Listening to people talk or watching them when they don't know they are being watched is spying."

"Miss Ashford knows I'm there. She walked over to the window, looked straight at me, and commented on what strange little birds lived in Texas. But there were no birds in that tree with me. They all flew away."

Gunter didn't dare look at his mother, knowing he would burst into laughter. How was he to discipline his daughter when he was laughing so? "I believe you owe Miss Ashford an apology because you were still listening to her. And none of the men knew you were there."

"Three of the men proposed to her. Even Herr Unger. He's an old cur-mug-eon. And no one wants to marry him."

Mutter gasped and held her hand over her mouth. Her eyes twinkled. "Do you know what a curmudgeon is, *Liebling*?"

"No, but it is really bad because Frau Temming said it. And I didn't spy. I was sitting right here eating a cookie like you told me to."

"Still, it isn't nice to talk rudely about people and use words if you don't know what they mean."

Greta turned to her father. "What is a cur-mug-eon?"

The only description that came to Gunter's mind was Herr Unger. "Someone who is old and argues."

"How is calling Herr Unger a cur-mug-eon rude if it is the truth?"

Gunter took his daughter's hand in his. "Not all truthful words are kind. Above all, we should try to be kind."

"Oh. Miss Ashford told him no. And he left very angry. Was that rude?"

At the stove, his mother looked heavenward. "I'm going to go set dinner on the table now."

"We should help Oma." Gunter stood.

"Your hands are dirty. And I need to tell you about the other men."

"You shouldn't. That is gossiping. It is not kind to talk about people when they are not there."

"But Oma and Frau Temming do it all the time."

"Go help Oma while I wash up."

By the time Gunter arrived in the dining room, all the callers had left. Miss Ashford sat in the far corner of the table, her lips tightly pinched. Greta took the seat next to her instead of her normal seat. Herr Schellenberger and the Kerksiek sisters were already seated. Gunter sat next to Mutter and prayed his daughter wouldn't say anything inappropriate at the meal.

Miss Ashford set food on her plate, then on Greta's. Unlike most nights, the residents spoke in English.

Even Herr Schellenberger joined in. "I saw Herr Unger here. It is not right for a German man to marry an American."

"We are all Americans now." The Kerksiek sisters' unified answer was rewarded with silence from the butcher.

Miss Ashford ate less than half her meal. Occasionally, she leaned over and cut something for Greta. Though she answered questions politely, Miss Ashford did not join in the conversation. When the meal was over, she helped Greta take the dishes to the kitchen and left through the back door.

Gunter gave her a few moments before leaving under the guise of needing to use the outhouse.

Miss Ashford sat on the bench behind the house, the one his mother often used when shelling peas. "Is it customary in Texas for men to propose when they have only just met a woman?"

"No. Although I heard that thirty years ago, men lined up when a new woman came to town to propose to her."

"Is Grünlauf thirty years old?"

"No, I was talking about Austin. But the story is probably exaggerated."

"I received five proposals this afternoon from men who'd barely introduced themselves. And a sixth. Well, not exactly a proposal—yesterday afternoon from a man who didn't introduce himself at all when I was returning from Mrs. Robert's house." She looked away but not before he noticed her cheeks redden. Her way home would have led her past Grünlauf's most notorious saloon. Gunter could imagine exactly what type of proposal she'd received. "I suggest next time you go visit Mrs. Roberts, you take the long way around."

"I don't understand it. First people trying to marry me off to a man I've never met. Then today it seems every eligible man between the ages of sixteen and sixty-five showed up on the doorstep to propose to me in at least two different languages, maybe three."

Not every eligible man had come. There were many more, like himself, who wouldn't propose to a stranger. Gunter understood part of the men's reasoning. She was new, and she was beautiful—fair skin, dark hair, and dark eyes—but beauty alone did not explain why any of the German men would have proposed. Most Germans married other Germans from one of the nearby communities if they didn't find someone in Grünlauf.

"Do you think the terms of your father's gift to your future husband became common knowledge?"

"Unfortunately, that is the only explanation I can find. I am not one of those women who has men falling at her feet. A sum of $15,000 will attract all sorts of men."

That much? Around here, $15,000 could set up a family for life. Gunter sat down on the other end of the bench. He could have contradicted her, but that was not the point of this conversation.

Miss Ashford continued talking. "I am assuming from the number of women who talked to you at church on Sunday that there are other single females in Grünlauf."

"Quite a few."

"I always knew someone would marry me for Father's money. I didn't mind much. That is how it is in society. Being a preacher's wife, at least the money would be going to a worthy cause. I always hoped men would be somewhat less obvious about it than they were today."

"Men are also probably looking at you for your housekeeping skills."

Miss Ashford laughed. "Then they would be extremely disappointed. I have learned many home skills, but I have yet to make a loaf of bread that isn't dough in the middle or burned at the ends."

"If you would like, I could tell that information to Greta. She is learning to gossip. I'm sure by sundown the news will be all over town."

"That may help. It will remove all the men who want to save money by not going to the bakery."

"Do you know when you'll need a ride to Austin?"

"No. Mrs. Roberts and I are leaving for Austin early Monday morning. She wants some ice and said she would help me sell some of my things. With any luck, I will earn enough for a ticket."

"I wish you the best of luck, then."

"Thank you and, Mr. Braunig, this may sound silly … but thank you for not proposing." Miss Ashford nodded and went back into the house.

From what little he knew of her, Miss Ashford would make a wonderful mother for Greta. However, she didn't belong here, and proposing would only make her miserable. Still, part of Gunter desperately wished he could propose—and not for the money or half-baked bread.

15

ast night's rain left huge muddy puddles in the road. Mrs. Roberts steered her chaise to avoid most of the splashes. Still, Amanda was glad she'd draped the oilcloth over her skirt. They crested the hill above Austin. Like last Saturday, the streets were full of wagons, carriages, and cowboys on horses.

"We've arrived at the perfect time. All the shops are just opening," said Mrs. Roberts. "There's a dressmaker we should go see first. If anyone will be interested in your white gown, she will be."

Amanda missed the cobbled roads of Boston. Most Texas roads were nothing more than hard-packed earth. The stench was the same. Only instead of street cleaners, she imagined much of the dung was ground into the mud.

Mrs. Roberts turned down one street and up the next, finally stopping in front of a well-kept store displaying dresses in the window. A delicately lettered sign declared that dresses of quality were made here.

"Mind where you step." Mrs. Roberts pointed to the road before getting out.

Amanda had already learned that lesson. She pulled her travel bag from under her seat and stepped smartly to avoid catastrophe.

Mrs. Roberts led the way into the store. The proprietress came out from a back room. "Mrs. Roberts, what brings you to town this time of year?"

"Ice. And an errand. Mrs. Maple, I would like to introduce Miss Amanda Ashford, recently arrived from Boston to marry our preacher. Unfortunately, he went to see the good Lord the day before her arrival."

"Oh, my poor dear." Mrs. Maple threw her arms around Amanda as if they were old friends. "How may I help you?"

Amanda opened her bag. "I would like to sell my wedding dress."

Mrs. Maple's face fell. "I'm afraid I have a full inventory of those. Many a new bride discovers that her fancy white dress won't do her any good out here. Let me see it anyway."

Careful not to snag the lace, Amanda lifted the dress from its confines.

Mrs. Maple fingered the material. "Why, this is exceptionally fine silk. Imported?"

Amanda nodded.

Mrs. Maple took the dress over to the light of the window. "The stitching is by machine, of course. And finely done. The lace...I've never seen it's like. Was it imported from Europe?"

"No. I crocheted it from a pattern one of my college friends shared with me."

"I can try to sell the dress on consignment, but I doubt it will fetch over four or five dollars. Of which you will keep half. However..." Mrs. Maple rubbed the lace between her fingers and lifted it away from the dress. "If you're willing to take the lace off the dress, I would buy it from you for three dollars."

Amanda considered the offer. "The lace is worth more than the dress?"

"White may be all the rage in bridal fashion, but it isn't very practical for a place as dusty as Texas. But I can use white lace on anything. It would surprise you how many members of Austin Society have me regularly remake their old gowns. The addition of lace such as this would be much sought after."

The dress would still be useful. Emily had talked about dying her white graduation dress a robin's-egg blue if she didn't find a husband. Without the lace Amanda made specifically for her wedding, the gown would be quite fashionable as a day dress in Boston, especially if she dyed it. A pale shade of green would be lovely. "I will sell you the lace."

"Are you sure, dear?" asked Mrs. Roberts.

"Quite. I made that lace especially for my wedding. I could not wear it if I ever marry again. It would feel like wearing secondhand goods." Amanda turned to Mrs. Maple. "Do you have a pair of scissors? I'll start on removing it right away."

"The lace should not be cut off in haste. If you want, I can have one of my girls remove it. Then we can give the dress back to you. Do you have other errands in town?"

Mrs. Roberts answered. "Besides fetching ice, there were a couple of things I thought you would like to see. Will you have the dress ready by three?"

"You plan to stay in town all day?"

"I wouldn't want Miss Ashford to return to Boston thinking we are backward in our tastes. I thought I would show her the best Austin has to offer." The bit of Southern accent in Mrs. Roberts's voice vanished completely during the last sentence, her Northern roots showing.

"We will have it done by one o'clock in case the day grows too warm and you return early."

"We shall see you then." Mrs. Roberts ushered Amanda out the doors.

Amanda put her bag back under the seat. It still contained one of her serviceable dresses and a few lace doilies. "I'm afraid everyone was right. I'll never make enough money selling my things to purchase the train ticket."

Mrs. Roberts turned the horses down the street. "The rest of your things will likely not bring much more than the lace."

"There has to be another way I can earn money."

"How long did it take you to make the lace on your dress?" Mrs. Roberts turned down a street that was not as well kept as the last.

"Weeks and weeks. I only worked on it some evenings after I'd completed my studies."

"Do you have much more of the thread?"

"Perhaps enough for another yard or two of lace. I thought it would be nice to put on our baby's christening dress." Amanda felt her cheeks heat, even in the warm sun. Perhaps more than being married to a minister, she dreamed of being a mother.

"Mrs. Maple might buy more lace from you if you made it. We might even find proper thread here in Austin. Or you could order it from the Montgomery Ward mail-order catalog."

"The mail-order catalog didn't have thread as fine as I needed. I ordered some last fall. It made nice doilies, however." Amanda calculated the cost. If she could get the thread as cheap here in Austin as she did in Massachusetts, she might be able to make money. But it would still take months to have enough for train fare. By then, Father would be home. While he may still be determined not to send her any money, Mother would insist upon her returning home. She needed only enough money to make her way until mid-September.

They passed a saloon where women wearing nothing more than their foundation garments and silk robes leaned out of the upper windows. How many of them had turned to the profession due to a lack of funds? A shiver crawled up Amanda's spine. She needed to find a solution before things became that dire.

⟭◆⟬

As Gunter hammered out the dent in the Sherman's old teapot, he couldn't help but wonder how the damage had occurred. The story that it fell off the stove had to be fiction. Another customer entered the smithy.

"*Guten Tag*." Herr Unger sat down on the bench inside the door.

"Good day. What brings you here?"

Herr Unger produced a bent set of tongs. "I stepped on these this morning when they fell on the floor."

Gunter took the iron tongs from the older man and turned them over in his hands. Apparently, today was the day for outlandish tales of how kitchen implements came to be damaged. It took some force to bend them in such a way. And to the best of his knowledge, Herr Unger weighed less than the average elephant. "I can have these repaired by tomorrow morning. I will need to heat them up and, as you can see, I've already cooled my forge for the day."

"That will do." Herr Unger frowned as he spoke.

Gunter was unsure whether it was his natural disposition or if the man didn't want to make a second trip to the forge. "The charge will be two bits."

Herr Unger played with the brim of his hat. "Seems like a lot for just bending back some metal."

Gunter held up the tongs. "Fixing them will take some time."

"All you got to do is bend them back."

Curmudgeon. The word fit. "Well, I guess it depends if you want me to do the job properly." Curiosity overcame Gunter. "I understand you were at the boardinghouse on Saturday."

"Ja."

"To visit Miss Ashford?"

"Ja."

"I am surprised. I didn't think you called on people."

"Ja."

This was harder than Gunter thought it would be. "I understand she had several visitors."

"Too many."

"Miss Ashford said several men proposed to her. Were you one of them?"

"None of your business."

Gunter shrugged.

"For $5,000, she could be nicer."

Gunter sat on the bench across from Herr Unger. "Five thousand, you say?"

"Ja. Her dowry."

Interesting. If Herr Unger had heard $5,000, who started the rumor, and what about the other $10,000? "Who says she's worth $5,000?"

"Everyone."

"I have not heard such a thing."

"You never go to the store."

"I don't often have need to go to the *Kaufmännisch*."

"No. Grünlauf Mercantile."

The store on the English side of town explained the mix of nationalities. Few non-Germans went to the German dry-goods store. "Are you sure it is $5,000?"

"Ja. Mr. Fife is terribly upset that he will not get the $5,000."

"Did you hear this from Mr. Fife?"

"Nein."

Gunter leaned forward. "Who told you?"

Herr Unger grunted and stood. "Too many questions."

"Miss Ashford asked why all the proposals. I am trying to find out who started the story that she has a dowry of $5,000."

"Are you calling me an old gossip?"

"No. I am trying to help a lady."

Herr Unger pointed a bony finger at Gunter. "You want the money too?"

"No. I don't."

"Well, she'll have to marry one of us."

"How so?"

"Her papa isn't going to give her the money to return home. I heard that too."

So the good people of Grünlauf had some of the story correct. "I'm sure she can find a way to get the money."

"Doubt it. She tried to sell her fancy clothes at the mercantile."

That was hardly surprising. Any number of people would have witnessed Miss Ashford at the store. Gunter was more concerned about who'd told the part about the contract with the bank. If the real value was known, every cowboy within a fifty-mile radius would be lined up at his mother's boardinghouse. "Well, I'll have your tongs fixed by morning."

"Are you going to propose too?"

"No. I owe Pauline more than marrying again for money."

"Man does not live by bread alone."

Not the way Gunter read the scripture. He walked over to the workbench and set the tongs down. "Tomorrow morning."

Herr Unger grunted as he left.

16

Mrs. Roberts stopped the carriage beside a large stone church. Amanda recognized the name of the denomination Ebenezer belonged to.

"There's someone we should speak to here." Mrs. Roberts walked into the church without waiting for Amanda. She hurried to catch up. The sanctuary was much cooler than outside due to the thick stone walls and high ceiling. Mrs. Roberts walked up the side aisle and down a hallway. She rapped on the frame of an open door.

A man in a clerical collar with gray hair around his temples looked up from his desk. "Well, well, Mrs. Roberts. What brings you to town?"

"Reverend Whitesides, I wanted to introduce you to Miss Amanda Ashford."

The reverend stood and came around his desk. "Ashford…Ashford…Ashford. Why is that name familiar to me?"

"She was Reverend Coolidge's fiancée."

"Was? Did one of you call it off?" He led them out of the cramped office and into the sanctuary.

He didn't know? Words wouldn't form in Amanda's mouth.

Mrs. Roberts answered instead. "Reverend Coolidge died a week ago Thursday night. Were you not informed?"

Reverend Whitesides's eyes grew wide at Mrs. Roberts's proclamation. Clearly, he had not heard the news.

"Miss Ashford had the sad distinction of arriving in town minutes after the burial concluded. Now she is in a most tricky situation. She doesn't have enough money to return to Boston."

"Not enough money? How is that even possible? Coolidge told me many times that his fiancée's family was quite well off." The reverend addressed Mrs. Roberts as if Amanda wasn't in the room.

"Pardon my rudeness, Miss Ashford. I simply do not understand how I could not have been told of Reverend Coolidge's passing. And how have you come to have no money when Ebenezer promised $5,000 to the church after your marriage? If it was anyone other than Mrs. Roberts telling me the news, I would not believe a word of it."

Amanda found some comfort in knowing that Eb had planned to do good with his windfall. "I cannot tell you why you were not informed. No one told me until I arrived at the church, and they tried to force me to marry Mr. Fife."

The reverend's jaw dropped momentarily. "Please tell me you did not marry that odious man. I know I should not talk of any human being in such terms, but I'm sure the Lord will forgive me in the case of Mr. Fife. He has been thrown out of not one but three of our seminaries. My superiors thought that a year as an assistant in some remote town might do him some good."

"No, I did not marry him. How could I marry another man when I expected to marry Reverend Coolidge?"

The rotund reverend sat down heavily on the front pew, gesturing for the ladies to join him. "Mrs. Roberts, do you know why I was not informed?"

"I can only imagine." She raised an eyebrow, indicating that the reverend might imagine the same thing.

"I will write immediately to headquarters and let them know. Do you know if the family has been notified?"

Amanda and Mrs. Roberts shook their heads in unison.

"I'm afraid I didn't even think of it. I assumed someone took care of notifications before my arrival," said Amanda.

"I will write to Reverend Coolidge's mother this very afternoon. In fact, I may even send a telegram. As you know, Ebenezer Coolidge was most attentive to his mother and wrote to her every week. She will be upset to not have received last week's letter."

"Thank you very much. I'm not sure I would know what to say." What did one write to the people who would no longer be her in-laws about their son's death? Not a topic in any etiquette book she'd ever read.

The reverend turned his full attention to Amanda. "How can I help you?"

"I don't have the funds to return to Boston. My father has gone to Europe with the rest of my family and cannot be reached. The funds Eb spoke of are not available to me."

Mrs. Roberts leaned forward. "It's necessary that she purchase a first-class ticket. I cannot imagine a young lady such as Miss Ashford traveling alone so far in second class. Currently, she is still short of even that fare, and you'll agree we cannot have Reverend Coolidge's bride traveling in the immigrant car."

"Are you asking for $50? If it was only a matter of ten or maybe fifteen dollars, I could donate it to you. However, we just completed a funding drive to build a new school over the summer. I couldn't approach even our most generous of donors so soon to raise an additional forty."

Amanda tried to smile for a moment. There had been hope that she would actually be able to purchase a ticket today.

The minister must have seen her disappointment. "You went to college, did you not, Miss Ashford? We are in need of teachers."

"I have thought about being a teacher, but I do wish to return home before a year is up."

"Well, it was worth asking. We will have a shortage of teachers next fall at three of our schools. Perhaps you may know of some teachers you could recommend?" He looked more hopeful than he had a right to.

Still, she could not deny helping him. "If you give me the information, I can pass it on to Bradford College. I am sure there are still those who graduated with me who are looking for something."

"Thank you. That is much appreciated. Now, as for your situation, you say the reverend died a week ago?" He looked at Mrs. Roberts for confirmation.

"Yes, he was found Friday morning."

"We are over halfway through the month, and he has not received any of his pay yet." The reverend pulled a piece of paper from his pocket and scratched some numbers on it. "I can give you $13.50 from what Reverend Coolidge was owed. I should send it to his mother, but you obviously have the greater need."

It was enough money to pay for a second-class ticket all the way home. She wouldn't be comfortable, but she would make it.

"Anything else, ladies?"

"Do you know where I might find the Rangers?"

⟞⊶◆⊷⟝

Although Gunter made weekly deliveries to Grünlauf Mercantile, he rarely shopped there or anyplace else. Mutter always picked up any little thing he needed. The bell rang over Gunter's head as he entered the store. The proprietor left the counter and came over to where he stood.

"Anything wrong? I wasn't expecting a shipment on a Monday."

"No. I am only—" Gunter spied a doll on a top shelf. "Looking for a present for my little girl."

"Is it her birthday?"

Gunter counted in his head and was shocked to realize how soon Greta would turn five. "Not until September 2. I have a few weeks yet."

"We carry a fine selection of dolls."

"Do you mind if I just look?" A conversation about a doll he had no intention of purchasing wouldn't get him near any gossip about Miss Ashford.

The bell over the door rang again, and three women entered. The proprietor's smile grew as he turned to them. "Let me know if you need my help, Braunig."

Gunter had no choice but to look at the shelf of dolls while the proprietor rushed to wait on the women.

There were only four dolls, each different in price and quality. A porcelain one with blonde ringlets reminded him of Pauline when they first met. Greta had a fair amount of her father and wasn't so delicate in coloring as her mother. The least expensive doll's painted eyes seemed to be at cross purposes, her brown dress faded and dusty. Of course, it was the only one in his price range.

Gunter became aware of the women talking behind him.

"I don't blame her for not marrying Mr. Fife. What were those men thinking?"

"I heard she is still in town, but she doesn't come to church. Imagine she was going to marry our reverend."

"She could be going to the German church. It may be too hard to go to where he taught."

"Oh, Dorcus, you are too kind. What I don't understand is why she is still here."

"Haven't you heard? She doesn't have enough money to leave, and the money her father sent is only for her husband. She has to marry to get it. My brother proposed to her, and she turned him down flat. He didn't have a chance at the $5,000. Even told her she could leave after a month, just like the bank contract says."

"How did your brother hear about the contract?"

"I'm not sure. What about this calico? Too much green?"

The conversation turned entirely to dresses.

Since the women stood between him and the exit, he had little to do but look at the dolls.

"Did you find a doll yet?" The proprietor's voice startled Gunter.

"I'm not sure. I need to ask my mother's advice. Won't the faces break easily?"

"Not if your girl is careful. The blonde one was made in Germany."

"Ja. It reminds me of Greta's mother."

"Is Miss Ashford still in town?"

"Ja." Gunter suspected the proprietor already knew.

"When is she planning on leaving?"

After the lectures on gossip he'd given to Greta, Gunter carefully weighed his answers. "Soon."

"Half the men who come through that door want to get a chance to propose to her. Have you?"

"No."

"Why not? She isn't bad to look at, and $5,000 for living with her for a month could pay for finer dolls than I stock. Is she a harpy?"

"So much money?"

"Her rich father wants her married off no matter what. Wrote up a contract and is paying the husband. I guess he figures if she is married for a month, she is not his problem anymore."

"Unbelievable."

"Mr. Denton confirmed the story. Some lucky man is going to get her and all that cash. If I wasn't married…"

The banker? Gunter needed to get out of the store and think. "I'll let you know about the doll."

"Come back anytime."

Weren't bankers supposed to be discreet? And if he was spreading the $5,000 story, what was he intending to do with the other $10,000?

⬥

Amanda entered the office alone. The men standing and sitting about the austere room all had the same hardened look. Perhaps she should have allowed Mrs. Roberts to accompany her into the building.

Amanda lifted her chin. "I'm looking for a ranger named George Washington."

The man closest to her gestured with his head to a man behind him.

Amanda turned her attention to the man. "Are you George Washington?"

Several of the men chuckled. When they smiled, the rangers were not so scary.

"My mother named me George Washington, but I go by GW." He stuck out his hand. "GW Morgan."

"Amanda Ashford."

"Reverend Coolidge's fiancée?" His question calmed her nerves. If he knew Eb, he had to be the right person.

"I was."

"Was?"

Amanda looked around the room. "May I talk to you privately?"

"Boys?" Mr. Morgan did the same funny head-point thing his friend had, only this time, the men left. Most of them nodded at her on the way out.

"How can I help you?"

"Did you know Ebenezer is dead?"

Mr. Morgan pulled a chair out from behind a desk and gestured for Amanda to sit.

"When? How?"

"The day before I arrived, on June 19. I just missed his funeral. He left me a letter telling me to give this to you." Amanda opened her travel bag, took out the worn Bible, and handed it to the ranger.

"A Bible? Why a Bible?"

"I don't know. His letter was very specific that I get this Bible to you and not trust anyone."

"Do you have the letter?"

"He told me to burn it."

"What do you remember?"

Amanda closed her eyes and pictured the letter in her mind. "Amanda, if you are reading this, then I was not able to remove this letter from the box before our wedding night. I fear I have fallen victim to a fanciful imagination these last few weeks. Twice, I have had the most unusual dreams. Please go home as fast as you can. Something is terribly wrong. I do not wish you to know what I suspect as you will be in danger too. I pray I am wrong. Tell your father he was right. Money had more reason for my choices than sense. I am deeply sorry. Hurry home, my friend. Ebenezer. PS. Burn this letter immediately. Take the Bible to the Texas Rangers and give it to George Washington. I met him and trust him. ONLY the Rangers." She opened her eyes. "That is every word."

"You memorized it?"

"Yes. I thought I should."

"Nothing more? Nothing about his dreams? Other letters?"

"No. I left Boston on June 12. The last letter I had from Eb was in May."

"Did anyone say how he died?"

"Only that he died in his sleep. I don't think the deputy sheriff thinks he was murdered."

"What is the deputy's name?

"Jasper Roberts."

"Out in Greenleaf?"

"Grünlauf." Her correction came automatically.

"That is right." He flipped through the pages of the Bible. "The reverend knows I already have a Bible. This is an odd gift."

"I thought it odd as well. It was inside a locked strongbox meant for my wedding gift…"

Mr. Morgan frowned. "Perhaps he left a clue. Are you returning to Boston soon?"

"As soon as I am able. There have been a few problems." Amanda let her voice trail off.

"I'll look at the Bible. I have a long train ride up north. My brother is a sheriff and has asked for my help."

"Thank you." Amanda rose to leave.

"Miss Ashford, if we happen to meet again, pretend you don't know me unless I recognize you first."

Amanda nodded at the strange request.

Mrs. Roberts waited outside in the carriage. "There you are. Did you finish your errand? I got our ice. It was so convenient that the icehouse was only three doors down."

"Yes, I did. Thank you." It may have been a mistake for Mrs. Roberts to even know she'd visited the rangers. The less Amanda said, the better.

"I've been thinking. I have a little money saved up. If I loan you the other forty dollars, will you pay me back when you get home?"

"Of course I will. I may have to wait for my parents to return…"

"Then let's hurry back to Grünlauf. You have some packing to do."

17

The early-morning work hours were hardest on his little one. Unable to leave her alone in the house, Gunter carried her to the boardinghouse and tapped on the door with his boot. Miss Ashford held open the kitchen door for them. Gunter carried Greta inside to his mother's bedroom.

Miss Ashford remained in the back hallway, her long hair in a single braid, her feet bare. Gunter slowed his steps. He hadn't seen a woman with her hair down or in bare feet since his wife…Gunter focused on her face.

"Can we talk? Privately?"

Gunter held open the kitchen door and led her around the house to the bench.

Miss Ashford sat trying to hide her pink toes under her skirt. "I have the money for the train."

"How?"

"The minister in Austin gave me Eb's back pay, I sold the lace off my white dress, and Mrs. Roberts has loaned me the remainder."

"When do you plan on leaving?"

"As soon as is convenient. When could you take me to Austin?"

"Do you have your ticket already?"

"No. I didn't have all my money with me yesterday."

Gunter wished he could drop today's obligations and take her. However, two of the bigger ranchers in the area had contracted him to shoe their horses. He couldn't let the jobs go. "I'm driving in on Friday morning to pick up some shipments for the kaufmännisch and the mercantile. Can you wait a few more days?"

"Friday will be fine. I don't have anything to rush back for. I'm hoping to repack my trunks so there's only one. There are many things I brought that I don't need. Perhaps your mother could help me find people who need them—*need*, not who might purchase them."

"I'll ask."

"Thank you so much, Mr. Braunig. Your kindness has made all the difference. I never expected to be in—" She waved her arm to encompass the world of trouble she'd found herself in.

"Life gives us things we don't expect."

Miss Ashford laughed. "I know what you mean. It doesn't quite ever go according to plan. My old dorm mom would tell us to look for brighter tomorrows. I'm not sure how that will be. I'm not expecting a very bright future at this point."

"Do you still think returning to Boston is for the best?"

"I don't know what I would do here. Other than making lace, I have no marketable skills. I could teach, but that means a year contract and moving to another place. I may not look it, but I am a coward at heart. I don't want to go through more changes."

Gunter looked down at his hands. "Did you have more proposals?"

"Greta must have spread that gossip about my cooking. Only one, but he wasn't serious. But at least he took off his hat while he proposed. I'm not exactly sure of his age, but there wasn't much hair under his hat, and he was missing enough teeth that it was hard to understand him."

Gunter returned her smile. "Was he wearing a faded red shirt?"

She nodded.

"He's been around these parts for more than forty years. Takes good care of his horse. You could do worse."

"I am better off not marrying in haste."

"What are you going to do until you leave?"

"Other than dodge proposals, I'm not sure. I'm reading a book with Greta. I promised her we would finish it, so I guess I will crochet lace, help your mother, and read."

"My wife used to read to both of our children." Gunter tried to push down the emotion in his voice.

Miss Ashford laid her ungloved hand on his arm. "I'm sorry. I did not realize you lost a child."

"A little boy."

"I used to say I'm sorry and not be sure what I meant. I know better now. There really isn't anything anyone can say, is there?"

"No. I tried to take some comfort in knowing that people care enough to try to say something."

"When I return to Boston, no one will know I was almost a widow. A few of my college friends, perhaps, but no one in particular. Mother and Father didn't tell many people where I was going or why. Most of their friends probably assume I went to Europe with my family. In a way, I am glad I had the time here to feel his death."

"Will it be a problem being in Boston alone?" Gunter needed to stop his questions, but her last comment made him want to gather her in his arms and give her comfort the same way he had in the back of the wagon. She was wrong. She wasn't a coward.

"No, not at all. I'll probably spend my days corresponding with friends and reading books at the library. When my mother and father get back, there'll be more than enough time for balls and outings and whatever else they suggest. I'd rather spend some time quietly. Mrs. Maple said I have a talent for making lace. Perhaps I will learn some new patterns. I won't need it for myself, but it will make good wedding gifts for my friends."

"None for you?"

"Why should I? Whoever marries me won't care what I look like as long as his bank account receives the proper influx of cash. I understand now that Eb was marrying me for my money. It hurts to realize even a minister wanted my bank account more than me." She wiped away a tear. "Although, I was marrying him because he was a minister, which is kind of the same." She pinched her lips. She looked across the yard.

"You could marry for love."

"Is that why you married?"

"Ja."

"You are a truly fortunate person. I see why her death still affects you. If possible, I wish for you to find something like that again." She put her hand to her mouth. "Oh, that was inappropriate. Greta told me you wanted a wife…"

Gunter chuckled, the sound bubbling inside him and becoming a full laugh. "What am I going to do with my daughter?"

"I don't know." The response to his question hadn't come from Miss Ashford.

Gunter and Ashford turned toward the little voice. Miss Ashford concealed a giggle.

Greta stood with her hands on both hips. "What are you going to do with me?"

Gunter held open his arms for Greta to run into. "Hug you."

18

Greta tossed a stick into the creek and watched it twirl and bounce off a few rocks. The water wasn't that deep. "I wish we could go in."

"Your grandmother told us to stay out of the river." There had also been a mention of snakes, something Amanda would rather not think about.

"Oma never wants me to have fun." Greta tossed a pebble in the water.

"I'm quite sure your grandma wants you to have fun but be safe at the same time. So, what were you going to show me?"

"It's this way." Greta pointed up the street. They continued to walk along the bank. Here and there, flowers grew in the shade, bright yellows mingling with pinks and whites. On either side of the creek, barbed wire stretched between posts protecting fields from wandering cattle and perhaps people.

Greta pointed to a blackened chimney standing not one hundred yards from the brook. If Amanda had known this was Greta's destination, she would never have allowed the child to bring her here. Wordlessly, Greta left the shade of the trees along the brook and walked in the direction of the chimney, Amanda hurrying after her.

As they drew closer, foundation stones and the crumbling chimney marked where the house once stood. Beyond the house stood a barn. Amanda didn't believe in hauntings, but the barn tried to change her mind. "We should leave."

Greta paid no attention. "This is the house where we used to live before the fire, the fire that killed Mama and Hans. Papa carried me out, then he went back in. I was afraid he wasn't going to come out."

As nervous as being there made her feel, Amanda knew she needed to let the child finish.

"Men came and tried to put out the fire. One of them helped Papa out. He was burning too. They dumped water on him. Mama and Hans never came out."

"Do you visit here often?"

"No. I'm not supposed to come up the creek this far alone. I like seeing where we lived. We were happy here."

"Aren't you happy in town?"

"I don't have a mama anymore."

"Do you want one?" Amanda knew she trod on dangerous ground.

"I want a pretty one like you. You smell pretty, like flowers."

"Well, thank you very much. Do you think we should turn back?"

"Please don't tell Papa where we've been. It always makes him sad when I ask him to come out here."

"I won't." Amanda made the promise knowing full well that if Gunter asked her directly, she would have no choice but to tell the truth. Amanda turned to look back at the house. Something moved in the barn. It had to be the wind. She hurried Greta toward the path near the creek. Once they reached the shade of the trees, Amanda looked back again.

She could clearly see the outline of a man through the loft window of the barn. Someone had been watching them. She might need to tell Gunter about their trip after all.

Soon the town came back into view. As the way into town was somewhat easier, Amanda decided they must be traversing slightly downhill.

"Was your father a farmer?"

"We had cows. He was also a blacksmith. Papa can build anything."

When they returned to the boardinghouse, Amanda had an idea to distract them both from the adventure to the house. "How would you like to smell like flowers?"

"Me? Smell like flowers?"

"Yes, I can give you a touch of my perfume."

"What's that?"

"It's something ladies wear to make them smell good."

"Fräulein Schulz needs some."

Amanda wasn't sure if she should correct Greta or not. "That is something for Fräulein Schultz to decide for herself. Each woman needs to choose her own perfume."

"Can I choose yours? Then I will smell all pretty for Papa."

They climbed the stairs to find Amanda's door ajar. She was sure she'd closed and locked it that morning. As she pushed it open, it caught on one of her nicest boots. Shredded scraps of gauzy white fabric rustled like fallen leaves teased by the breeze coming through the open window. Her wedding veil and every article of clothing, books, linens, doilies, and shoes lay strewn from one end of the room to the other.

"You have a very messy room."

"I did not do this. Someone's been in here and gone through my trunks," Amanda picked up her best corset from the floor near the door and tossed it onto the bed. "We need to go talk to your grandma."

Amanda hurried back downstairs with Greta trailing behind. They found Mrs. Braunig in the kitchen. "Do you know if anyone has been in my room?"

"I just returned from the kaufmännisch."

"Someone's pulled everything out of my trunks and strewn my belongings all over my room."

"Is anything missing?"

"I don't know. I didn't want to go through it yet. Do I need to send for the police? I mean, the sheriff?"

Mrs. Braunig put a hand on her hip. "The deputy will do you no good. Still, you should tell him if something was stolen. Greta, help me make strudel while Miss Ashford cleans her room."

"But she was going to give me something to make me smell like flowers. It's called par foam."

"Perfume. However, I need to find it." Amanda hadn't smelled it when she entered the room, so she doubted the bottle was broken. She retraced her steps upstairs. Last night, she'd separated the things that could stay in Grünlauf from the things that needed to return to Boston. Now she'd have to start all over. Whoever had been in the room had tossed every single stocking and handkerchief.

Money. The money for the ticket. Was it still there?

She'd put all her money in a bag inside the locked drawer of her small trunk. In between the bed and the window, the trunk stood on its end, the locked drawer hanging open and empty.

Gone.

Everything she needed for her trip. Well, not quite everything. A handful of the dimes remained. Amanda collapsed on the bed between her bustle and a pair of stockings. Why? Why did this have to happen now?

❖

"Papa! Papa!" Greta slid to a stop just inside the door to the smithy.

Gunter's first impulse was to chastise his daughter, but before he could say anything, she held out a piece of paper to him.

"Oma sent this."

Gunter read through his mother's hastily scribbled words. "Is Miss Ashford well?"

"She was crying. And her room is very messy."

"Oma's note says I'm to find the sheriff. What happened?"

"You told me not to listen."

Another time, Gunter might have laughed. "I'm not asking you to listen; I'm asking you to tell me what you know."

"All of Miss Ashford's money was stolen."

"Stolen?"

Greta's head bobbed up and down.

"Oma wants me to get the deputy sheriff. I'll take you back to the boardinghouse first."

"Papa? I'm sorry I ran in here. I know I'm not supposed to."

Gunter hugged his daughter. "You stopped before you were in any danger. Sit here while I close things up for the day."

He'd completed his farrier work an hour ago, and his forge had cooled. They walked as fast as Greta's little legs would carry her and entered through the kitchen door.

"Oma, I brought Papa."

"Very good, Liebling. Go see if Miss Ashford needs any help, but don't touch anything unless she asks."

Before going upstairs, Greta looked at both of them as if she understood she was being banished from the area.

"Someone came in while I was at the market. They dumped all of Miss Ashford's things. She says her money is gone except for some coins." Mutter told him no more than Greta had. "The Kerksiek sisters had walked to the post office, so no one was here."

More was gone than Miss Ashford's money. Any hope she had of leaving Grünlauf was also gone. Gunter doubted Mrs. Roberts could afford to loan Miss Ashford the entirety of a ticket.

Gunter turned to the stairs, but his mother's voice stopped him. "Not now, son. Go fetch the deputy first, like she asked."

Gunter nodded, though they both knew that contacting the deputy would do little to recover the lost funds.

He found Jasper in the jailhouse with his feet up on the desk.

"Miss Ashford's room was vandalized and her money stolen."

"I thought your mother put locks on her doors."

"She does. I am reporting a burglary."

Jasper eased his legs down from the desk as if it were the most difficult thing he had done all day. "What am I supposed to do about it?"

Gunter clenched his jaw. "Miss Ashford would like you to come investigate and preferably find the culprit."

Jasper stood and made a point of checking his gun. He took his hat off the desk and placed it on his head. "Not for me to disappoint the lady."

They walked down the street at a pace not much faster than the Kerksiek sisters on a Sunday stroll. Gunter squelched an inclination to hurry the deputy along. He knew from experience that anything less than a tornado had little effect on the speed at which Jasper Roberts moved. At the boardinghouse, Jasper let himself in and headed upstairs.

Gunter followed. Miss Ashford didn't need the deputy in her room if she was alone.

"No need to follow, Braunig."

Gunter resisted swearing, knowing that the words were perhaps the only German Jasper knew.

Outside the door, the Kerksiek sisters stood commenting on the tragedy. Gunter didn't need to worry about Miss Ashford being alone with the deputy.

"Move aside." The deputy shoved his way into the room. Gunter was tall enough that he could easily see over the sisters' bobbing heads. Greta had not exaggerated. Whoever had broken in had not been subtle about it. It looked as if they had taken every single one of Miss Ashford's things and spread them to each corner of the room.

"Why are you cleaning up?" demanded the sheriff's deputy.

Miss Ashford spun around, arms full of clothes, eyes narrowed. "Because I'm trying to determine what is missing."

"So what is missing?"

"I had $120. I found a few dimes, but everything is strewn about, so it's hard to tell what else they have taken."

"Was your room locked when you left it?"

Miss Ashford dumped the clothes she was holding into a trunk. "I believe so."

"Believe so?"

"Yes. It is my habit to lock my room when I leave the boardinghouse."

"Habit? You've only been here a few days. You may have forgotten."

"Deputy Roberts, I lived at college for four years, and I assure you I am in the habit of locking my door when I leave."

"You could have left it open?"

"I could have done a lot of things, like climbing down that tree." She pointed out the window. "However, it is most likely I left my door locked. Just as it is likely I haven't been climbing trees!"

Jasper walked over to the door and inspected the knob. "It doesn't seem to be broke, so no one used force to enter. It could have been anyone—a woman with a hatpin."

Miss Ashford put her hands on her hips. "A woman with a hatpin? I suppose a woman with a hatpin had the strength to upend my trunks too."

"She had a friend." The deputy looked at the Kerksiek sisters.

"Are you insinuating the Kerksiek sisters did this? They would have difficulty lifting a large bucket between them, let alone my trunk. No offense, Miss Kerksiek and Miss Kerksiek."

"None taken." The sisters answered in unison.

"I was pointing out that it could be anyone. "

"It can't be just anyone because there's probably only one person in town who's had a windfall of $120. Go find them. I need my money back."

"Investigating isn't that easy, ma'am," Jasper said ma'am with a certain amount of snideness that had even Miss Ashford balling her fists at her side. "You're cleaning up all the clues."

"I'm sure there wasn't a clue in any of my petticoats. Either you want me to tell you what's missing or you want me to not clean up. Which is it?"

Maybe it was the size difference, but watching Miss Ashford reminded Gunter of Frau Temming's little terror that chased all the big dogs in town. Reverend Ellerbrock's shepherd wouldn't go near the little ball of barking fur.

"If you find anything that's not yours in all this mess, it could be a clue and you should report it immediately."

Miss Ashford didn't answer. She was too busy staring at the ceiling.

Jasper turned to leave the room and had the nerve to tip his hat, which he had forgotten to remove, as he passed the Kerksiek sisters.

Everyone stood in their places until they heard the front door close.

Miss Ashford growled. "The nerve of that man. I hope you didn't vote for him."

"He's a deputy sheriff. No one voted for him. He was appointed."

"Then I hope you didn't vote for the man who appointed him."

"I did not." Only because, like all the German men in town, they'd been denied entrance to the school on the day of the vote.

"Good. If women could vote, men like him wouldn't be in positions of power." Miss Ashford stood with her hands on her hips. "Unfortunately, Mr. Braunig, it looks like I will not be leaving tomorrow. I hope I can scrape up enough dimes to pay your mother."

"If you can't, I'm sure we can work something out."

Miss Ashford appeared at dinnertime looking composed. Herr Schellenberger said the prayer in English this time. The residents of the boardinghouse made polite conversation.

Miss Ashford cleared her throat. "I know you are all wanting to ask. The bandit, or whatever you want to call him, left with all but $18.50 in dimes. None of my clothes are missing, although a few are ripped beyond repair. As for my other personal effects, I can find nothing missing. The hatbox containing the reverend's personal effects has been smashed, and the contents are gone. I had barely started to look through his things. I suppose I will have to ask Mrs. Roberts."

Condolences were given all around. The sisters offered to help repair what clothing they could.

"Mr. Braunig, will you accompany me to the jailhouse after supper? I would like to amend my original statement of loss. Whoever was in my room wanted Ebenezer's things."

"I'd be happy to."

"Can I go too, Papa?"

"Not this time, Liebling."

Everyone seemed to spend the rest of the meal avoiding the topic of the theft.

Immediately after the meal, Gunter left with Miss Ashford. Near the bridge, she stopped and looked around. "They did not find my jewelry. I don't know if it will bring me enough for a new ticket or not. I'm afraid to take it into town for fear I might lose it too."

"While in Austin tomorrow, would you like me to ask the jewelers to see what you might get for it?"

"My parents will have me locked away for selling these things, but I know of no other way. The pearl earrings were my grandmother's. If she was alive, she'd yell at me. However, I have run out of all other avenues. But if it is not enough to buy me at least a second-class ticket, don't sell any of it."

"You have my word."

They crossed the bridge on a predictably fruitless trip. Jasper sat at his desk, no more interested in finding Amanda's things than in finding the arsonist who'd killed Gunter's wife.

B oth Emily and the dorm matron at Bradford were fond of quoting a long-dead ancestor. "Your problems will look smaller in the sunshine. Problems, like shadows, are always bigger at dusk."

They'd lied. Morning did not make anything look better. Things still looked quite impossible. After giving the jewelry to Gunter last night, Amanda spent most of the night tossing and turning, worrying about what her parents would say. Was it still legal in Massachusetts to put somebody in the stocks? If so, her parents would have a set erected in the center of Boston Common and hand out rotten fruits and vegetables to every passerby. And that would just be the start. They would fire the upstairs maid and have Amanda do her work instead. Not that Amanda had anything against doing hard work; she'd already offered to do the same for Mrs. Braunig, who said she really didn't need her help, even though her hand had healed.

She needed to visit Mrs. Roberts. The woman deserved to know that the money she had loaned Amanda was gone. Jasper said he would consult his mother about the missing items in the hatbox. Amanda had remembered that her photo and one of Ebenezer's parents had been in there as well. Who would want that?

Not wanting to talk to anyone, she deliberately missed breakfast. The dining room was empty by the time she made her way downstairs.

Greta sat on the porch. "There you are! I waited and waited. Oma told me I couldn't go upstairs and bother you. I wasn't going to bother you, though. I was going to bring you this." Greta pulled a flattened slice of bread and butter from the pocket of her pinafore. It had likely looked edible when it had first gone into her pocket.

Mrs. Braunig came outside. "Miss Ashford, I told Greta I'd save you a piece of bread and a boiled egg. Greta, go put that with the slop bin so Herr Unger can feed it to his pigs.

"Yes, Oma." Greta ran around the house.

"Come, you should eat, even if you do not want to be around people," said Mrs. Braunig. "Gunter has already left for town. He'd forgotten that today was your American Independence Day and there would be crowds of people in Austin, celebrating the holiday."

Amanda had forgotten as well. "Is there a parade?"

"Not in Grünlauf. Most of the families on the other side of the river go to Austin for the celebration."

The parade was one of her favorite things as a child. Once, there had been an old man, at least one hundred years old, who was one of the last living men to fight in the Revolution. Father had tears in his eyes when the man passed them in a carriage decorated with red-white-and-blue bunting. As she grew older, she appreciated the concerts more than the picnics. Ice cream, however, was a tradition she'd miss. Mrs. Roberts hadn't brought back enough ice to make any.

"We will have a picnic at the church tonight to celebrate."

"Really? I didn't think you would."

"Ve are proud to be in America. But we have learned that people on the other side of the river don't understand that we can be American and German at the same time, so it is best to celebrate quietly."

Amanda was not sure what to say, so she smiled.

"You are welcome to come with us. We only have one rule—no sauerkraut." Mrs. Braunig laughed.

"I would love to go. I need to go tell Mrs. Roberts about the burglary, then I will come back and help."

"I have apples. Can you make pies?"

"Yes, that is something I do well."

Greta clapped her hands. "I love apple pie almost as much as strudel."

Amanda walked to Mrs. Roberts's home, careful to take the longer route that kept her far from the saloon. Most of the businesses on the American side of the river flew small flags or were decorated with bunting. Mrs. Roberts had bunting wrapped along her board rail. Amanda knocked on the door.

The deputy answered.

"Is Mrs. Roberts in?"

The man pushed past her. "As ornery as ever."

"Come in, Amanda." Mrs. Roberts called from the kitchen. "Pay him no mind."

Amanda found her there, chipping at a block of ice. "Did he tell you about the burglary?"

"In his own way. Wanted to know what I kept from the reverend's house. Apparently, a Bible is missing."

Amanda gulped. "So you know someone went through everything in my room and took my train ticket money?"

"What?" Mrs. Roberts stopped chipping ice.

"Someone took all of Eb's things from the hatbox, and they took my money. I'll still pay you back for the loan."

"I'm not worried about the money, dear. Was there a Bible in the hatbox? I don't remember one."

"No, just letters and papers and a photograph of his parents and one of me. I didn't go through much else, but there was nothing as big as a Bible. You mentioned there was a watch in there. It must have been under the papers. I never saw it."

"That is what I told Jasper. But Mr. Fife insists there is a missing Bible." Mrs. Roberts set two glasses of iced lemonade on the table.

"Eb may have had more than one. Mr. Fife kept all the study books. Although after meeting with Reverend Whitesides, I regret letting him have them."

"Perhaps they will be what Mr. Fife requires to become the preacher he needs to be." Mrs. Roberts was much kinder than Amanda in her thoughts.

Amanda sipped the lemonade, letting the cool drink rest on her tongue. "This is heaven. I'll never take ice for granted again. I can't remember a summer when we didn't have it at most meals."

"It is a miraculous time we live in where machines can make ice."

"There are so many new inventions every day."

"Half of them don't work. I saw one supposed to help a bald man grow hair. Quackery."

"What about the sewing machine?" asked Amanda.

"I haven't used one myself, but most women rave about them."

"My roommate Emily loved the ones we had at Bradford. She could sew anything."

"We do live in wondrous times. And train travel saves weeks and weeks."

Amanda finished her lemonade. "Thank you so much. I promised I would help Mrs. Braunig bake some pies."

"How are you going to return home now?"

"I'm not sure."

"I've heard a rumor that if you marry, you can get money."

"My husband gets it all."

"He might be willing to let you leave."

"Then what would I do?"

"Go home."

Amanda knew it wouldn't be that easy. "If I get a divorce, I'll never be welcome home."

"Keep separate bedrooms. Get an annulment. Your society friends will never know."

Amanda pinched her lips. "I'm not desperate enough for that."

⬥

Three separate jewelers told Gunter the same thing. "Paste."

Every single jewel was fake—excellent fakes according to all three jewelers he consulted. The pieces were worth some money but not nearly enough for a train ticket. Miss Ashford's hopes were to be dashed yet again.

He'd stopped by his bank in Austin to find it closed for the day. There was enough money in his savings to purchase Miss Ashford a ticket. But if she didn't pay him back in time, the mortgage on the boardinghouse would be in danger— the mortgage the sale of the land could cover. But Mutter said many times she would rather have the land than the boardinghouse.

Gunter pulled up to the ice makers for his last pickup.

"Braunig, I expected you almost two hours ago." The man greeted Gunter in German. He ran one of many businesses the kaufmännisch conducted business with simply because of the ties to the old world.

"I had other errands."

"You better hope your horses can fly. The day is getting hot."

"I know." Gunter helped them load the ice into his wagon and covered it with sawdust. Packed in sawdust, it would still melt on his way back home but not as fast.

"We are ready to close up. I have an extra block I will give you, but it is already partly melted. You must have enough for ice cream tonight."

"Danke."

On the return trip, Gunter passed several wagons full of Grünlauf residents. He waved at the ones he knew.

The majority of the wagons contained families. Mrs. Roberts drove her own carriage, Mr. Fife beside her. Mr. Denton and Deputy Roberts both rode horses near a wagon of saloon girls. Miss Ashford wasn't in any of the wagons or carriages.

Gunter resisted the urge to pick up his horse's pace. With the town mostly empty, the German celebration would soon begin. If he had only believed the first jeweler, he'd be home by now.

⟞⟝◆⟞⟝

Amanda set the last of the pies on the table to cool. As the kitchen felt only a few degrees cooler than the oven, it probably wouldn't help. The boardinghouse needed a summer kitchen like those she'd seen behind other buildings. Amanda slipped out the back door, hoping to cool herself off. Mrs. Roberts's iced lemonade was too many hours long ago. She leaned against a post and closed her eyes, trying to discern if she was only imagining movement in the thick afternoon air. The boards of the porch squeaked under someone's steps.

Amanda opened her eyes to find a man she'd never seen staring down at her. He hadn't shaved for days and possibly not bathed in twice as long. A hat shaded his eyes.

"Miss Ashford?"

Manners be hung from the attic rafters. "Who is asking?"

"I am." He stepped closer, trapping Amanda in the corner of the porch.

Mrs. Braunig had left several minutes ago to take some tablecloths to the church. Where was Herr Schellenberger? "I mean, what is your name?"

"You can call me Joe when you are lying in my bed."

Bile rose in her throat.

"Excuse me. I need to go."

He easily blocked her way. "Not so fast. When are we getting hitched?"

"Hitched?"

"Gotta make it legal to get that money."

"What money?"

"The $5,000. Usually I pay to sleep with those women. But your father is going to pay me to wed and bed you. Are you any good?" He leaned forward.

Amanda dodged him. He went to grab her and missed but got close enough that she smelled the liquor on his breath.

Her hand brushed against something. Greta's broom. She gripped the handle and swung it up, catching the man between his legs. When the man grunted and doubled over the banister, Amanda hurried past him, following the wraparound porch to the front of the house and praying someone was around. The Kerksiek sisters sat on the porch swing, eating pieces of pie.

"It smelled so good we couldn't wait." Their united response calmed her.

Amanda hurried over to them. She'd hoped for someone stronger, but two witnesses would have to do.

With a roar, the man hobbled around the corner, stopping at the sight of them. He pointed at Amanda. "You will marry me."

"No. I won't."

He limped toward her. At the sound of an approaching wagon, he stopped. "This is not over."

The man stepped off the veranda as Mr. Braunig pulled his wagon to a stop. Amanda took the first deep breath she had since the stranger's appearance. With Mr. Braunig near, no one would pester her with proposals or innuendos.

"Mutter is wondering how the pies are."

The sisters held up their plates. "*Köstlich wunderbar!*"

Amanda didn't need a translation to know the sisters approved.

Mr. Braunig jumped onto the veranda. "I hope you saved me some."

The sisters laughed huge, full-body laughs as jolly as they were.

Amanda followed everyone into the kitchen, where the sisters had eaten half of one of the five pies.

Mr. Braunig looked at the half-finished pie. "I should taste it first. It might not be good."

"We should lock up and go to the church." Amanda picked up two of the pies to take to the wagon.

"Mmmm." Mr. Braunig nodded with his mouth full as he ate pie directly from the tin. He set the remainder of the pie and fork in the pie safe. "I'll finish this later."

The sisters set their plates in the dry sink. "Did you tell the man no to his proposal?"

"Another one?" Mr. Braunig picked up the other pies.

"He never asked." Amanda turned to leave before anyone inquired what the man said.

Gunter brought out the remaining pies and went back into the boardinghouse. The Kerksiek sisters climbed into the wagon bed. The one in blue stepped over the seat and settled herself on it, the movement rocking the entire wagon. The other sat on a crate.

The door to the kitchen banged, and Gunter came out carrying a crank-handled ice cream freezer in each arm.

"We are making ice cream?" Having already settled on not eating ice cream this Independence Day, the surprise delighted her more than she could express.

"Ja. The ice is already at the church. The Volmer's ice cream maker broke." Gunter set them in the back of the wagon.

With no other place to sit, Amanda walked past Gunter to the road.

"Miss Ashford, sit here." Gunter pointed to the empty spot at the back of the wagon. "You can protect your pies."

Amanda tried to pull herself up the way the Kerksiek sisters had, but her bustled skirt was too tight.

"Turn around. It will be easier." Gunter picked her up at the waist.

To balance herself, she placed her hands on his arms. He didn't let go once she was seated. Her gaze locked with his. There was something in it she didn't understand.

"Hold on tight." He released her and took his place on the wagon seat.

Amanda clutched the sideboard with one hand. The other covered her midsection in a vain attempt to calm the fireworks exploding inside.

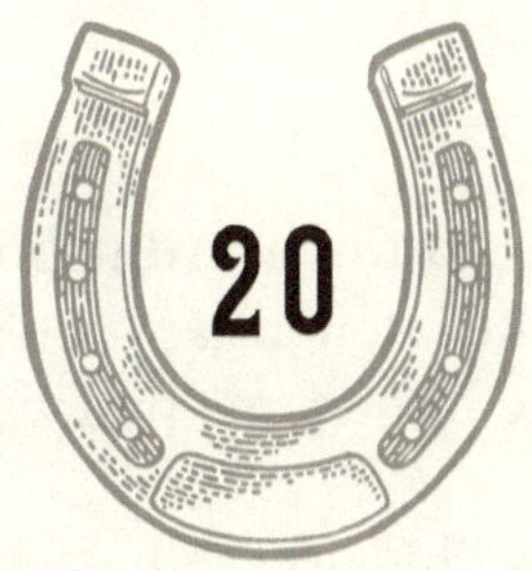

20

Papa, when do we go to Oma's?" Greta pushed her plate back on the table.

"Don't you like my cooking?" They'd slept late this morning after last night's celebration.

"Oma's is better."

Gunter laughed. "You're right."

"You could share Miss Ashford's pie." Greta looked at Gunter's plate.

He'd hoped she wouldn't notice. Miss Ashford told him she couldn't cook. If this was bad, she'd lied twice. The other time was last night, when she insisted nothing was bothering her. The man who'd proposed yesterday was his best guess.

Gunter divided the remaining pie.

"Danke." The word was garbled around the food in Greta's mouth.

"After we are done, we can go to Oma's. I need to talk with Miss Ashford." The bag of fake jewelry weighed heavily in his pocket. He hadn't had the heart to say anything last night.

"What else are we doing?"

"I need to check the horses' shoes today."

"Can I come?"

"What if we go for a ride after?"

"On a horse?"

"Yes, on a horse."

"Yeah!"

They walked over to the boardinghouse. Herr Schellenberger dug around the kitchen garden. "Guten Tag. Fräulein Greta, did you come to help me pull weeds?"

"May I, Papa?"

Herr Schellenberger hid his laugh. "Better say yes, Gunter."

"I'll tell Oma you are helping in the garden."

Inside, Gunter set the pie plate in the cupboard.

Mutter came in from the dining room. "Ah, that is where my missing pan went."

"Is Miss Ashford here?"

"In the washroom, washing the sheets."

Gunter tapped on the open door.

Miss Ashford stood and wiped her hands on her apron.

Gunter pulled the leather bag out of his pocket.

"They didn't sell?" She held out her hand, and he dropped the bag into it.

"No. The jewelers all agreed—they are paste."

"Paste?"

"One of them called them the best fakes he'd ever seen."

"But they've been in the family forever." Miss Ashford sat on the stool, opened the bag, and pulled out a broach.

"I went to three different jewelers."

"Is that why you were late getting back with the ice?" She poured her jewelry into her lap, inspecting each piece.

"Yes."

"I'm so sorry. I never expected my parents would do this too."

"Do what?"

"My grandmother left most of these jewels to me. I saw the appraisals. They were real. My parents must have switched them on me so I couldn't destroy the legacy by selling the Ashford family jewels." She dropped the jewelry back into the bag and the bag into the pocket of her apron. "What do I do now?"

"I can't tell you."

"Mail is here!" Greta bounced into the room. "The sisters brought it back from the store. You have a letter, Miss Ashford."

"Thank you." She read the direction. "It is from my friend Emily in Hiramsville. Maybe she'll have an idea."

Gunter turned to leave.

"Thank you for trying to sell the jewelry. I am sorry to have wasted your time."

"It wasn't wasted." He couldn't think of anything else to say, so he left.

Greta stood on a stool in the kitchen playing at the dry sink while Mutter kneaded bread. He waved before heading out.

There must be something more he could do.

"Gunter?"

He turned back to his mother's voice.

"This was in the mail." She handed him a paper.

The message from the Grünlauf bank was short. "They are calling the mortgage? We have six more months."

"Ja."

"I may need to sell the land."

"No. You can't."

"Mutter. If we don't, we might not have either the land or the boardinghouse. We could sell and move someplace where you wouldn't have to work all day, every day."

"I don't want to move. What are we going to do?"

How was he supposed to know? Everyone needed answers and help he didn't know how to give.

The sheets hung limply on the line, confirming what Amanda already knew—no breeze to cool the hot Texas day. Even without wind, the laundry would dry quickly. Amanda retreated to the shade of the veranda and opened Emily's letter.

Halfway through the first page, she stopped and reread the paragraph after the one where Emily wished Amanda well in her marriage.

> "My teaching job was not what was promised, as the school was a house of ill repute. I hope that is not too shocking, but as you are in Texas also, you might understand these things. I was fortunate the sheriff rescued me before . . . Presently I am living with a kind widow and working as a laundress. Fortunately, life with my aunt prepared me for such a job . . . I am seeking better employment. If you learn of any teaching positions at a real school, I welcome the referral . . ."

Amanda took a deep breath. She couldn't believe it. Emily didn't have a job at a school? Thank heavens Hiramsville had a good sheriff. If the same thing had happened here, the deputy would have forced Emily into prostitution. Texas wasn't working out the way either of them anticipated.

Any thoughts she had of trying to get to Hiramsville were off the list.

"Miss Ashford?" Greta's voice came from above her.

Amanda stepped off the porch and looked up at her window. "Outside, Greta."

Greta's head popped over the windowsill. "Oma says you have a visitor in the parlor."

Not another one. Another man who just wanted her for her money? If he was anything like the man yesterday, he would drink through the money before the thirty-two days were over.

At least with Eb, she chose where the money could go, knowing most would end up with the church.

Amanda crossed the yard and turned into the alley. Whoever was proposing could wait.

Amanda passed between the two trees at the side of the river. The cooler air washed over her, solidifying her thoughts. The only way to obtain the funds to return to Boston was to marry, and the only man she could marry in good faith was Gunter. But he held absolutely no interest in her or her money. Then there was the letter from the bank Mrs. Braunig had left on the table. At the very least, he could pay off the mortgage on his mother's boardinghouse with Amanda's money. Something good could come of her father's stubbornness.

He could pay her back. It was a business deal and nothing more. Thirty-two days. That's as long as they had to be together—thirty-two days. Then he could give her $200 and she would disappear from his life forever. The $15,000 Father had given for the dowry should more than recompense him.

Breathing deeply, Amanda squared her shoulders and headed in the direction of Gunter's forge. The clanging of metal on metal filled the air. The doors stood wide open. With all the courage she could muster, she approached. The sun was in her eyes. As she stepped through the doorway and into the shade, her jaw dropped.

Under his leather apron, Mr. Braunig wore no shirt. She'd once seen her brother's back—well, more than once as he was fond of swimming in the ocean. But her brother's back was only half as wide as Mr. Braunig's. Her brother's arms were nowhere near as muscular either. Muscles rippled in a rhythm that made her breath catch and heart beat an unfamiliar cadence. The skin above the blacksmith's right shoulder puckered and wrinkled with each hammer strike in a way that made her wince. As the fire popped, Amanda's eyes traced the outline of the largest burn scar she'd ever seen.

Turning away, while necessary, seemed impossible. Finally, she closed her eyes and stepped back, bumping into the door as she did so. Mr. Braunig wheeled around, the leather apron covering his shoulders and chest.

As he set his hammer down and reached for a shirt, Amanda looked at her feet.

"Miss Ashford, I wasn't expecting you today. Did Mutter send you?"

"No. I shouldn't have come." She turned to leave. This was a terribly bad idea.

"Stay." He came closer. His shirt hung over the apron.

"I only came to ask you a question."

Gunter inclined his head but didn't answer.

Amanda cleared her throat. "I have a business proposal for you."

"Do you need something made?"

"No, I need a husband."

"A husband?"

"Yes. Only for thirty-two days, and then I will leave. You can get an annulment based on the grounds that I didn't fulfill my wifely duties." Her face burned as hot as the coals in the forge.

Mr. Braunig stepped forward. "So we pretend to be married for a month and then what?"

"I leave. You keep all but the money necessary to send me home safely, and I go home."

"I've been teaching Greta not to lie. How do I explain a business marriage to her?"

"It is the only way I can get the money. I have barely enough to subsist on for a month as it is. A dozen men want to marry me for my money. Most want me for other things too. I'd never be able to go home if I married them."

"Miss Ashford—"

"Amanda. If we're going to be married, you should at least call me by my Christian name."

"Miss Ashford, we are not going to be married. I cannot live a lie."

"Tell Greta and your mother the truth but no one else." Her voice betrayed all the desperation she held inside.

"Greta will not understand. I can't marry you and have you leave. It will break her heart."

"I saw the letter from the bank. The dowry can save your mother's boardinghouse."

Mr. Braunig crossed his arms. "That is none of your business."

He was her only chance. "Please, Mr. Braunig. You are the only man in town I can trust. You know as well as I do that the men who've been proposing to me…well, they won't let me leave…I won't be able to claim an annulment. Father made it so I can't get to my dowry, but I can choose who gets it. Please marry me?"

He stood close enough to touch her, pity etched in every line of his face. "I can't."

Waves of embarrassment washed over her. The fragile bond of friendship between them was broken, severed by a question she should have never asked. "I'm sorry I bothered you."

Amanda waited until she was in the alley to let the tears fall. There was some irony that the only man she could trust to be honest was the only one who wouldn't marry her for the money. He was too honest.

21

No matter how many times he rolled over, Gunter couldn't find a comfortable sleeping position. Refusing Miss Ashford was the right thing to do. Even if her idea solved so many problems. The little girl in the next room would never understand what a pretend marriage meant for her. She'd already lost one mother.

He'd already lost one wife.

Miss Ashford might trust him to live so the marriage could be annulled, but Gunter didn't trust himself. Maybe because she was grieving for the Reverend Coolidge, she hadn't noticed the times they'd touched. But her expression was so reserved. She'd hardly reacted to seeing him without his shirt on. Or maybe she pretended not to notice like he had pretended not to notice the other morning. The image of her long braid and bare feet had replayed in his mind every night since then.

And there had been the moment when he'd lifted her onto the back of the wagon the night of the Independence Day celebration and struggled to let go of her waist. That night, she'd looked at him, and their eyes had connected.

He thought he'd seen the same surprise in her eyes that he felt. If they had been alone, he might have leaned in and kissed her.

A month of pretending that he wasn't interested in her inside the house and happily married outside would be a form of torture that would have Dante create a new circle in the depths of hell.

Gunter threw off the light sheet and sat on the edge of the bed, then reached for the letter from the bank. Miss Ashford's dowry would solve all the money problems they'd ever had. He could purchase the cattle and fulfill his father's dream of having a ranch. They could sell the boardinghouse, and Mutter wouldn't have to work day and night as she had most of her life.

He could change his answer and quietly wed Miss Ashford. If he slept in the small bedroom and kept the photograph of Pauline in its place…He reached for the photo in its smoky glass frame. It had been among the few things that survived the fire. Greta had taken it from the shelf to look at and then hidden it under the cushion of the davenport to keep from getting in trouble—a small act of disobedience that proved to be a blessing.

As the birds commenced their morning chatter in the trees, Gunter dragged his hand down his face. He best wash up before Greta arose. This Sunday, they would prepare for church without Mutter's help. It was better for him to stay as far from Miss Ashford as possible.

⊰◦⊱

Only as she arrived at the white church did Amanda remember that services started a half hour later than the German church. She wandered into the cemetery and over to Eb's grave. The pinned paper and wooden cross had been replaced with stone. Amanda traced his carved name with a finger. Seeing the blue of her sleeve against the stone seemed odd. In Boston, Mother would have insisted Amanda wear black at least for a few weeks. No one had mentioned that here. Not even Mrs. Roberts, who wore blacks and grays daily, mentioned wearing mourning clothes.

"Would our love of ministering have been enough?" The whispered question went unanswered.

"I saw part of your letter to your mother. Don't feel bad because you wanted my money. I wanted to be a minister's wife. If I had found a man willing to minister in China, I would have..." She allowed her hand to drop from the headstone in a small circle, a gesture meant to encompass all she couldn't say. "I am sorry it ended this way. I'm trying to be faithful to God, but it is hard. I feel abandoned by everyone. Everything is so wrong."

Wagon wheels rattled behind her. Amanda stepped back, hating to be caught talking to a gravestone. One last thought came, so she whispered it. "I forgive you for not loving me. Can you forgive me?"

Voices grew louder behind her. Amanda turned.

"Miss Ashford? I thought you were gone already." Reverend Whitesides advanced through the graveyard, a tall skinny minister at his heels.

"Mishaps seem to be my lot. My room was burgled and my ticket money stolen."

"Has any attempt been made to find it?" asked the tall man.

"Yes."

"Oh, forgive my manners. This is Reverend Parks, newly arrived. Reverend, this is Miss Ashford. I am here to install him as the new minister for this congregation."

"My condolences to you." Reverend Parks dipped his head. Obviously, he knew of her plight.

"Have you given any more consideration to teaching school for us, Miss Ashford?"

She breathed a sigh of relief that Reverend Whitesides didn't suggest she marry the new minister. "No. However, I have a friend, valedictorian of our class, who is in need of a job. The position she was offered in Hiramsville was a false promise."

"Valedictorian?" asked Reverend Whitesides.

"She always wanted to be a teacher and is very competent in all forms of academia."

Reverend Whiteside's brow knit. "Give me her name, and I will send her an offer. I have heard much about Bradford College. Any graduate willing to teach is worth hiring. You are sure you will not reconsider?"

"May I think about it another week? If I have not found a way to return to Boston, I may have to consider the option of teaching more carefully." It was honest, respectable work, which was more than she was finding elsewhere.

"By all means."

The first notes of a hymn flowed through the open windows of the church, and Reverend Parks cleared his throat. Reverend Whitesides extended his arm to Amanda. "We should go in. It would be poor form for us to be late for Reverend Parks's first week."

At the door, Amanda left the two reverends and slipped into the back pew. Mr. Fife sat behind the pulpit. His face fell as he watched the two ministers advance on him.

Reverend Whitesides spoke so that his voice didn't carry, obviously introducing Reverend Parks. Mr. Fife's face reddened. His mouth flapped like a fish, yet no sound reached Amanda's ears. He stood for a moment more before turning on his heel and exiting through the back door.

A moment later, Reverend Whitesides started the meeting and Reverend Parks delivered the sermon. His voice was strong, but the text of Daniel facing Goliath seemed more appropriate for Sunday school, a fact he recognized in his conclusion. "You must pardon me for speaking to the children today. I have been away from my wife and children for more than a month and look forward to them joining me this week. I am afraid my little ones were on my mind when I wrote my sermon."

A worry Amanda hadn't realized she'd even thought of faded from her mind. No one would ask her to wed this minister.

At the conclusion of the meeting, Mrs. Roberts approached. "Amanda, had I known you were going to attend today, I would have asked you to sit with me."

"It was a last-minute decision but most fortuitous. I was able to pass on the name of a friend for one of those teaching positions Reverend Whiteside mentioned."

"Have you found a way home yet?"

"No."

"I've been thinking. You could marry Jasper, then get an annulment in a month."

Amanda forced a frown away. "Why Jasper? I didn't think you approved of him."

The man in question stood not twenty feet away, talking with Mr. Fife. He was not of the same cloth as the sheriff who'd helped Emily. Somehow, she knew marriage to a man like Jasper would end in misery.

"Well, he hasn't proposed yet, and you have turned down almost every eligible man in town twice..." Mrs. Roberts's voice faded. "Oh, what am I saying? It is the worst idea I've ever had. Would you like to come over for some iced lemonade?"

"Thank you for the offer. Perhaps another day. Now, if you'll excuse me. I must talk with Reverend Whitesides."

As she neared the reverends, Mr. Fife joined them. Amanda paused, not wanting to interrupt, but she needed to get the slip of paper with Emily's name to them, so she resumed her course.

"Where am I to live?"

"That is not the church's concern. The house is for the use of the reverend."

"But Coolidge let me stay."

"Reverend Coolidge was unwed. Surely you had plans to move upon his wed—" Reverend Whitesides stopped midsentence when his eyes fell on Amanda.

She held out the slip of paper. "Sorry to interrupt. This is my friend's name and direction. She only wrote Hiramsville on the envelope, so I trust that is enough for the post office."

"Thank you, Miss Ashford. Write soon to let me know of your decision."

"I will. Good day."

As she reached the bridge, Amanda heard her name called in a high, whiny voice. Taking a deep breath, she turned to face Mr. Fife.

"You must reconsider and marry me."

"Mr. Fife. The answer is still no."

"Because of you, I don't have a place to live now."

"I don't see how that is my fault." Amanda turned to cross the bridge.

Mr. Fife grabbed her arm with more force than she thought him capable. "You owe me."

"Let me go." Amanda reached up for her hatpin.

Feet pounded on the bridge. "Let her go!"

⬦

Mr. Fife dropped Miss Ashford's arm and stepped back. Gunter heard the pounding of his own blood in his ears. He filled his lungs to cool his urge to hit the man on the Lord's day.

As Miss Ashford dropped her hand from her hat, keeping her focus on Mr. Fife, something glinted in the light.

"You need to marry me." Mr. Fife reached for her.

"Do not ever touch me again." She used a long hatpin to punctuate her words.

Gunter found himself stepping back from the woman with the miniature sword.

"But—" Mr. Fife reached for her left hand and was met with the working side of the hatpin. "Ouch!" He pulled his hand back, revealing a pool of blood in the palm of his hand.

"I warned you. Leave. Me. Alone." She stood her ground, and Mr. Fife turned and dashed away, cradling his bleeding hand.

Still holding the hatpin, Miss Ashford spun around to face Gunter. "Thank you for your assistance, Mr. Braunig. As you can see, it was not necessary."

"That is a remarkable hatpin."

"Mrs. Smythe insisted we have them for the train." Miss Ashford poked the pin back into her hat.

"Very wise." Gunter didn't know what to say next, but it seemed wrong to turn his back on her and walk away.

"I would like to apologize for my forward behavior yesterday. I didn't think through the repercussions for you or Greta. You were right to refuse me. I need to find another way. I've heard all my life that when God closes a door, He opens a window somewhere. I hope the window isn't so high up in the wall I need a ladder to reach it."

"Nothing to forgive. If you have received other proposals like Mr. Fife's, I can understand." Gunter walked toward the boardinghouse.

"Only one. I didn't have my hatpin."

"Do you have any other plans?"

"The dimes I have left will pay for another few weeks. I am writing to my father and his secretary this afternoon. If that fails, Reverend Whitesides in Austin has asked me to teach. I've never thought of myself as a teacher, but isn't that much of what a missionary does? I could save enough money by teaching during the school year to return home."

Relief filled Gunter; her desperate proposal was not the only avenue available to her. He paused at the gate to the boardinghouse. "I wish you the best of luck."

Miss Ashford turned into the yard.

Gunter continued on. A walk would do him good. The gate squeaked behind him, and the quick steps of Miss Ashford caused him to turn around.

She caught up with him. "There is something I need to tell you, something I should have told you days ago. Greta and I went on a walk along the river…brook…creek, whatever you call it. Anyway, she wanted to show me…If I'd known where we were going, I would have never agreed."

"She took you to the house?"

"Yes."

"You shouldn't have gone there." A growl entered his voice. The cellar was exposed. Greta could have fallen in.

"I didn't know. Honestly, I didn't know until I saw the chimney."

"Thank you for telling me. In the future, don't take my daughter on any walks." Gunter turned around again, intent on escaping her.

"Wait." She touched his sleeve.

"What?"

"There was a man in the barn watching us. I thought you should know."

"So you weren't telling me because you accompanied my daughter to a place she is forbidden to go?" He fisted his hands at his side and glared down at her.

Instead of cowering, she raised her chin. "Forbidden? No one ever said anything about it being forbidden. Your mother said I could take her on a walk. Last week, you even told her she could walk with me by the water as long as we didn't go in."

Looking down into her eyes was as perilous as the inferno that had consumed the house. The warring emotions of wanting to lash out at her for endangering his daughter and wanting to see if Miss Ashford's fiery nature would extend to her kiss blazed within him. Gunter stepped back. "Burned-out shells of houses aren't play places."

"I know that. I didn't let her go in." Her voice raised, and she folded her arms.

"Then why are you telling me this?"

"I only thought you should know there was a squatter in the barn."

"And you didn't tell me the moment you got back?"

"I forgot."

"Forgot?"

Her hands moved to her hips. "When we returned, I found my room ransacked, and the strange man watching us from the barn loft escaped my mind."

"He watched you? You're sure it wasn't a shadow?"

"I wasn't at first, but I looked back twice. I thought you should know. I get the feeling Greta has been there on her own. She knew the path too well. And I've met some men who—" Miss Ashford looked away. "I only thought you should know."

Gunter watched her return to the boardinghouse before changing his route to the livery. The same foreboding he'd felt at the wagon tracks stopped him. If it wasn't Sunday, he might ask another man to ride out with him. If he walked near the river, he would have the cover of the trees. He changed direction again. That woman had him walking in circles.

22

Amanda reread the letter she'd written to her father yesterday afternoon. She'd included as little detail as possible, listing just facts and dates. Father preferred lists to long, prosy letters. On paper, the two weeks and three days she'd been in Texas seemed much shorter than the eternity she felt she'd been here. She enclosed an account of the money she'd spent and what had been stolen. She addressed a duplicate letter to Mr. Dewey in hopes that the more detailed letter would succeed where the telegrams had failed and spur the man into advancing funds for her return trip.

The letter to Emily started out concise but grew as Amanda poured out emotions she didn't realize needed an outlet.

She read the last page of her letter, wondering if it was too shocking.

> *The most embarrassing thing I have done was propose a tempo-rary marriage to Mr. Braunig. I cannot tell you how desperate I felt then or degraded I feel now to have done such a thing. He is, however, a man of the highest integrity and refused me on*

principle—an action that has improved him in my estimation. There is also his daughter to consider. For her sake, I can bear his refusal.

Do not read, my friend, too much into my words. He is far from a perfect specimen of manhood. His anger is quick to flair but as quickly contained. He also hides behind his German heritage. The town is very divided, more so than Boston with our Italians and Irish.

Do you think I ever loved Eb? I know I argued with some of our friends. But I find I am not missing him as much as the death of being a minister's wife. I cannot be satisfied to return to Boston and marry as my parents wish, yet I fear trying to find another man when I know I will never be the next great missionary to have her portrait displayed in the Bradford gallery. If only we did not require husbands to do the work, I could come to Hiramsville and help you revive it. Although I believe the American side of town here needs a revival of the spirit as much. Very radical ideas. Perhaps I should become a suffragette.

I am, as you see, quite adrift. I will write again soon. Perhaps I won't be as scattered.

Amanda folded the papers together. After taking them to the post office, she returned to the boardinghouse and began the list of chores Mrs. Braunig gave her. None of them had to do with reading to Greta. Mr. Braunig must have had words with his mother about how unstable she was for a chaperone for a four-year-old girl.

⊰•◦•⊱

Tuesday morning, Kurt and Peter arrived at the smithy as requested. Their friendship had waned after the fire, and Gunter hadn't been sure they'd come.

"Vat is the problem?" Kurt stood outside the smithy door.

"Someone said there is a squatter in the barn out by my old house, and there are wagon tracks cutting through my land. Will you come with me to check it out?"

"If you can't look after your land on your own, you should sell," said Peter. A rancher at heart, Peter had strong opinions about Gunter's land sitting fallow for nearly two years.

"I told you what happened the night of the fire…"

"Ja, and the sheriff said you were wrong. No one else was there."

"Someone started the fire outside the kitchen. There were men in the dale that night. The wagon tracks go into the dale. I want a witness this time." He had some support for his story from the German community, but even they had had doubts when the deputy sheriff announced the fire had been an accident.

The old friends looked at each other. "One hour, then we must return to our work."

They rode out to the house and barn first. Surrounded by wildflowers, the burned-out foundation continued to weather and rot.

The barn stood empty. A dried flower lay on the ground inside the door. Miss Ashford may have rightly guessed his daughter visited on her own.

Peter came down the ladder from the barn loft. "Someone's been here." He opened his fisted hand to reveal several cigarette butts.

"Anything else?" asked Gunter

Kurt crouched in the middle of the floor. "Mouse droppings. More than I'd expect for an empty barn. I'd also say a wagon has been here, but not since the last rain. No tracks outside."

They crossed the land through the center of the parcel to the place where Gunter had found the wagon tracks. Fresher horse tracks covered them.

Gunter dismounted for a closer look. "These are new."

Kurt joined him. "How much farther until we are on high ground?"

Gunter pointed to a large mesquite tree two hundred yards away.

"We'll have the sun behind us. If there is anyone in the hollow, they might see us." Peter led his horse a few feet. "We should go by foot."

The men walked silently. Peter stopped them as they neared the tree. "Kurt, stay with the horses."

Keeping low, Gunter and Peter moved forward. Gunter imagined cattle thieves or bandits using the small valley on the end of his land as a hideout. He wasn't prepared to see rows upon rows of plants growing. He stood with Peter, hidden in the shade of the old mesquite. Someone was farming on his land.

"What are they growing?"

Peter shook his head in answer to Gunter's question and turned back toward where Kurt was. They mounted their horses and headed back to town. Near the fence line, Peter slowed. "When was the last time you were out there?"

"Not since right after the fire."

"Is that where you saw men?" asked Kurt.

"They were headed in that direction. The hollow was on my father's land. He thought it would be good for growing things with the natural springs. But it is too far out to build on."

"Did your cattle ever go there?"

"I got my ten head only days before. They never were out of the range, and I sold them right after the fire."

Peter lifted his hat and wiped his brow. "I owe you an apology for not believing you these last two years. Never thought you meant to kill my sister. I only thought you were covering up a mistake."

Hearing the words he'd waited nearly two years to be spoken didn't heal anything. "What do I do now?"

"If the deputy was worth anything, I'd say tell him, but—" Kurt left the answer hanging.

"I can't think of what they are growing. It didn't look like any crop I've ever seen." Peter had worked several years on the farms and ranches in a forty-mile radius as part of his plan to learn the American ways before he started his own place. "What about the barn? When is the last time you've been out to it?"

"Last fall. I came out to pull down the chimney, but I built the thing too well."

"Why haven't you sold?"

"Because the only offers I've received are at half the value. And none of them are from German families. Why haven't you offered?" Gunter looked at Peter.

"I told you last time. It's good land, but the parcel between yours and mine isn't for sale. I want a continuous range."

"Well, I may have to sell soon or have nothing. The bank called the mortgage on the boardinghouse."

"I thought you owned that free and clear."

"My father mortgaged it to purchase his part of the land. Mutter insists the land is more important. She wants me to live Vater's legacy, but the land doesn't call to me like it does to you and my father. I never wanted to be a farmer or rancher."

Kurt turned in his saddle. "Living up to our fathers' expectations is not so easy. I would have liked to be a clockmaker like my grandfather. Instead, I stand behind the counter of the kaufmännisch and balance ledgers."

Peter laughed. "I told you to run away with me years ago."

"I am the eldest. I couldn't." Kurt's answer was good-natured. He had no desire to farm either.

"So what do we do?" asked Gunter.

"First thing is to figure out what they are growing. I'll ask around. Even if you wanted to, you probably couldn't sell the land without getting rid of the squatters."

"If I can get the sheriff to remove them." Gunter stopped at the smithy. "Thanks for riding out with me."

"Thanks for the excuse to ride." Kurt continued to the livery.

"I need to get back out to my spread. I'll let you know what I learn. You were wise to ask us to come." Peter raised a hand in farewell.

Gunter checked Riese's hooves before returning him to the livery. His friends believed him. The silent recrimination was gone, and part of his old self had returned.

23

Amanda's fingers cramped. Every minute she wasn't needed to help Mrs. Braunig, she spent crocheting. She measured the length again. Deducting her costs, she sadly realized that four days of mindless work would not even pay for room and board.

Every time she closed her eyes, she counted stitches. When she ate, she counted stitches. The constant round of numbers in her head was never-ending. Now she realized that all the finely spun cotton and time in the world meant she would only starve more slowly. Amanda rubbed and stretched her fingers. Her neck and back ached. The only bright spot was when Greta came to recite rhymes out of the book, pretending to read.

They no longer went on walks. Amanda wasn't sure if the little girl was being punished or not, but it wasn't her place to ask.

Mrs. Braunig came out onto the back porch. "Have you seen Greta?"

"Not since noon."

"Gunter told her she must stay here."

"Would you like me to look for her?"

"Please."

"I'll start upstairs."

The attic windows had been thrown open to allow the heat to escape the house. Still, the room was too warm to stay in. Amanda checked the empty bedrooms, even under the beds. As she passed her room, the scent of her perfume wafted out. The dab Amanda put behind her ears each morning would not smell so strong. She opened the door and found Greta sitting at her dressing table, tears streaming down her face.

"What happened?"

Greta pointed to the broken glass bottle on the floor. "It fell. Oma said never to walk on the floor if there is broken glass."

"Are you hurt?"

Greta shook her head.

Amanda lifted her off the chair. "Come, your grandmother is looking for you." Amanda walked through the empty rooms. "Mrs. Braunig?"

The door to the cellar opened. "You found—" Mrs. Braunig sniffed.

Amanda set Greta down.

"I didn't mean to break it. I just wanted to smell pretty for Papa." Greta hid in Mrs. Braunig's skirt.

"The whole bottle?"

"I'm afraid so. I'll work to air out the room. We may all smell like flowers for a week."

A half hour later, there was nothing more Amanda could do to clean out her room. The smell was still overpowering.

Gunter knocked on her open door. It was the first time she'd seen him since Sunday. They'd both avoided each other well.

She smoothed her skirt. "Mr. Braunig."

"How much do I owe you?"

"Nothing. It was an accident."

"It must have been expensive."

Likely very expensive since her mother had given it to her as a birthday gift. "I have no intention of replacing it."

"She knows better—"

"She is a little girl. I promised I would let her have some last week. But the break-in…I forgot. It seems I forgot many things that day." Amanda shifted her weight under his gaze.

"I shouldn't have gotten upset with you Sunday night."

"I should have told you sooner."

"You are making it very hard to apologize." His accent sounded more German than usual. "Vat can I do to fix this?"

"Not everything needs to be fixed."

He raised a brow.

"This room is going to smell like this for months, so I caused just as much damage by not following through on my promise."

"Really?"

"I broke a bottle of my mother's perfume once. We went to the Cape for the summer, and when we came back, you could still smell it—not as bad, but Father still complained. Mother never wore that kind of perfume again."

Mr. Braunig smiled. "Are you sure I can't do anything?"

"Is Greta not allowed to walk with me anymore?"

He looked at the palms of his hands. "Ja. I thought it best."

"I understand. May I still read to her?"

"She should not spend so much time with you. She likes you too much."

Amanda swallowed. "I understand. I will try and—I will find a way to leave soon."

"Danke."

Amanda waited for him to leave before turning to the window. Tears blurred her vision. Losing Greta as a friend hurt more than losing Eb.

Gunter muttered several choice words under his breath in German as he returned to the smithy. He'd expected Miss Ashford to be upset with Greta or name some exorbitant price for the perfume. Instead, she'd put Greta at the center of the conversation. It would be so much easier if she smelled like Fräulein Volmer or didn't cook delicious pies or ignored Greta.

If she'd never proposed, he wouldn't think about her as a wife. The more he didn't think about it, the more confused he got. It would be so easy to marry her and hope she changed her mind about leaving. With $15,000, they could travel to Boston every year.

They could be happy.

Only in his dreams.

After two years, he'd met a woman he could think of marrying.

A woman he shouldn't marry.

A woman he couldn't marry.

A woman he wouldn't marry.

24

Amanda stared at the pages of the agenda she'd used her last semester of college. She hadn't written a single appointment since the day they'd left. She filled in dates. A month ago, she'd boarded the train for Austin. Three weeks ago, she'd arrived...

Father raised her to have a plan. The blank pages of the calendar mocked her. Last year she told her parents she was old enough to choose her own path. That path had led to an edge of a cliff. Waiting for them to rescue her wasn't going to solve anything. It would be easier if they did, but if they did, she would lose all her choices. Amanda wasn't sure how she hadn't seen that before. Returning to Boston would be easier and more comfortable, staying in Texas more uncertain.

Amanda pulled out the list of schools from Reverend Whitesides. Perhaps she and Emily could teach at the same school and room together. She turned the agenda to September. Unsure of when school started in Texas, she wrote, "First day of school" on Monday the first.

Then she recounted her dimes. Mrs. Braunig had dropped her room and board by a dollar a week for the work she was doing to help. If she continued to make and sell lace, she would have enough money to survive the rest of the summer.

She pulled out a piece of paper.

Dear Reverend Whitesides,
I would like to apply.

An hour later, Amanda walked to the post office, her heart lighter than it had been in weeks.

Father was right; creating a plan changed everything.

She set the letter on the counter and counted out the postage. "Anything for me or the boardinghouse today?"

"No, I have two letters for Mr. Braunig. Will you deliver them?"

"He doesn't live at the boardinghouse."

"They look important."

Amanda held out her hand. "I'll stop by the smithy."

"Thank you, Miss Ashford."

Amanda crossed the bridge and turned toward the livery. The doors were open on either end. The horses must suffer from the heat too.

The smithy was quiet. Amanda found Mr. Braunig sharpening knives in the shade of the tree behind the smithy.

He stopped as she drew near.

Amanda held out the letters. "The postmistress asked me to deliver these. They looked important, so I thought I would bring them here."

"Thanks."

"I wanted you to know that I applied for a teaching position, so you don't need to worry about getting me back to Boston anymore."

"You didn't want to teach."

"I don't. But if I go home, I will never be able to choose anything again. I'm not choosing to teach as much as I am choosing to be independent."

"In the meantime?"

"I work for your mother, crochet lace to sell, and avoid men who want to marry me for the dowry."

"Have they stopped asking?"

Amanda tipped her head to the side. She hadn't thought about the proposals. No one had asked in days. "No one since Mr. Fife."

"Maybe he told everyone about your hatpin."

Amanda laughed with him. "I should get back to the boardinghouse."

"Miss Ashford, I was wrong to ask you not to read to Greta. I'm finished for the day. If you'll wait, I'll walk you back and talk with Mutter."

Something in his look froze her heart. A man correcting his own mistake. If he had said yes last week, she might have fallen in love with him. Good old-fashioned read-in-the-book love. "I should go now."

Amanda hurried into the alley next to the livery. Mr. Braunig could never know her feelings. He'd shown her pity when he turned her down. It would be far worse for him to show her pity and accept.

Before she realized what had happened, a hand clamped over her mouth. Then an arm wrapped around her waist and she was pulled against a man's chest. He smelled of tobacco and whisky. He lifted her off the ground and carried her into the darkness of the massive barn. Amanda kicked, hitting only air. She scratched the man's arm. Her hatpin. She reached up.

"Hatpin," said a whiny voice off to the side.

The man holding her let go of her mouth and clamped his hand around her wrist.

Amanda screamed.

Gunter froze. Had a woman screamed? Another sound came. A horse kicked its stall in the livery. There shouldn't be any horses in the livery. Nick had taken them out to the pasture a while ago. Gunter grabbed the knife he'd just sharpened and hurried to see what was wrong.

Jumping the corral fence, he flattened himself against the barn wall.

"Tie her hands."

Thump.

Gunter crouched low and entered the barn.

"She kicked me." Mr. Fife's whiny voice came from a stall on the other side of the barn.

"Hurry."

"Go stand guard. This will only take a minute. Then she'll have to marry you."

Thump.

Mr. Fife ran out of the stall and to the front of the barn. Gunter would deal with him later.

"Listen here, little hussy. You are making me mad. Boss wants this done. You only have to be alive enough to say 'I do.'"

Gunter crept closer.

A slap.

A whimper.

The stall door wasn't closed all the way. Through the crack, he could see Amanda lying in the straw. A large cowboy stood over her, removing his belt. Gunter kicked the door open. The cowboy spun around, his fist ready to connect with Gunter's head, but Gunter ducked and slashed. The man's pants fell. Gunter punched him in the gut, doubling him over. In the corner, Miss Ashford struggled to stand. Gunter wished the fight was over so he could help her. The cowboy charged him but tripped on his pants.

"What is—" Mr. Fife stopped at the stall door. "I have a gun."

Gunter stopped thinking, throwing caution aside. He punched and slashed, moving between the men and Amanda.

Fife aimed with shaky hands. Gunter shoved the cowboy in Fife's direction as the gun went off, both assailants falling to the ground.

Shouts of men and footsteps came from the front of the barn.

"What is going on here?" For once the deputy was where he needed to be.

Gunter opened his mouth, but Miss Ashford's voice came out. "That man and Mr. Fife tried to—and Mr. Braunig stopped them! Mr. Fife shot him."

Jasper pushed the cowboy off Mr. Fife. Blood covered them both.

"It looks like Mr. Fife saved you, ma'am."

"Mr. Fife was helping him." Miss Ashford stood tall, even with her hands bound. Her hat was no longer on her head, and part of her hair was mussed.

Jasper stood, and another man took his place next to the bleeding cowboy.

"How do I know they weren't trying to stop Braunig?" asked Jasper.

"Idiot." Miss Ashford held up her bound wrists. "I know who attacked me and who saved me. And unless you are going to let that man bleed to death, I suggest you start acting like a lawman should. Mr. Braunig, if you would please put that knife to good use."

Gunter held the knife to the poorly tied rope binding her wrists. Her hands were shaking. He steadied her arm with his other hand to avoid cutting her and sliced the rope.

Once her hands were free, she tried to push her hair back in place. "I demand you arrest that cowboy and Mr. Fife for attempting to force themselves on me."

"Too late," said the man kneeling over the cowboy. "He's dead."

"I didn't do anything." Mr. Fife shook from head to toe.

"You tied me up and told the cowboy I had a hatpin."

"I-I couldn't hurt a fly." Mr. Fife's lie wasn't believable with the dead cowboy at his feet.

Jasper crossed his arms. "I think the woman is confused. No doubt this drifter attacked Miss Ashford, and it looks as if Braunig fought the cowboy and poor Fife got the lucky shot that dispensed justice."

Miss Ashford stepped forward, no doubt to argue, but Gunter put a hand on her shoulder to stop her. "Let me walk you home while these men clean up."

Her eyes flashed, but she agreed. She scooped up her hat, the hatpin still secured to a chunk of her brunette hair. Gunter escorted her out through the closest door and turned her back toward the smithy. They needed to talk before Mutter saw her.

As soon as she reached the door, she spun to face him. "Why did you not tell the truth that Mr. Fife was an accomplice?"

"Because Jasper wasn't going to arrest him no matter what I said. The version that will be all over town in an hour is that Mr. Fife saved you."

"That is wrong"

"Not important."

"Justice is always important."

"So is your life."

Miss Ashford covered her mouth with both hands and started to shake. "They tried—"

"Sit." The wooden bench wasn't the most comfortable, but it was better than her fainting when her brain, heart, and body stopped fighting. He had no idea what it was called. He'd seen it in many people: the mother who saved her child from drowning, the man who killed a rattler before it struck his friend. And he'd felt it as a father who saved his only daughter from his burning home.

He fetched a dipper of water for Miss Ashford.

"They were going to force me to—to—marry Mr. Fife."

If the men hadn't slowed down to tie her hands, Gunter wouldn't have gotten there in time. He needed his own drink of water.

"You saved me."

"I am glad I heard you scream."

"Who was that man?" Miss Ashford took another drink.

"I don't know."

"I am trying to understand. Is my money so valuable that forcing me into marriage is the only option?"

"It must be."

Miss Ashford closed her eyes. "The love of money is the root of all evil."

"Yes, it is."

Straw stuck out of her hair. When Gunter reached for it, Amanda's eyes widened. He dropped his hand. "You have straw—"

Her hands flew to her hair. "I must look a mess."

Now was a suitable time for a judicious lie. "If you get the straw out of your hair and your hat back on, it will hide most of the damage."

"Do you have a mirror?"

"Sorry, no."

Amanda pulled several pieces of straw from her hair. "Better?"

"There is still more. May I?"

Amanda nodded and bowed her head, and Gunter worked out the few remaining pieces and a dangling hairpin. He handed her the pin. Amanda coiled the largest piece of dangling hair and stuck the pin in it. Her hat was dented on one side. She worked on it for a moment, removing the hatpin and hostage clump of hair. "Do I have a bald spot?"

"Not that I can see."

Placing the hat on her head, she held the hatpin in her hand, staring at it. "I couldn't get to my hatpin."

Gunter waited silently for her to make the next move. At last she secured her hat.

"Come. Let's get you back to the boardinghouse." Miraculously, she didn't fight him.

25

After they washed her hair, Mrs. Braunig left Amanda to soak in the tub. There wasn't a bald spot, only a rather thin and tender area on the back of her head. She relished the chance to scrub the smells of the barn off her skin. Eventually, her fingers puckered and the water reached an uncomfortable temperature that either needed to be warmed to be enjoyable or cooled to be invigorating. She dressed in a clean blouse and skirt without a bustle. It was time to help Mrs. Braunig with dinner preparations.

"Are you feeling better?"

"Much. Thank you. I know what a bother it is to have to prepare a bath."

Mrs. Braunig waved her hand as if batting away a fly. "My son would like to speak with you. He is in my private sitting room."

She'd never cleaned Mrs. Braunig's personal rooms, and, like other guests, had never had reason to be in them. The sitting room contained a single chair and a settee. Mr. Braunig stood near the lace-covered window.

"You wanted to talk with me?"

Not leaving his post, Gunter turned toward her. "Are you well? Were you injured?"

"The worst of it is the bruise on my face." The attempt to smile caused her to wince.

"I am worried someone might try to …" he took a deep breath, "harm you again. They spoke of a boss …"

Though the room was as warm as any other retreat from the Texas sun, she felt cold. She clasped her arms tightly around her. "There is so much I don't understand. The few men who have mentioned my dowry believe it is only $5,000. My dowry is much more. I saw the documents."

Mr. Braunig gestured to the chair. "Please sit."

The overstuffed chair was as comfortable as it looked.

"I have been rethinking your business proposal. I accept."

"But—" Of all the things she expected him to say, this was not one of them.

"Please hear me out before you say anything. Until you either leave or marry, men will continue to try to marry you, and unscrupulous men will apparently use force. I don't have the means to loan you the money to return home. If you choose to teach, there is enough time to annul before the school year starts since married women can't teach. Upon our annulment, I will give all the money to you."

"No. You were correct about Greta. She would never understand."

"She will. In time."

"You said marriage for convenience is wrong. Again, you were correct."

"I can protect you."

"That isn't your job. You have played the part of the Good Samaritan and more. I was wrong to ask you to marry me. I let my desperation cloud my judgment."

"This is—" A knock at the door stopped him midsentence.

Mrs. Braunig opened the door. "Sorry to interrupt. Mrs.

Roberts is here with the deputy to see Miss Ashford."

Amanda stood. "I should go."

Mr. Braunig nodded. She half expected him to continue his plea.

Mrs. Roberts engulfed Amanda in her arms as soon as she entered the parlor. "You poor child. You don't need to say a word. Jasper told me all that happened."

Not wanting to show weakness in front of the deputy, Amanda stepped back from the motherly embrace. "As you see, I am well."

The deputy sheriff stepped between Amanda and his stepmother. "I have a few more questions for you."

Amanda sat down in her favorite chair. If she was going to face an inquisition, she would not do so standing in the center of the room like a child. Mrs. Roberts sat down on the davenport on the other side of the room.

The deputy didn't sit. Instead, he stood near enough to keep Amanda from rising gracefully from her chair. "Have you ever seen that drifter before?"

"Not that I recall." Amanda had to crane her neck to answer him. Sitting had been a poor choice.

"Did he say anything about where he was from?"

Amanda folded her hands in her lap. "It wasn't a picnic conversation. He did know Mr. Fife. Have you asked him?"

"Mr. Fife says he never saw him before he shot him."

"That is a lie. Mr. Fife helped him by tying up my hands. Then the man told Mr. Fife to stand guard."

"That story doesn't match Mr. Fife's." The sheriff took a step back, giving her room to breathe.

"Of course not. Mr. Fife is hardly likely to implicate himself."

"He claims Mr. Braunig was the man's accomplice."

Amanda leapt to her feet. "Absurdity! Mr. Braunig fought the man off."

"Well, these tales don't match. Mr. Fife has a long-standing reputation, and you have caused nothing but trouble since you arrived. My question is, should I arrest Mr. Braunig for his part in the assault?"

"He rescued me!"

"So you wouldn't testify against him?"

"Of course not."

"Then, with the death of the cowboy, I will have to declare this event over."

Amanda put her hands on her hips, not sure what to say. It was clear Mr. Fife was not to be prosecuted. The idea that they would arrest Mr. Braunig was more than ridiculous.

The deputy put his hat back on and left the room.

Mrs. Roberts patted the cushion next to her. "Come sit."

Amanda sat next to her friend. "I can't believe he is your son."

"Stepson. I had no hand in raising him."

"I should complain to the sheriff."

Mrs. Roberts patted Amanda's hand. "I know how confusing this must be for you. It is normal for a woman who has been violated to create—"

"I wasn't violated."

"—to make up stories, even when there are witnesses. I've seen it before."

"I'm not making anything up. Mr. Fife was the one who bound my wrists. He may even have a bruise where I kicked him."

The hug Mrs. Roberts gave her wasn't as motherly as the first. "I know this is difficult, dear. Women have endured this shame for centuries."

"What shame?"

"Being forced." Mrs. Roberts's hushed words echoed like cannon shot in the small room.

"I wasn't. Mr. Braunig rescued me before that could happen."

The polite nod and smile on Mrs. Robert's face were the same her mother had used in cajoling Amanda as a child. "Even with your dowry, this will lessen your chances with most men."

"I wasn't violated." Amanda struggled to keep her tone even.

"Fortunately, Mr. Fife said he will still marry you. In a few weeks, everyone will forget the attack, and if you are with child—"

The ludicrous suggestion hung between them. Amanda slid away from Mrs. Roberts's embrace and rose with all the dignity of her mother. "Thank you for visiting."

"Oh, anytime dear." Mrs. Roberts took the hint and stood too. "Just don't wait too long. If there is a child…"

"I wasn't—" Amanda couldn't find a polite word to use.

"Of course you weren't." Mrs. Roberts patted Amanda's arm.

How did the woman not believe her? Gritting her teeth, Amanda saw the woman to the door.

Greta sat on the porch. Amanda hoped she hadn't heard or understood the conversation. "Do you know where your father is?"

"Around the back, chopping wood."

Amanda stepped back into the parlor. If Mrs. Roberts repeated the rumor to Reverend Whitesides, the school would never hire her. That morning, all Amanda wanted was to make her own choices. Now lies dwindled even that. Amanda checked her appearance in the hallway mirror. She had only one choice left.

chopping wood did not release as much tension as hammer to anvil, but Gunter was not leaving the boardinghouse until he knew there was a plan to keep Miss Ashford safe. His loose shirt stuck to his skin. As tempting as it was to remove the sodden cloth, he kept it on in case Miss Ashford sought him out. He kept one eye on the house. The deputy had left several minutes ago. If she didn't appear soon, he would go find her.

He balanced another log on the stump.

Miss Ashford descended the porch steps and hurried across the yard, stopping five feet away. "How soon can we be wed?"

Gunter set aside the ax. "We need a license from the courthouse."

"In Austin?"

"Yes. We could go to that one."

"Can we get there before it closes? I rather not wait until Monday."

"If we hurry." It would be close. "Are you sure?"

"On two conditions. One, you keep the money."

"It is not my money."

"Then enough to pay off your mother's mortgage."

He could argue the money later. He wouldn't keep what wasn't his. "What is the second?"

"You will write to my father about what happened today. Mrs. Roberts believes—" she looked away, her cheeks turning scarlet. "I was violated. If there is to be an annulment—"

"I understand."

Miss Ashford nodded but didn't look at him. "When can we leave?"

"I need to change and get the team. Fifteen minutes?"

"I'll be ready."

He would have to explain to Mutter and Greta when they got back.

On the way to the livery, he stopped at the smithy. He didn't have time to make a ring for her, but he did have several silver bands he'd used for practice. One had a delicate silver rose and several rosebuds. He took it from his hiding place, hoping it would fit.

A quarter hour later, he pulled the light carriage he'd borrowed from Kurt to the side of the boardinghouse. Miss Ashford exited in the dress she'd worn to church her first Sunday.

His mother followed holding Greta's hand, a look of concern on her face. "Vill you be back tonight, or are you having the judge marry you?"

He hadn't planned that far ahead. Reverend Ellerbrock would refuse to perform a sham wedding. Gunter looked to Amanda for an answer.

"A judge, but we will be back tonight."

Mutter shook her head. "It would not look right for you to return until tomorrow. Sunday night would be better."

"Where are you going, Papa? Can I go too?"

"Liebling, you are going to stay with me. Your papa must go to Austin to take care of some business. He will be gone until ..."

Next to Mutter's shoulder, Miss Ashford mouthed, "I told her."

"Sunday."

Miss Ashford's eyes grew wide, but she nodded. "I don't have a bag packed."

"We will make do. We must hurry before they close."

"Goodbye, Liebling, Mutter. We must hurry." Gunter helped Miss Ashford into the carriage. Neither of them spoke until they were out of town.

"I told your mother as quickly as I could. I hope you don't mind."

"I gathered. I had not planned on staying in town for two days."

"It will be expected."

Much would be expected. "Gunter. You should call me Gunter."

"I like your name. It makes the same sound as the hammer in the smithy. Gun-ter. Gun-ter." The way she said it did remind him of the clanging of the hammer on the anvil.

"Are you sure about this, Amanda?" He tested her name on his tongue, liking the sweet sound more than he should.

"Yes."

⊰◆⊱

Amanda twisted the rose ring around her finger, in awe that Gunter had made such a beautiful thing. It was slightly too big when worn next to her skin, but over the gloves, it fit perfectly.

Gunter chose one of the nicer hotels.

"We could stay somewhere less expensive." She made the argument again.

"No. Mutter is right. This must look like it is real. We don't know who might be observing."

The proprietor said nothing about their lack of luggage as he showed them the large corner room. She felt a blush creep up her face when the man pointed out the large bed. Gunter hurried the man out of the room. Amanda ran her finger along the back of the settee. "This will be my bed."

"I can sleep on the floor."

"Nonsense. This is the perfect size for me. We can't start our marriage arguing when the answer is obvious."

Gunter rubbed the back of his neck. "I suppose you're right."

Second, third, and fourth thoughts ran through Amanda's mind again. When she'd said yes, spending two nights in a hotel room had not been part of the plan. "Do you really believe we are being watched?"

"I don't know if *watched* is the correct word. The more I think about the events since Reverend Coolidge's death, the more I wonder."

"The only thing I have of value is my dowry. I don't know why this is so important."

"I should write that letter to your father." Gunter sat down at the table under the far window.

During the ride to Austin, they realized they'd need a bit of diversion for two days. Amanda unwrapped the dime novel she'd purchased at the mercantile down the street while Gunter purchased a checkers board and a doll for Greta's birthday.

Amanda removed her gloves and replaced the ring on her finger. She should get used to wearing it.

Gunter's voice interrupted chapter 2. "Who do you think the boss is?"

"The who?"

"When I was sneaking into the barn, the cowboy was threatening you and mentioned the boss."

Amanda tried to recall the words. Suddenly, her senses were overwhelmed with the man's words, his look, the smells, and the hand that had pushed up her skirt. She closed her eyes to block out the memory but didn't succeed.

"Amanda?" Gunter's voice was closer. "Open your eyes."

He was kneeling in front of her. "I'm sorry. I didn't think…"

"I remember he said something about a boss. But there were only the two of them there. Weren't there?" She buried her shaking hands in her skirt.

"I didn't see anyone else." He held out his hand, and she grasped it. "I'm sorry."

"I need a moment. Sit with me?"

He stood slowly. Amanda scooted as close to the arm of the couch as possible. Only a few inches separated them, not much closer than they had been in the buggy. Strength radiated from him. If she could only hold it and soak it in. What had they been discussing? Oh, yes. "Mr. Fife works for the church. At least partially. Reverend Whitesides couldn't be his boss, could he?"

"Fife works for the church?"

"Yes. Reverend Whitesides was upset that Mr. Fife was trying to take over the congregation. Last Sunday on the bridge, Mr. Fife was upset because he couldn't live in the parsonage anymore."

"Hmm …I thought he was a solicitor of some kind. Did Reverend Coolidge ever mention him in his letters?"

Amanda thought. "No. He wrote about Jimmy often."

Gunter rubbed his jaw. "No last name?"

"Sorry, no. We are no closer to knowing who the boss is." Amanda turned over her book. "Too bad we are not detectives like in *The Leavenworth Case*. I read it last year."

"How do detectives work?"

"They figure out the clues. Observe. Write things down."

Gunter returned to the table. "We have time and paper."

27

Three sheets of paper lay on the table, yet Gunter was no closer to the answers than yesterday when they started trying to piece together the clues they had so far. Being a detective was much easier in the books. Gunter reached for a fourth page and added the oddities on his land and the fire two years ago.

Amanda sat on the couch reading *The Weekly Democratic Statesman*. "This is the least important news I've ever read: 'It is estimated that every American boy would eat 350 pounds of candy a year if given the chance.' Of course they would. I would if it was chocolate. I could easily eat a pound a day."

"Is the entire newspaper like that?"

"No, most of it has to do with politics, though there is an article on the increasing numbers of opium eaters in the state."

"I've never met one."

"Me either."

Gunter pushed his chair back from the table. "I don't see how any of this is related. We've written down every weird fact I can think of except Herr Unger's dog going crazy last spring."

"Could that be significant?"

"No. We are making up things. None of it is related. Men want your money—no big mystery there. Whether it is $5,000 or $15,000, there is a lot of money at stake. Ebenezer isn't the first man to die mysteriously, but neither the deputy nor the doctor thought anything was wrong. And while I don't trust the deputy, the doctor is a decent fellow. And neither of those ties to the squatters or cattle rustlers on my land."

"There is one more thing…" Amanda bit her lip. "Never mind. I shouldn't have mentioned it."

"What?"

Amanda shook her head and went back to reading the paper.

Gunter stared at her for a long time. If they were really married, he would press her for an answer. His mind catapulted to what marriage to her would be like. He hadn't realized until last night how long her hair was. He'd returned from the washroom to find her brushing it in the mirror. It looked as smooth as melted chocolate cascading down her back. When she caught him staring, she quickly braided it. It hadn't been easy sleeping in the same room either. His mind imagined her little snores coming from the bed, next to him, not from across the room. At least at home they would not be sharing a room at night. No matter how much his bride insisted he stay in the larger room and bed, he'd put a cot in the empty room.

The rustle of the paper made him look up.

"I need to talk to someone, and I cannot tell you who or why. But I need you to drive me there."

"Who do you know in Austin?"

Amanda pinned on her hat. "I am not sure what I can say other than that he is a Texas Ranger."

An old man sat at the desk in the otherwise empty office. Amanda looked back through the window to where Gunter sat in the buggy. He wasn't pleased but had trusted her enough to bring her and not follow her inside for ten full minutes.

"Excuse me. Is George Washington Morgan here?"

"Sorry, ma'am, he isn't."

"When do you expect him?"

"Don't rightly know. Can I help you?"

"No. I'll try again."

"What is your name? I'll let him know you came in."

"Miss Amanda Ashford. I mean Mrs. Amanda Braunig of Grünlauf."

"Why didn't you say so?" The man behind the desk opened a drawer. "Here it is. GW left a message before he headed north. I was supposed to ride out and give it to you, but they had an incident…Anyway, this is for you."

Amanda took the crumpled yet sealed paper from the man. Reasoning that GW trusted the man to leave it for her, she opened it on the spot.

> Miss Ashford,
>
> I have been called to urgent business in the north. After reviewing what you said and my last interaction with Reverend Coolidge, I advise you to leave Texas as soon as possible. Whatever you do, don't get married. Your life will be in danger.
>
> GWM

"Anything helpful?"

"It might have been yesterday. If he comes back, will you tell him I married Gunter Braunig the day before I received his message?"

Unsure what to do with the note, Amanda stuffed it up her sleeve.

28

The house was decidedly cleaner, and Greta was happier now that she no longer needed to be woken up before dawn. If not for those two changes, Gunter would hardly know he had been married for ten days. One-third of their time. He'd walked the long way around so as not to pass the boardinghouse where Amanda and Greta waited for him each afternoon to start their new and rather dull life.

During the day, Amanda continued to help clean at the boardinghouse, where she took Greta. When he finished his work, he would bring them both home for dinner, which was usually the same thing as served at the boardinghouse. After Amanda read to Greta, Gunter would tuck his daughter into bed. During this time, Amanda would take herself to the small bedroom where he'd put the cot, and shut the door. Thus, in a week of marriage, they had managed to talk hardly at all. He had envisioned them sitting together at night, reading or discussing possibilities as they had at the hotel. Until they went to visit the Rangers, they'd had some semblance of a friendship.

Amanda wouldn't tell him what happened.

The door was locked, as it should be. Gunter took the key out of his pocket and let himself in. A new smell—something tangy and sweet at the same time—teased his nose. Gunter followed it into the kitchen, where Amanda sat at the table, reading a letter. She fumbled with it as she stood, putting it in the pocket of her apron.

"Where is Greta?"

"When I left, she was sleeping in your mother's parlor."

"You are supposed to stay with her."

"I came over to check on dinner. Herr Schellenberger brought the post. I've only been here a few minutes."

"We talked about this. You shouldn't be alone."

"I can see the door of the boardinghouse from here. I kept the house locked, and no one has been by."

"You could have waited."

"No, I need to check on the beans so they don't burn."

"How am I to keep you safe if you don't follow the rules?"

Amanda pointed out the window. "Herr Schellenberger is watching the house. Someone is watching me every minute!"

Something about the way she lifted her chin and raised her voice warned Gunter to back off. He didn't listen to the warning. He'd take a fight over the polite silence of the last few days. "You could have cooked at Mutter's."

"I'm making baked beans. It isn't a German recipe."

"So it won't cook in a German oven? I didn't think you thought of us that way."

Amanda's hands fell to her hips. "What are you saying? Your mother's customers want their schnitzel, strudel, and sauerkraut. I don't want to cook something they wouldn't like, so I made it over here."

"Don't you like German food?"

"Not sauerkraut."

"But you should eat it."

"Why? Because I married a German?"

"Ja."

"Greta doesn't like it, and her first language is German."

Gunter opened his mouth to fire back and out came laughter. "Are we fighting over not eating sauerkraut?"

Amanda pushed a wisp of hair out of her face. "No, we are fighting because I—" She burst into tears and ran from the room. The sound of her footsteps slowed when she reached the little bedroom upstairs and shut the door.

He'd been wishing for a conversation, not whatever this was.

Through the window he saw Herr Schellenberger sitting on the front porch, talking to Greta. He should get his daughter. He opened the front door and walked to the gate.

Greta noticed and did the same in the boardinghouse yard. Gunter waved her across the street. Mutter waved from her kitchen. Before last week, he'd often had Greta come home that way. Just a wave and look to make sure no wagons barreled down the street.

"How is my girl?"

"Good. Where is Miss Amanda?"

"Upstairs."

Greta wrinkled her nose. "What is that smell?"

"Baked beans."

"Oma made Wiener schnitzel. Can I eat over there?"

"We should try some of what Miss Amanda made for us."

Greta wrinkled her nose again.

A creaking board above them alerted him to Amanda's return.

"What a long nap. You must be growing taller."

Greta tipped her head. "What do you mean?"

"My old nursemaid used to tell us that whenever we took long naps, we were trying to grow taller. Once, my brother Charles slept for an entire day. And sure enough, when he woke up, his pants were too short."

"What is a nursemaid?"

"A person who is paid to take care of children when their parents can't."

"Are you my nursemaid?"

Amanda looked at Gunter with wide eyes.

"No, *Liebling,* she is your friend," Gunter replied for her.

<hr>

Amanda scraped the baked beans into a crock. There would be enough for Gunter's lunch tomorrow if he wanted them. Greta only ate half her portion but had declared them better than sauerkraut—praise that put the meal barely above pig slop. She wouldn't be entirely surprised to discover that Gunter had detoured past Herr Unger's pig pen with his lunch. Cold beans didn't taste good anyway. Amanda took the crock and marched outside to the covered bucket Mrs. Braunig put her scraps in. It was half full. Herr Unger hadn't collected it yet tonight. The contents of the crock slid into the bucket, a chunk of salt pork sliding over the remains of a corn cob. Was it wrong to feed pigs pork?

As she replaced the lid, a hand clamped around her arm. Amanda whirled around, the crock held high, ready to strike her assailant. She stopped just in time, sending a fine spray of sauce onto Gunter's shirt.

From her perch on her father's back, Greta giggled.

Gunter dropped his hand. Amanda clenched her jaw to hold in all the words she wanted to say that Greta needn't hear.

"We'll talk later." From the way the muscles worked in his jaw, Gunter suffered from the same problem she did.

"Of course." Amanda crossed the road with Gunter close behind. Anxious to have the discussion over, she headed straight for the book she'd been reading with Greta.

"Will you sing tonight instead?"

"Sing?"

"The song you used to sing while washing. You haven't sung in so long."

Amanda bit her lip. She hadn't realized she sang while doing the wash. "What song is that?"

"Oh, George, my George." Greta muttered the next couple of words. "Flirting on the ice!"

The song had been popular at Bradford, especially in the winter when there were ice-skating parties. Amanda had sung it because it reminded her of everything cold. The choice between fulfilling Greta's wish and singing a love song in front of Gunter twisted within her. "Perhaps another song."

"Please. I like the ice one."

Amanda bit her lip. "As soon as you are in your nightgown, I'll sing."

Greta clapped her hands and ran upstairs, stopping halfway and coming back for her dress to be unbuttoned.

Amanda didn't look at Gunter as she walked into the kitchen to wash the crock. She was still drying it when she heard Greta's bare feet padding across the floor into the kitchen. "I brought my hairbrush. Papa said I needed to have you brush my hair too."

Usually the most difficult part of the day. Perhaps a song would be worth it if the little girl would stand still. Amanda took Greta's hand and led her into the parlor, singing as she brushed, thankful to focus on something other than Gunter's presence.

To Central Park one day,
I took my love with me
To pass the time away
In skating merrily.
When on the gliding steel,

She whispered once or twice—
Oh! George, my George, pray don't reveal
Our flirting on the ice.

For this is so entrancing.
Better than dancing,
Softly smoothly gliding,
Yes. Pleasant words no chiding,
Oh, so fascinating.
What can equal skating?
For nothing surely is so nice,
When flirting on the ice.

Greta joined in the second time Amanda sang the chorus. "I don't understand how you can dance on ice."

Grateful not to have to sing the other verses, Amanda tried to explain frozen-over ponds and ice skates.

"Ice like they put in the ice cream freezer on Independence Day?"

"Yes."

Greta spread her arms out as if measuring an ice block. "That is too small to dance on."

Gunter laughed. Amanda hadn't heard him laugh since she'd trounced him in a game of checkers at the hotel. "Liebling, it is true. When I was a little boy in Germany, I went ice skating."

"Did you flirt on the ice?"

"No, I didn't."

"Why not?"

"Little boys don't flirt." The tips of his ears turned red. Good, he needed to feel some of the embarrassment too. "Come, it is time for bed."

"There is still more song." Greta folded her arms and stomped her little foot.

"Pouting is not the way to ask Miss Amanda to sing. Perhaps tomorrow." Gunter held out his hand, and Greta stuck out her tongue.

Gunter scooped the child up. "Liebling, it is time to say good night."

Greta's bottom lip stuck out as far as she could make it. Amanda couldn't resist quoting Mrs. Smythe. "Better be careful or a bird will come along and poop on that lip."

Under furrowed brows, Greta's lip retreated. Gunter's lips quivered as if he tried not to smile.

"Good night, Greta," Amanda called as Gunter carried her away.

Knowing she had some time, Amanda opened Emily's letter to finish reading it. Nothing prepared her for the unbelievable and harrowing tale Emily wrote of. None of the dime novels Amanda read came close to what Emily had survived the past month. And now she was getting married. Emily, who claimed no one could ever tempt her into matrimony, would be married in ten days. Emily begged Amanda to come stand with her, but she knew Gunter wouldn't let her out of his sight for that long. Amanda returned to reading the details of Emily's escape, so intent on the story she didn't hear Gunter come back downstairs.

"Is that from your father?"

She folded the letter. "No."

"Do you want to finish reading it?"

"I've already read it once. It is from my friend Emily. She's getting married on August 8. She invited me to come to Hiramsville and stand up with her."

"Out of the question."

"That is what I thought you'd say."

"I'm trying to keep you safe."

"We don't know that there is any danger." From George Washington's warning, Gunter was the danger. Or could be.

How was she to know? Eb's warning didn't include Gunter on either side. He had left the Bible with him, so he trusted Gunter to get it and the letter to her unopened.

"You don't know there isn't."

"We married to keep me safe. Instead, I am smothered. At the hotel when you told me you thought Mr. Fife and whoever are working with the boss were watching me, I felt the same way I did when I read Edger Allen Poe. Now I know someone's watching me every moment for my safety, and I still feel as if I can't breathe right."

"What do you mean?"

"It is hard to explain. I can't even go to the outhouse without permission. I feel like I am your prisoner."

"I am keeping you safe."

"Think about it. It doesn't make sense to do anything to me now. If they want the money, they have to wait until we are married for thirty-two days. You are in more danger than I am. Making me a widow would better serve their purposes—or waiting until the money is yours and trying to steal it."

"When did I become your enemy?"

"You aren't my enemy."

"It sure doesn't seem like I am your friend."

"Only twenty-one more days. Then I'll leave, and your life can be normal." What was normal? For him it would be whatever life had been before she came to Texas. For her? She had no idea.

"I thought you said they would be after the money then."

"Gunter, don't you understand there is no way to know what the future will be? If the last weeks have taught me anything, it is that plans are revised."

"That they are." He stood. "We should get to bed."

"I need to use the outhouse."

"I wish I had a toilet like the hotel and boardinghouse do."

"Well, after I am gone, you'll be able to buy one so Greta doesn't have to go outside in the middle of a rainstorm."

"I hadn't thought about that."

"Twenty-one more days. We can be through." Amanda wasn't sure if the positive voice was for her or him.

29

Usually Gunter enjoyed his Friday morning freight runs to Austin. Today, too many thoughts weighed on his mind to do anything but focus on the team. Nothing in their relationship. The message from the school board that she was ineligible to teach now that she was married had set Amanda in a peculiar mood. She'd mentioned going to Boston again with a certain sadness to Greta, not him.

Then she made a *Potthucke* almost as good as Mutter's. None of the boardinghouse residents had even noticed it wasn't Mutter's. Gunter wouldn't have known either if Greta hadn't announced it. Why bother learning to cook his favorite foods if only to leave?

The calendar that hung on the kitchen wall now had Xs counting down the days. Amanda hadn't spoken an unnecessary word to him, and she'd complied with every restriction he put on her.

He should be happy.

He wasn't.

The entire situation was miserable. There had to be a way to repair it even if they only had to survive another two weeks.

The freight pickup went smoothly, with every single crate accounted for. Gunter walked over to the train-station office and looked at the schedules. Traveling to Hiramsville required three train switches, taking most of the day. If they could travel in a straight line, it would take half the time. No matter how he calculated the trip, it would take three days—two for travel and one for the wedding. Mutter would take care of Greta. Or they could take her with them. A four-year-old child's ticket was only a quarter fare. Gunter studied the chart and pondered the possibilities.

Three train switches meant it would be easy to spot anyone following them.

"Sir? Are you going to purchase a ticket?"

A line had formed behind Gunter while he looked at the chart. "I'm not sure."

"Stand aside, then."

"Two round trip tickets to Hiramsville for next Thursday's departure." Gunter set his money on the counter. "And a quarter-fare ticket as well."

Gunter tucked the tickets safely into his pocket and headed for his last stop, the icehouse.

The entire hour-and-half ride back home, Gunter second-guessed his rash decision. The combined fares took most of the money he'd brought into town. If his father was alive, he would chide Gunter for spending so recklessly. First, the hotel room and meals for his pretend honeymoon cost a total of twenty dollars. Now, this trip to a wedding would require more meals and another hotel stay. It was money that could go toward mortgages. He was counting on money he didn't deserve.

Strudel dough was much more difficult than pie dough. When Amanda thought it was almost thin enough, it ripped. She huffed and wiped her forehead with the back of her hand.

Greta giggled.

"What did I do wrong this time?" Amanda forced a smile for the little girl.

"You have flour." Greta pointed to the center of her forehead.

"Proof that I am working hard." She rolled the dough into a ball and tried again.

Mrs. Braunig entered the kitchen and stared at the worktable. "Nein. It is no good. If you roll out too many times, it will be hard. Throw the dough away and try again."

This glob of dough joined the other one in the slop bin. "Perhaps you should do it. I am going through all the flour."

"Don't give up. You try to learn how to make strudel in only a few days. I've been making it for thirty years."

"I could watch you." Amanda had yet to see the entire process from beginning to end, only parts she caught as she came into the kitchen from some other duty.

"Time for watching is over. Time to learn by doing." Mrs. Braunig picked up the cloth covering the worktable. "There is too much flour here. Greta, go outside and shake it."

Greta returned looking much like Amanda imagined a ghost would. "Greta, what happened?"

"The flour flew into the air and landed on me."

"Never mind. We will wash you up before dinner. "

Amanda worked the flour, eggs, and oil together as she had before, then formed it into a log shape and rolled it out.

"Stop. The dough needs some time to rest." Mrs. Braunig hummed a little tune. "Now, roll a little more. Then we stretch the dough with the backs of our hands, like this. Do not use your fingers; they will make holes."

Amanda slid her hands under the dough and moved them as Mrs. Braunig did. "I thought I could roll the entire thing out."

"No, it isn't like pie. Strudel must stretch." Mrs. Braunig demonstrated the step Amanda had tried to do with the rolling pin.

Soon the dough covered the entire table. "Is it thin enough to read the Bible through?"

Amanda studied the thin skin of dough covering the cloth. "Yes."

"Now it is ready."

"I thought I could use my rolling pin."

"No. Must not cut corners when making strudel."

"Why didn't you correct me earlier?"

"Because it is easier to learn from failure than success. You needed to understand how the dough must be stretched and not rolled like pie." Mrs. Braunig added a meat filling using the large cloth to assist her in rolling and folding the strudel. "Greta, go wash up."

Mrs. Braunig waited until the washroom door shut behind her granddaughter. "Why do you want to learn to make strudel if you are leaving my son in two weeks?"

Two weeks too soon and too far at the same time. "Gunter likes it."

"Will you make it when you go to Boston?"

"My mother has a cook. I will not be allowed in the kitchen." Amanda washed out the bowl.

"How did you learn to cook?"

"We had culinary classes at the school. I knew that if I married a minister, I might not be able to hire a cook or maid, so I learned."

Greta returned to the room, a light coating of flour still evident in her hair.

"Looks like someone is taking a bath tonight," said Amanda.

"Saturday is tomorrow." Greta held up her hands for inspection.

"You are dirty today."

"But Saturday is bath day."

"True. We will see after dinner. If I can brush the flour out of your hair, it can wait."

"Yippee!" Greta clapped her hands and ran to the parlor.

"You let her off too easily," said Mrs. Braunig.

"I don't want to haul out the tub two nights in a row."

"You could bathe her here."

The indoor water pump did make things go faster.

Mrs. Braunig fanned herself. "No more cooking. I hope Gunter brings ice today. Some days I wonder if we would have left Germany if we knew it was so hot in Texas."

Amanda finished cleaning the dishes. "Not all parts of America are warm. Boston gets warm in the summer, but not like this."

"We arrived in September. Not so bad then. My husband hurried to build the boardinghouse. I told him we should make an outdoor kitchen, but he said one kitchen was enough. For seventeen summers I have cooked in this kitchen. My husband was wrong." Mrs. Braunig hung her apron on a hook on her way out the back door.

"Why did you build a boardinghouse?" Amanda grabbed the mending basket and followed Mrs. Braunig around the back to the shade of the trees.

"My family ran an inn three times the size of this. My Herman knew blacksmithing. He built the forge first. We worked hard to save money to buy land. Herman was sure that farming was the way to our future, but some days I am not so sure. I am too old to learn to farm, but I promised my husband I wouldn't sell the land."

Bringing up the mortgage would be impolite, especially since Mrs. Braunig probably didn't know she knew.

"Do you think it would be wrong of me to break my word to my husband?"

"When did he die?"

"Almost three years this September 2."

"What are you going to do with the land?"

"Nothing. I am too old to learn to farm. I wouldn't like it. No one to talk to out there. Gunter was never interested in farming or ranching, but he is a good boy and has followed his father's wishes. Since losing Pauline, he doesn't want to farm either."

"You could sell the land."

"We tried, but someone wants to purchase it for less than what we bought it for. And none of our German friends can afford it even at the low price. We worry if we sell it to someone who is not German, it will make it harder for us. Herman and I had money when we arrived. Other families didn't. Some were promised land they never received. I would like to sell but not to some rancher who already has more land than he needs."

Gunter pulled his wagon into the side yard. Greta flew out of the door. "Papa!"

He brushed the top of her head. "What have you been doing?"

"Helping."

Amanda watched the interchange. She couldn't remember ever rushing to greet her father when he came home from work. Each night, she and Charles had been paraded into the parlor before her parents had dinner. Father would ask them questions about what they did. After answering, they would be sent off to bed. Sometimes Mother would come hear them pray. How wonderfully odd to have a father who played with you. If she'd had the choice, she would have chosen a father like Gunter.

"Oh, the strudel!" Mrs. Braunig jumped up from the bench.

"I'll go get it. You can see if your son brought any ice." Amanda hurried into the house, glad to have something to do other than wish for a life she hadn't had.

30

As planned, Gunter met Kurt and Peter at the smithy early Saturday morning.

Peter dismounted his horse. "I don't get a chance to talk with you after church. I am surprised you married an American. Was it for her money?"

Gunter wished to skip the subject of his hasty marriage. "Did you find out what they are growing in the hollow?"

"First, you answer my question. You married very quickly. I thought you loved Pauline better than to make a rash choice."

Telling either brother the truth would be the same as telling Kurt's wife and Peter's mother. In a few days, everyone would know everything about his life. "Not every hasty decision is rash. Are we going to talk all morning or ride out?"

Peter climbed back onto his horse. "Let's get moving. I need a closer look at the crop they are growing. None of my farmer friends knew what it could be from my description."

"Should we circle around and come from a different direction?" asked Kurt.

Gunter pointed out the only argument he could find. "It will take longer."

"If we do, our faces will be in the sun," said Peter. "If there is anyone down there, we will have the sun on our side."

"Then we should go around." Kurt led out.

Gunter wasn't sure who exactly had put Kurt in charge, but at least while riding, they couldn't ask him any questions about his new wife. They didn't pass any signs of human life as they cut through Gunter's father's land.

The north end of the hollow sloped gently.

Peter made a clucking noise with his tongue and pointed to a large mesquite grove. Someone had built a lean-to near the base of the tree. Kurt signaled for the men to dismount. "We should walk in from here."

"I'll go. You stay here with the horses," said Peter.

"It's my land. I should go," said Gunter.

"No offense, but I'm skinnier and faster. I'll go." Peter didn't wait for the men to agree before he struck off.

Kurt pointed to a cluster of scrub bushes. "Let's take the horses over there. It gives us better cover.

The minutes dragged by as the sun rose higher and higher in the sky. A shout and the report of a gun broke the morning stillness. Gunter and Kurt mounted their horses to be ready. They had to wait only a few moments for Peter to appear, running at top speed. He waved both men forward, then jumped on his own horse with the skill of a man who'd worked on farms and ranches for years.

Peter caught up and signaled them to turn west, away from town. Gunter was torn between arguing and following, but Peter had more experience on the range and knew the hill country better. If someone followed, it was best not to lead them to his home.

They rode hard for a mile before they met a well-traveled road. Peter continued riding away from Gunter's land, then turned at a gate to one of the largest ranches in the area and slowed. "The foreman knows me. We can water our horses and walk them from here."

Gunter recognized the man who exited the barn as a frequent customer.

"What brings y'all out this way?"

Peter answered. "I wanted to show my friends that spread over yonder, only Kurt needs to get home, and we rode our mounts too hard. Can we cool them off?"

"They don't look too bad, but you were always the cautious one."

"Better cautious than stranded." Peter led the men over to the horse trough.

"Are you still working on your own spread, then?" asked the foreman.

"Yup. Hoping to expand."

"I heard there is some land between here and Greenleaf. Ain't no good, though. One of the dogs chased a rabbit in. When he came home, he was as loco as a rabid coon. Thought we were going to have to put him down. A couple of weeks later, there were some coyotes just as crazy as the dog near there. Ran all over the road, chasing their tails."

"Ever seen anything like it before?"

"Nope. Some of my hands say it is haunted on account of all the natives we chased off." The foreman looked at Gunter. "Blacksmith, don't you own that spread?"

"I do. Never heard it was haunted, though."

"It did kill your wife."

No one spoke after the foreman's declaration. He removed his hat. "Pardon me. I shouldn't have said that."

Gunter made a point of checking his horse. "I think Riese is recovered."

"My horse too. Thanks for letting us stop," said Peter.

"Do y'all need anything else?"

"Thank you, no. We'll get on our way." Peter waved in farewell. Gunter nodded at the foreman, as did Kurt.

They rode out, keeping their horses at a leisurely pace.

Peter set his horse in the center. "I've heard a lot of crazy things around the campfire, but never crazy dogs."

"What about haunted land?" asked Kurt.

"As near as I can tell, there isn't a cave, hill, or valley in Texas that hasn't been cursed by some tribe or haunted by some ghost killed in some battle." Peter's flippant answer wasn't nearly as reassuring as he likely meant it to be.

They passed a wagon headed in the opposite direction, but the road was otherwise empty.

Peter kept scanning the countryside. "It was one man. From the way he walked, he was drunker than any man I've ever seen. I was lucky he didn't shoot me on accident with that rifle of his."

"So what are they growing?" asked Gunter.

"Flowers."

⋙◆⋘

One of the more useless pieces of information Amanda learned at college was in the astronomy course. Dog days of summer had nothing to do with panting dogs looking for shade. Rather, Sirius, the Dog Star, could be seen rising about the same time as the sun. Some speculated that this phenomenon somehow created the hottest days of the year. Her teacher had argued that Sirius didn't cause the hot weather. However, finding herself panting like a dog from just pumping Greta's bathwater, Amanda wondered if her teacher had been wrong.

"I don't want to wash my hair."

"Greta, we talked about this. Yesterday it was flour, and today you managed to get enough twigs and leaves in it that I am surprised nothing has taken up residence. Tomorrow is Sunday, and your hair needs to be clean."

"What does 'taken up residence' mean?"

"It means I wouldn't be surprised if a mouse were living here." Amanda brought out her lavender-scented soap to entice the girl. "Smell this."

Greta sniffed it and climbed into the tub. "You can wash my hair with that soap. It smells pretty."

Once she was in the tub, bathing Greta wasn't difficult, other than the splashing.

Amanda stood, her apron soaked through. "All done. You even have enough time to let it dry before bed."

"Will you sing the ice-skating song again?"

"I know other songs."

"But I like it."

"Give me a moment to do something with the water." Amanda dipped an empty bucket into the tub.

Gunter knocked on the wall. "Don't take it out. I'll use it to bathe."

"You might change your mind when you see the water. Greta had enough flour still on her that if she'd been caught in a rainstorm, she would have turned to glue."

He crossed the room and looked into the metal tub. "I'll dump it so you can go sing to her."

Unlike Amanda, Gunter was able to lift the entire tub and carry it out the door.

Amanda brought her comb with her to the parlor. "What shall I sing while we comb?"

"Combing hurts."

"I know. I used to hate it. But if hair dries before it is combed, it hurts more. How about I'll sing as long as you let me comb?"

"The ice song."

Knowing Gunter would hear the love ballad made it difficult to sing. After the second round of the song, Greta requested it a third time.

"Aren't you tired of that song yet?"

"No."

"There are so many other lovely songs. Have you ever heard of 'The Angel and the Child'?"

Greta shook her head, nearly getting the comb caught in a curl.

"It is by Henry Wadsworth Longfellow—a famous poet who lives in Cambridge, Massachusetts, which is across the river from Boston, where I live."

"You don't live in Boston. You live here."

"I mean where I grew up."

"You can sing that song, then."

Amanda launched into the song, which had nothing to do with flirting or marriage. Halfway through, though, she remembered the ending was anything but happy, especially for a girl whose younger brother and mother had passed. She repeated the first verse and ended the song while braiding Greta's hair. "There you go."

"Why do you braid my hair at night?"

"So it doesn't tangle when you sleep."

"Do you braid your hair at night?"

"Yes."

Gunter entered the room. "Time to tuck you in, Liebling."

Greta hugged Amanda before skipping upstairs. Gunter nodded toward the kitchen. "I emptied the tub and put in fresh water if you need it."

"Thank you." Last week, she'd bathed at the boardinghouse to avoid needing to bathe in the same house as Gunter. Today there wasn't time. Amanda ran upstairs and got her dressing gown. Gunter had set the tub in the corner and hung a quilt from hooks in the rafters, dividing the room. Amanda had wondered what purpose the hooks held. Still, she hurried through washing her hair, self-conscious of any movement above her. Sharing a bathroom at Bradford had taught her efficiency in bathing. Dressed in her dressing gown, with her hair wrapped in a towel and holding her soiled clothing tightly to her chest, she darted for her room. The towel around her head shifted, and she ducked to keep it from falling.

"Whoa." Gunter caught her by the shoulders before she barreled into him.

Amanda stepped back, and the towel slid from her head. She bent to retrieve it at the same time as Gunter. They bumped heads, and Amanda fell backward, dropping her clothes. Gunter also lost his balance, landing next to her—only inches away. It was the closest they had been since the brief kiss in front of the judge, a kiss she had pushed from her mind. It had been nothing like the one she'd shared with Eb so long ago.

Gunter reached to help her. Her hand lingered on his arm. "Did I hurt you?"

"No." Not entirely true—her posterior ached, but something inside warmed her, canceling out the pain.

His hand moved up her arm and captured a lock of her hair as he spoke softly. "*Die Schöne.*"

Amanda had no idea what the words meant and didn't dare ask because her heart was beating so fast she feared her voice would not work.

Gunter dropped her hair and stood. He was a giant of a man. An image of the last time a man stood over her flashed through her mind. Then there was fear. But as Gunter lifted her to her feet, she felt protected. She had the irrational thought that if her dressing gown was not covering her, Gunter would still treat her with care and respect.

He stepped back slowly, his eyes never leaving hers. "You are sure I didn't hurt you?"

"I am well."

"I wanted to talk with you last night, but I didn't have a chance. Will you stay and talk with me tonight?"

She should say no, gather her clothes, and run to her room. Instead, she nodded.

"Sit, please." With Gunter's hand still on her arm, she sat at the end of the couch, tucking her bare feet out of sight. Gunter gathered her clothes and set them on the chair, save the towel, which he handed her as he took his place on the other end of the couch.

Gladly, she took the towel, mostly to have something to focus on other than Gunter.

"I stopped at the train station yesterday." Gunter took a folded paper from his pocket and handed it to her.

Amanda unfolded the paper, reviewing the train tickets to Hiramsville. Tears sprang to her eyes. Emily! Only this morning she'd posted the letter congratulating her friend and sent her apologies for not being able to attend.

"I know I should have consulted you first, especially since I decided to bring Greta." He shifted on his end of the couch.

Looking through a veil of happy tears, Amanda felt her heart overflow. He was too good, too kind. "I'm sorry."

<hr>

Gunter gripped the back of the couch to keep himself from gathering Amanda into his arms. The urge to kiss her that he'd felt landing beside her on the floor grew more intense. Only two more weeks and she would be gone. "Sorry?"

"For being upset with you the other night. I know we did this to keep me safe and living this way cannot be easy for you either. I know you didn't want to live a lie. And then tickets—I never imagined. Greta too. I'll pay you back."

"You don't need to pay me back."

"Oh, I guess that is true. My dowry should more than cover the expense."

"I wasn't thinking of your money. I was harsh the other night. I wanted to say I was sorry."

Amanda wrapped her hands in the towel. "When I proposed to you, I didn't realize how difficult this would be. I shouldn't have put you in this position. I heard Herr Schellenberger's comment about Germans marrying Germans. I hope they are not unkind at church tomorrow."

Gunter smiled. Some would share the views of Kurt and Peter. Others would be kind. After she left was when the unkindness would start, though, where Amanda had attended the German church most Sundays, she was less of an outsider than she could have been. "Queen Victoria married a German. I will tell them I found my queen."

"I am not anything close to a queen."

She was in so many ways, like the way she carried herself and never gave up. As much as he loved Pauline, she would have cried and wailed for days if she'd faced even half of what Amanda had the past month.

"I know they believe you did it for the money and think poorly of you. When I leave, I want to tell them the truth—about how noble and gallant you have been and how kind and how you even refused me. Gunter Braunig, the woman who gets you for a real husband will be incredibly lucky indeed." Amanda rose. "Thank you so much for the tickets and for including Greta."

Gunter sat on the couch for a long time after she went to her room. He wouldn't let her tell anyone the truth. No one needed to know how much he would miss her.

The bathwater was cool and lightly tinted with Amanda's lavender soap. It had always been more practical to share bathwater with Pauline as in the scorching summer the creek ran low and some wells failed. If Amanda could read his thoughts as he stepped into the bathwater, she would not believe him so noble.

31

re we there yet?" Greta asked again. In the front seat of the buggy, Herr Schellenberger grunted and mumbled something in German to Gunter. He'd been so kind to wake up early and drive them to the station; Amanda didn't want Greta to annoy him.

"I have an idea. How many nursery rhymes can we recite?"

Greta shrugged her shoulders.

Amanda kept her voice low. "Mary had a little lamb ..."

In the seat in front of them, Gunter spoke to Herr Schellenberger in German. Whatever he said seemed to calm the older man. Perhaps he was telling him it could be worse. Greta could have requested "Flirting on the Ice." Again. Gunter was the most patient of men, especially when it came to his daughter. And Amanda.

Sixteen rhymes later, Greta pointed outside the buggy. "Look at all the people, Miss Amanda. Are they all going on the train?"

"No. They have other things to do."

At the station, Gunter kept a firm grip on his daughter's hand and the two valises they'd packed for the trip. As they hurried to their train, Amanda noticed a man standing in the shadows. He seemed familiar. Amanda looked back to see that he'd followed them, his hat low over his face so she couldn't see his features. She stayed close to Gunter as they looked for their train. Twice she looked back, and the man was still near. When they boarded the train, she searched, not finding him. It must be her imagination. There was no reason for anyone to follow them to Hiramsville. All of their detective notes from the hotel were making her think like a dime novelist.

They claimed a pair of cushioned bench seats, and Gunter sat in the back-facing one. Greta took the space near the windows, and Amanda sat next to her in the forward-facing seat. Greta pressed her hands to the window and watched the people hurry to and from their destinations.

When the conductor yelled the final "All aboard," Greta turned to Gunter, her eyes wide as the train inched away from the station. "Papa we are moving!"

Through the window, Amanda saw the man sprint to board their train.

⟫◈⟪

Someone was watching them. Gunter stood and rearranged the bags on the shelf overhead, trying to figure out who. A tall man in the last seat looked away, as did a cowboy across the aisle. He should have never read that dime novel of Amanda's. Not only was he looking for outlaws in Grünlauf, he was looking for train robbers—not that they had much to steal. Amanda's ring and the twenty dollars he brought for meals and the hotel were about it. And Amanda's wedding gift of handcrafted lace wasn't worth a robber's time. He glanced at both men again before sitting down. Greta still looked out the windows in wonder. Amanda had her crochet needle out. Gunter moved closer to the window to answer

Greta's questions, not wanting his daughter drawing any more attention to them than necessary.

The train slowed for its first stop.

Greta stood. "Are we there?"

"Not yet. There will be many stations that are not ours. And we will be on two other trains before we are in the right place."

"How many stations?" Greta didn't take her eyes away from the window.

"I don't know. I didn't count them."

"Then I'll count. This is one."

The conductor yelled and rang his bell and the train rolled out again.

"Is this seat taken?" The tall man stood in the aisle.

Before Gunter could tell the man to move on, Amanda answered. "No, sir, it is not."

Something about her voice caused Gunter to search her face. It could be nothing, but he thought she welcomed the man. She sat relaxed, in contrast to how he felt.

"Thank you kindly." As the man set his hat and bag on the shelf, Gunter could see a gun in a holster at his side. He sat at the end of Gunter's bench and stretched his legs, blocking the family in. "Name's GW Morgan. Nice to meet you, folks."

Greta cupped her hand around her mouth. "Papa, he has a gun."

"Yes, I do. Do you know why?" answered Mr. Morgan.

Greta shook her head. Gunter's muscles tightened. If the man so much as moved a finger to that gun...

"I'm a Texas Ranger."

Amanda smiled. Gunter looked from his supposed wife to the man who'd joined them. How did they know each other?

"This is my papa. He is a blacksmith. This is Miss Amanda. She lives with us, but she isn't a nursemaid. She is a friend." Greta's introductions, while accurate, were not sufficient.

"Gunter Braunig, my new wife, Mrs. Braunig, and my daughter." Gunter shook hands with the ranger and looked him in the eye. They sized each other up and came to the silent understanding that neither was a threat.

"Mrs. Braunig, is this the blacksmith who made your former fiancé's box?"

"Yes."

GW relaxed in his seat. "Congratulations on your nuptials, then. You married the one man who is the exception to my note."

Amanda looked from the ranger to him and back again. "You don't know how relieved I am to hear that."

Gunter watched his wife, not sure what to think. He knew she'd talked with a ranger in Austin.

"Papa, I need to go." Greta hopped up and down.

"I'll take her. There is a ladies' retiring room in the car ahead of us." Amanda looked at the ranger for permission rather than at him.

"The train is safe."

Gunter watched over the seat as Amanda and Greta made their way down the aisle.

"How do you know my wife, and why am I an exception?"

"What was in the box you gave her?"

"None of your business."

"Actually, it is."

Gunter locked eyes with the ranger. "A book and a letter."

"That letter directed Miss Ashford to me. I have the book— or had the book. It is now with my brother. His bride-to-be is exceptionally good at deciphering code."

"I don't understand."

"I can't tell you everything now, but I will when we are in Hiramsville."

"How do you know we are going to Hiramsville?"

"Because my brother is marrying your wife's friend. I do need to apologize to her. I left her a message not to marry anyone, but she got it too late."

Amanda's change of attitude toward him suddenly made sense. It also hurt. She had trusted him enough to marry him but not enough to tell him about the Texas Ranger or the message.

"Why shouldn't she marry?"

"Because smugglers have set their sights on her money." GW kept his voice low.

"We knew someone did."

"When your wife and daughter return, we should find a private place to talk."

"I can't leave them."

"I have three friends on this train as far as Fort Worth. She'll be safe."

Gunter studied the man. Being a ranger wasn't enough reason to trust him. After all, Jasper was a deputy. That Ebenezer Coolidge had trusted the ranger enough to send Amanda to him was a comfort. But he was dead. Amanda trusted him enough that she didn't trust Gunter. The vicious circle enraged and comforted Gunter at the same time. "You sure about that?"

"They will keep her safe. I promise."

Greta hopped down the aisle to their seats. "Miss Amanda and I didn't get lost."

GW stood to let the women into the seats.

Gunter joined him. "I'm going to stretch my legs. We'll be back in a few minutes."

He followed the ranger to the back of the train.

GW stopped at a private room in the next car. "We can talk here."

Gunter entered. If the ranger intended to kill him, the private booth was an excellent place to do so.

"I understand you don't trust me. Ebenezer's Bible is helping us put some clues together, along with some things my spy in Grünlauf has told me. I know you rescued Miss Ashford from her attackers. And I have some theories about the house fire that killed your wife, as well as who murdered the reverend. Would it surprise you if I said they were connected?"

Gunter stared at the man. "How?"

"What do you know about opium?"

❖

After lunch, Greta fell asleep with her head on Amanda's lap. The ranger nodded to Gunter. The men had hardly spoken since their return even when they switched trains. Gunter stood. "Walk to the dining car with me?"

Amanda slid out from under Greta without disturbing her slumber. The dining car was mostly empty. Gunter chose a seat near the center of the car with no one near them. "GW says we should try the lemon cake."

The anticipation to discover why Gunter brought her to the dining car when Mrs. Braunig had packed them a lunch made the wait for the food seem twice as long.

Finally the cake arrived.

"I wish you had trusted me, but I understand."

"I wanted to tell you about the letter." Amanda took a bite of her cake, knowing that eating would keep her from sharing all of her thoughts.

"GW says your friend Emily is good at deciphering. The reverend used code in the Bible to write out his suspicions."

"He isn't just going to the wedding, then, is he?"

"No. Do you remember the article you read in the newspaper?"

"The one about the boys and candy?"

"No, the one about the opium eaters."

"Yes." Amanda took another bite. Listening was easier with her mouth full.

"Did the article say where they were getting the opium?"

"No. I assume India or China. Isn't that where most opium comes from?"

"According to GW, there are people growing it in Texas."

"Where?"

"On my land."

Amanda dropped her fork on the plate. It clattered and fell to the floor.

Gunter handed her his unused fork since he hadn't eaten any of his cake. "They aren't sure yet. After the wedding, you should stay in Hiramsville."

"Why?"

"Because if something happens to me, you'll be safe. They may come after you again."

"Why?"

"Your money."

"Why does it always come back to that? I'm so tired of only being good for my money." Amanda stood abruptly, knocking her leg on the table. She made her way to the ladies retiring room before bursting into tears.

32

"All the problems of a real marriage with none of the blessings," Gunter explained his haggard look to the shaving mirror. He'd spent the night on the floor pallet the hotel had brought in for Greta. Which was not nearly long or wide enough to sleep comfortably. He'd learned during his first year of marriage to Pauline not to accuse a wife of being unreasonable, but it didn't mean he didn't think about it. Tonight after the wedding, he would meet with GW again and figure out a plan. GW would have the Bible back by then and hopefully all of the decoded messages.

He returned to the room and knocked first, knowing Amanda needed to dress.

Greta opened the door. "It's Papa."

"I am almost ready."

He'd never seen the pale-green dress before. "*Die Schöne.*" The words slipped out before he could stop them.

"Papa, you said it was rude to speak German in front of Miss Amanda." Greta put her hands on her hips and glared, something she'd learned from Amanda. "He said you look beautiful."

Amanda blushed.

Gunter swallowed and turned away. "Are you ready, Liebling?"

"Yes, do you like my new ribbon? Miss Amanda says it is a reminder to act very grown up. Which means I won't wiggle or talk during the wedding."

"I'm glad you returned early. I am invited to the house to help Emily get ready. Apparently, the woman who helped us last night sent a message that I am here."

"Then we should go."

Gunter got directions from Hannah, who was also dressed for the wedding. The house was only a few blocks away; however, walking that far would damage Amanda's dress.

"My buggy is waiting outside. It is big enough for all four of us and the driver. He's been loading my pies. Miss Emily loves my pies."

"Oh, Emily wrote to me about you." Amanda hugged the woman. "I'm sorry I didn't realize who you were last night."

"She told me about you too, chil', but she didn't tell me you married such a handsome man. I didn't recognize who you were either. We'd better get moving. That TJ is ready to be hitched, and he might arrest anyone who makes him wait for his wedding." Hannah's deep laughter told the opposite story. TJ would wait through a tornado if he had to. Gunter couldn't help but feel a bit jealous of the man.

⟨⇒◆⇐⟩

An excitable girl of sixteen led Amanda into the room where Emily stood in her dressing gown.

Amanda was immediately enveloped in the arms of her friend. "I can't believe you are here. I got your letter two days ago saying you couldn't, then GW tells TJ over dinner last night that you were on the train with him and married."

"Becky, let's give the two of them a minute." An older woman shooed the girl out of the room.

Emily let go of Amanda. "Five minutes, Becky, then you can help me dress."

The door clicked, and Emily whirled back to Amanda. "Your letter didn't say a word about a husband. You have five minutes. Talk fast."

"He isn't really my husband."

Emily pulled Amanda onto the bed with her. "What?"

Amanda told the story as briefly as possible. "So you see, we are not really married."

Emily hugged Amanda again. "Why didn't you tell me? I could have purchased you a ticket."

"How?"

"My uncles had an argument about my inheritance. My cousin Percy is here and brought me the money they felt I was owed. It is over $8,000. I can loan you the money, and you can go back with Percy. He'd be happy to chaperone you."

"I don't want to go back."

"What?"

"Yesterday when Gunter was trying to get me to stay here, I realized that I love him. Real love—not what I thought I had with Eb. I see that I was marrying Eb because of his job, which is silly because that's why my parents want me to marry in Boston society—because of a position. I don't care that Gunter is a blacksmith. He is the kindest—" Amanda stopped to calm her nerves. Now was not the time to cry.

"This is going to sound terrible, but I am glad you didn't marry Eb."

"You did try to warn me. What am I going to do?"

"You could tell him how you feel?"

Someone knocked on the door.

"Open that, will you? If I don't get dressed, TJ might arrest me for disturbing his peace of mind."

Amanda opened the door, admitting Becky and the older woman. "You're the second one to make a joke about TJ arresting people today. Do I need to worry?"

"TJ doesn't arrest anyone without cause. When he arrested Emily, it wasn't for real. And we are all glad he did." Becky picked up the dress bodice. "Now, can we put it on? TJ is talking about criminals with his brother. You need to get married before it gets serious."

Emily laughed. "If he runs away, I'll go arrest him."

The graduation-dress-turned-wedding-gown was almost as beautiful as Emily. Amanda stepped back into the corner and allowed Becky to fuss with her friend.

"Amanda, come put on my veil. Mrs. Reese and Becky, please send everyone over to the church."

White silk roses adorned the crown of the veil. "Oh my, if Barbara could see you now, she'd be green with envy."

"Have you seen my husband? She'd be more than green."

"I can't believe you are getting married. You always said you wouldn't." Amanda shook out the gauzy material.

"TJ showed me I was lovable. Other than you, Percy, and Uncle Carl, I hadn't felt wanted for so long. Promise me you won't miss out on the chance to have the same thing in your life."

Amanda centered the veil and fastened it in place with hairpins. "What if he is only being gallant?"

"Then at least you tried. I've never known you to give up on anything you wanted. Don't start now."

Becky opened the door. "TJ is gone, and so is almost everyone else. Miss Hannah is out front with your husband, ma'am."

Amanda kissed Emily on the cheek. "I better hurry. Can't get to the church after the bride."

The church overflowed with well-wishers. Gunter found a seat for them near the back. Greta sat on Gunter's lap and behaved perfectly. Tears welled again in Amanda's eyes as she watched her friend kiss her new husband. He couldn't take his eyes off her, and Emily likely had no idea that a hundred or more people were crowded into the chapel until some boy cheered and others joined him.

Soon the celebration spilled out onto the church lawn, where tables laden with food awaited. Amanda watched her friend from the shade of a magnolia tree and wondered how she could keep her promise to tell Gunter the truth.

GW approached with a plate piled high with food. "Where is Gunter?"

Amanda nodded to a table where Gunter helped Greta with a slice of pie.

"I have the Bible back. I need to talk to you two. Can I meet you at the hotel around six?"

"We'll need to do something with Greta. She shouldn't hear whatever you have to say."

"My mother can watch her or will know someone who can."

"Then Gunter and I will meet you at six."

33

Gunter rolled over on the floor pallet and listened. A sniffle. Greta was crying. He rolled onto his knees and stood. He slept in his pants but had hung up the shirt. Not wanting to wake Amanda, he didn't make any unnecessary movements as he crossed the room in the moonlight, and he didn't put his shirt on. His daughter slept peacefully across the top of the bed and both pillows. Amanda wasn't in the bed at all. Another sniffle came from behind him.

Gunter turned. Amanda sat in the corner, hugging her knees, her face buried in the tented nightgown.

He crouched down beside her. When she didn't move, Gunter placed his hand on her shoulder, and she raised her head. "What is wrong?"

She shook her head and pointed to Greta.

"She's asleep. She won't hear us."

Amanda wiped her eyes on the sleeve of her nightgown.

"I don't like the plan."

"Why not?"

"Something feels wrong. Jasper isn't the boss."

"So, you are crying over that?"

"No. I'm not."

"Then why are you crying?" Gunter moved until they were shoulder to shoulder—more like shoulder to midarm with their height difference

She wiped her face on her sleeve again. "Because of Emily."

"Do you cry after weddings instead of during them?" Gunter debated about getting his handkerchief.

"Not usually. I don't know. I haven't been to a wedding before—well, other than ours, and ours was so…so…" She sniffed and leaned her head against his shoulder.

"Ours was business, like we agreed."

"I should have never asked you to. Watching them today…Anyway, I feel like I have created a disaster, and now we have the rangers riding into town, fields of poppies growing on your land, and a huge debt that my dowry somehow became the easiest way to pay off. Eb is most likely dead because he figured it out or refused to hand it over to them."

Now he understood. "This isn't your fault. The smuggling ring existed before you met Ebenezer. If only I had stood up to Jasper's threat and sent you back the moment you arrived."

"I wouldn't have had money for the ticket."

"I could have sent you to Emily."

"She was in jail." Amanda's voice lightened.

"I could have thought of something."

She slipped her hand—small, warm, and perfect—into his. "You did everything you could for me."

"No, I didn't. I could have accepted your proposal immediately. Then they would have never attacked you."

"Why didn't you?" She leaned her head back, searching his eyes. The tears had left a trail, but it was dry now. A strand of hair escaped her braid.

Words in either language couldn't explain his refusal to marry her.

With his free hand, he tucked the strand of hair behind her ear. She didn't flinch or look away, so he cupped her cheek and leaned in closer. She turned toward him, her lips meeting his. Gunter moved slowly. The brief kiss at the courthouse proved she was inexperienced. Whatever the reverend had done to win her hand in marriage, it had not been to kiss her as she deserved. He tasted and tested, turning his body for a better angle. Her hand fluttered over his bare chest, stopping on his shoulder at the edge of the burn scar. She tried to pull him closer. Gunter groaned. The position was far too awkward. He pulled back and unwound their hands. Amanda blinked up at him and tried to lean in. Gunter freed her feet from the hem of the nightgown and lifted her into his lap, then captured her lips again and wrapped his arm around her, holding her close. And miracle of miracles, she returned his kisses with equal passion, her hand exploring his chest until it rested on his heart.

His own hands wished to explore as hers had, but he restrained himself, ending the kiss and cradling her to his chest. Were his daughter not in the room, he doubted he would have such control. He'd fallen in love with this woman and never wanted to let her go. If she was willing, he would make her his wife in a way that could not be annulled.

"*Ich glaube ich habe mich in dich verliebt.*"

⤜⬥⬦⬥⤐

Amanda wasn't sure if she should move or not. Gunter's heart raced with her own. Watching Emily kiss TJ at the church, she'd thought she'd witnessed a kiss beyond all kisses. Now, she had no words for what just happened or to explain how it was possible to feel like she was floating and on fire at the same time.

"*Ich glaube ich habe mich in dich verliebt.*" Gunter whispered the words into her hair.

"What does that mean?"

"It is the reason I said no the first time."

Amanda lifted her head from his heart and tried to see into his eyes. "Why?"

"I have fallen in love with you." He traced her jaw with one finger.

"*Itch globe, itch hab*—oh, I can't say it. I have fallen in love with you too. That was why I was crying. Because the plan means I go back to Boston, and I don't want to."

"You want to stay with me?"

"Please? I'm learning to make strudel."

Gunter lowered his lips to hers. "You don't…" kiss, "need to…" kiss, "make strudel." Kiss. "I'll eat your baked…" kiss "beans."

Amanda couldn't help giggling.

"Papa?"

Gunter froze. "I'm here, little one."

"Why are you on the floor with Miss Amanda?"

"We were having a discussion."

"About what?"

"About Miss Amanda becoming your mother."

Amanda buried her head in Gunter's very bare chest—oh, my! Now that the room was lighter, she could see better.

Greta hopped out of bed and joined them on the floor, then took Amanda's face between her hands. "Do you want to be my mutter?"

"Yes, I do. Would you like that?"

"Yes!" Greta tried to hug them both and ended up falling into a fit of giggles.

Sunlight brightened the room.

Amanda wondered at the time. "We need to catch the train."

After a false start, they managed to rise. Amanda looked down at the night dress, then at Gunter's back. He grabbed his shirt and headed to the washroom. Heat flooded her cheeks. She'd been sitting in his lap—an action not off-limits to a married woman. They had a marriage certificate, after all. But goodness! She'd been sitting in his lap! If Greta hadn't been in the room…

Amanda tied on her bustle.

"Greta, take off your night dress first."

"You didn't."

Amanda looked down. "I am all heads and feathers this morning. She removed the bustle and her nightgown and started dressing again. She was still fastening her boot buttons when Gunter returned, dressed and shaved. "Hannah says she has a bit of leftover pie for us if we hurry down to breakfast."

"I need help with my boot." Greta sat on the end of the bed with one boot half on. Gunter helped Greta swap them to the right feet. "Ready for breakfast?"

"Yes!" She hopped off the bed.

"Nearly. You may go down without me." Amanda needed a moment in the washroom.

Greta took Gunter's hand. "Papa? When are you having a wedding?"

Gunter's eyes met Amanda's. "We will need to discuss that."

The door closed behind them. A wedding. She thought Greta understood they were already married, although a real wedding would be nice. The lace she'd worked on in the train and in the last week would be enough to dress up her graduation gown a bit.

Amanda hurried to the washroom. The door was closed. It was an odd thing waiting for a washroom, standing in a hallway and looking like one was doing anything other than waiting. The door opened and Emily stepped out. "Emily, whatever are you doing here?"

"My new home is below the jail across the street. Hannah insisted we spend our first night here instead of in a room below the cells." Emily blushed. "And you? Have you kept your promise to talk with him?"

"We spoke."

"You are blushing. He is agreeable, then?"

"Yes."

Emily hugged her friend. "I am so happy for you."

"Only, Greta wants us to have a wedding."

"Oh, my." Emily put her hand to her heart, and her ring caught the light.

"It would be nice to have a real wedding. Reverend Ellerbrock might understand once we explain. I have new lace to add to my dress, though my veil was ruined when I had the break-in."

"Take mine. Please read the article in the magazine. It is all the rage to have something borrowed."

"Yes, and something blue. My dress is both old and new."

"There, then. You will only need silver in your shoe. Come get my veil."

Amanda pointed to the washroom "As soon as I—"

"Oh, of course."

⋙◆⋘

Greta didn't fall asleep until after the sixth station stop. Gunter moved her to the back-facing seat so he could sit next to Amanda. He laced his fingers through hers. "I can't believe she managed to talk about weddings for that long."

"I wonder…maybe we could have a wedding. If we explain to Reverend Ellerbrock that we haven't really been married, maybe he would let us…"

"I'll talk with him as soon as we get home. He'll probably insist you stay at the boardinghouse until we say our vows.

"How soon will he let us get married?"

Gunter dragged his finger across the back of Amanda's hand, tracing an invisible pattern. "I want to tomorrow. But

I think he will want us to wait a week."

"Why?"

"He likes to talk to couples to make sure they understand what marriage is."

"Well, you have been married before, and I have learned a few things in the last three weeks."

"That you have. We have a few fights to repair." Gunter brought her hand to his lips and kissed it.

Amanda blushed.

"If we had more privacy…" he whispered.

Amanda playfully slapped his arm. "Mr. Braunig, behave."

"What about the plan?"

"We are supposed to go about our normal business."

"We are supposed to be married. A second wedding will bring attention to us." Gunter couldn't decide if that would be helpful or not.

Amanda frowned. "So we need to wait until…?"

"I don't know. We may have to wait unless GW finds what he needs first. But he may appreciate us giving the town something to do."

Amanda rested her head on his shoulder. For a while, they traveled in silence, watching out the window.

"Tell me about the scar," she coaxed.

"When I went back into the house to find Pauline and Hans, a beam fell on me, pinning me to the floor. Kurt rescued me, but by then it was too late. Peter tried to go in through the front door and couldn't." He paused.

"I'm sorry. I shouldn't have asked."

"I want you to know…some nights I dream about the fire. I wake up screaming her name. I don't want you to be scared. I'll always love her."

"I know you will." Just as she would have a place in her heart for Eb, though it was different since she'd never felt for Eb what she felt for Gunter.

"That doesn't mean I can't love you too."

"I know. It would be very selfish of me to expect you to forget her. I hope you tell Greta stories about her so she can remember Pauline."

"She would have liked you, especially how you stand up to me and Mutter." Gunter kissed her where her forehead met her hairline. "I do have one request between now and our wedding."

"What is that?"

"More of an ultimatum, really."

She turned to face him. "Gunter—"

His eyes burned with a fire she didn't quite understand. "The next time I see you in your nightgown, I am not going to stop kissing you until we are truly man and wife."

Amanda swallowed, her entire being suddenly heating to match the intensity of his eyes.

"I only have so much self-control. And these three weeks of marriage..."

"I understand, and the same applies to the next time I see you without a shirt."

Gunter chuckled. "My Amanda, I can see we are going to have to convince Reverend Ellerbrock—the sooner, the better."

34

As arranged, Herr Schellenberger awaited them at the depot. Although he drove a two-seated buggy rather than an open wagon, the poor man looked done in from the sun. Amanda understood. She could hardly wait to get home to change out of her traveling suit with its many layers and bustle.

Home.

The word tumbled through her mind, no longer bringing up visions of Boston but instead a brook, a boardinghouse, and Greta and Gunter.

Gunter took his seat up front with Herr Schellenberger. As much as she wished to sit next to her husband, moving the older man to the back seat with Greta would not have returned his kindness; Greta had tired of her adventure and was in a sour mood since waking up from her nap.

The two men conversed in an odd mixture of German and English. Four years ago, she had the option of taking German or French. She'd chosen French, since it was spoken in more of the foreign missions. Perhaps if she wrote the school, she could acquire an old textbook. Learning German would better suit her life now.

Greta leaned into her side.

"Are you still tired?"

"We have been sitting forever."

"That is one of the problems with traveling. When we get home, we can walk around before bath time."

"Again? I just had a bath."

"Tomorrow is Sunday."

"But we went to church yesterday."

"That was special."

"Humpf." Greta folded her arms. "I don't need another bath."

"We shall see." Amanda didn't want to fight the rest of the ride home. They'd left the city now. "Why don't you count how many animals you can see?"

Greta leaned to the side of the buggy and watched the ground. Amanda kept a hand on Greta's skirt in case she leaned too far in her quest.

The men continued to talk.

"Your mutter's boardinghouse is full, as is the American hotel."

Amanda hadn't been paying much attention to the conversation in the front seat, but Herr Schellenberger's comment made her lean forward to listen.

"Full?" Gunter's voice carried a hint of disbelief.

"Ja. Five families from Bavaria have arrived. They thought there would be homes for them to move into. Your mutter doesn't have room for them all. One went to the American hotel and was told there was no room."

"For Germans or no rooms?" asked Gunter.

"No rooms. Your mutter had them pitch a tent on your land, near the smithy."

So much for Amanda's plan to stay at the boardinghouse until her second wedding—although she could sleep in Mrs.

Braunig's sitting room. Mrs. Braunig would surely need her help with all the rooms full.

"I saw a *Panzerschwein*." Greta pointed to a rock.

"What is a pantserswan?" asked Amanda.

"Papa, what is English for *Panzerschwein*? I forgot."

"Armadillo. In German, we call them armored pigs."

Amanda tried to look back at the rock, but it was no longer in view. "I've never seen an armadillo."

"Sometimes I see them on walks with Oma before bedtime. The Panzerschwein jumps higher than my head if you scare it."

Amanda didn't entirely believe Greta. However, since her mood had improved, she wouldn't argue.

"Is that Grünlauf?"

"Yes, it is."

"Yay!" Greta bounced in her seat. Amanda tightened her grip on Greta's skirt.

As they neared the boardinghouse, they could see several people on the porch. Three men in dark suits and bowler hats stood near the door. They looked terribly out of place. One looked up as they passed.

It wasn't possible.

Gunter stopped the buggy in front of his house. The three men crossed the street.

"Gunter, that is my father."

Gunter spoke German to Herr Schellenberger and gave him the reins, then turned to Greta. "Liebling, Herr Schellenberger is going to take you to see Oma. You need to stay with her until I come, understand?"

Amanda breathed a sigh of relief. Having Greta near would only complicate matters.

Gunter helped Amanda down, and Herr Schellenberger guided the buggy away. Gunter settled his hand on Amanda's waist.

"There you are! I have come to take you home." As usual, her father wasted no time with greetings.

"Gunter, this is my father, Quincy Ashford. Mr. Dewey his secretary." Amanda didn't know the third man. "And you are?"

"John Lewis, attorney at law, from Dallas."

"Gentlemen, this is my husband, Gunter Braunig. Would you like to come inside so we can discuss matters?" Every etiquette lesson and every observance of her mother's teas gave Amanda the words she needed to speak.

"I don't see the need." Her father's voice boomed loudly enough Amanda wondered if the American side of town could hear him.

"Please come inside." Amanda struggled to not yell back as she turned toward the house, forcing the men to follow.

Gunter walked her up the steps and to the front door. A blast of warm air greeted them. "I'll open the windows upstairs."

Amanda pulled the curtains back and opened the parlor windows. "Would you care for something to drink? The water from our well is usually quite cool."

Father stood near the middle of the room. "Get your things."

"Can we discuss this, please? Have a seat."

The attorney sat immediately. Mr. Dewey looked at Father and remained standing.

"What is there to discuss? Your letter was quite clear."

"Things have changed since I wrote to you." Amanda sat down, hoping her good manners would encourage the other men to sit.

"Yes, I know about your sham marriage. And you," Father pointed at Gunter, "will not receive a penny of her money."

"I don't want it."

Father stepped closer to Gunter. "What did you say?"

"I didn't marry your daughter for the money, even when she proposed to me."

"You proposed to this man?" Father turned on Amanda. "Your mother was right. Texas has turned you into a—I can't even say the word. Good women don't propose."

Amanda swallowed. "I was desperate. It was obvious that every bachelor in town wanted my dowry. And I didn't have the funds to leave. Although I begged Mr. Dewey to order the bank to give me money to leave. You are the one who put me in a position where the money was worth more than my life. Eb was murdered for it."

"What?" Her father stepped back, his voice now a normal tone.

Gunter laid a protective hand on Amanda's back. "If you will please sit, my wife and I will explain."

Father and Mr. Dewey sat down on the couch, while Gunter sat down on a ladder-backed chair from the kitchen.

Amanda turned to Gunter. "Is there anyone outside who can hear?"

"I will go get a bucket of freshwater and see." Going to the well was a good excuse to check.

Father pulled a folded paper from his pocket. "Your letter didn't mention murder."

"We didn't know he had been murdered then." Amanda wondered how to make her father understand without it sounding like a dime-novel plot. "As I wrote, Eb died the night before I arrived. Sometime last spring, he discovered an opium ring."

Father interrupted. "Opium in Texas? Preposterous."

The attorney nodded. "We have an increasing opium problem here."

"I am not clear on the details, but Eb ended up promising them $10,000 in exchange for his life. Money from my dowry. Anyway, Eb had a change of heart. Maybe he realized that the men would kill him and me as soon as they got the money. We don't know. So he underlined letters in his Bible to tell the story, or part of it, using some sort of code. The day he was murdered, he left the Bible and a letter with Gunter under the guise of needing a better lock on the box Eb commissioned for my wedding gift."

"How long have you known all this?" asked the attorney.

"I gave the rangers the Bible. They figured it out and told us last night."

Gunter returned with a pitcher of water and five cups. "There is no one outside, but I will keep watch."

Father's eyes followed Gunter as he took up a position leaning on the wall where he could see out the windows on both sides of the room. "Why does he need to keep watch?"

"Can I finish the story so you'll understand?"

Father crossed his arms and nodded. Amanda related all that happened to her uninterrupted until she told of the burglary.

"What did your policemen do?"

"We have a deputy sheriff, but he is part of the ring. The rangers actually think he is the ringleader. I don't agree, but, anyway, he did nothing. They can't get my dowry money if I leave town. But I didn't know that at the time. All I knew was that my only chance of leaving Texas was if I got my dowry, so I proposed a business deal to Mr. Braunig—Gunter. He would get to keep the dowry and file for an annulment, and I could go back to Boston. He turned me down."

"But you are married?"

"Father, please let me finish. That week, I realized Eb had only married me for my dowry, which I think you knew. All the men here only wanted to marry me for my money, and if I returned to Boston, all the men you and Mother would try to marry me off to would be about money as well. It was sickening to realize that I was only worth dollars and dimes. We fought a war to end slavery, but I was still being sold, in a sense. Only, someone was being paid to take me. So I applied for a teaching job, determined to make my own way." Amanda took a drink of water. She needed courage to tell this next part.

Gunter left his post and came to stand behind her, resting a hand on her shoulder. "*Schatz*, let me finish the story."

She had no idea what the German word meant, but he'd said it with such tenderness it could only be a term of endearment.

"Would you like to leave?"

"No, I can stay."

35

We did not know how desperate the men were for the money. Two men attacked Amanda with the intent to ruin her. I arrived in time to save her from being defiled." Gunter looked Amanda's father in the eye and waited for the full meaning of his words to take hold. Before continuing, he looked down at Amanda to make sure his words had not hurt her. She grasped his hand with her own.

"Although I do not agree with marriage being used as a means to an end, it was the only way I could think of returning your daughter safely to you. So I convinced her to marry me. We kept the same terms as her proposal. At the end of the thirty-two days, she would leave and I would file for an annulment on the grounds that she refused to fully be my wife. And although she keeps insisting I use the money to pay off my mortgage, my intent is to return it to you."

The attorney scribbled a note on a paper he'd been writing on.

"So it is true it's a sham marriage?" asked Mr. Ashford.

Gunter looked his father-in-law in the eye. "Not anymore."

Mr. Ashford jumped up from his seat. "What?"

"Father, please sit down. Gunter and I realized we want to be husband and wife."

"Have you—" Mr. Ashford's face turned red.

His attorney lowered his notebook. "I believe what Mr. Ashford is trying to ask is, has the marriage been consummated?"

Gunter felt his neck heat. "Not yet."

"Good," said the attorney. "We can proceed as planned, Mr. Ashford, and file the annulment on your daughter's behalf."

Amanda shifted, lifting Gunter's hand from her shoulder and standing. "We cannot proceed with an annulment because we do not wish one. I love Mr. Braunig."

"Poppycock! Love is the greatest lie of this century, all those novels filling young women's heads with drivel. You think I am going to allow you to stay in a place where men are trying to kill you and a corrupt deputy runs the town? I was insane for ever letting you follow this crazy plan to marry a minister. I only agreed because I thought you would come to your senses. I should have sent you to Wesley instead of Bradford."

"Father, I have come to my senses. You were right, I was marrying Eb only because I wanted so badly to have adventure and help people—something I thought I could only do as a missionary to a foreign land. I thought that was the only way I could be happy. I was wrong. Happiness is learning to make my husband's favorite food. Happiness is singing with Greta. Happiness is having my mother-in-law compliment my cleaning. It has nothing to do with money or having people look up to you as a benefactor." Amanda stopped and took a deep breath. "I wanted to be a missionary so people would love me for helping them, not because I wanted to help people. I wanted future generations to know I mattered and to tell stories about me. I should thank you. It took me losing everything to realize that I was just like you, only it wasn't money I wanted. I don't think you can ever understand what I am trying to say. I always said I wanted to be a minister's wife to help others, but I was wrong. I don't need to do grandiose things or have my portrait on the wall of some school. All I wanted, even from the time I was little, was to be loved and approved of. I've found that here. Greta loves me because I spend time with her. Mrs. Braunig lets me learn from my mistakes and does not chide me. And Gunter loves me in a way I am still learning to fathom. And I love them. I am not leaving."

Gunter wanted to gather his fiery wife in his arms and kiss her. Since he couldn't do so at the moment, he settled for holding her close to his side.

The attorney leaned over and whispered to Mr. Ashford. Mr. Dewey leaned his head in. At Mr. Ashford's nod, the attorney said, "From what has been said here, I don't believe Miss Ashford is of a sound mind; she obviously suffered from her fiancé's death and has fallen into a pattern of making rash decisions and creating fantastical stories. A corrupt deputy, opium rings, burglary, and the rangers—each of these stories is fodder for the dime novels Miss Ashford indulges in. Reading novels has proven to be most dangerous to a woman's mind. Since you both admit the marriage was only performed as a matter of convenience and Miss Ashford is not yet twenty-one, I advise Mr. Ashford to take custody of his daughter and consider committing her to a mental institution, where she may recover."

"Amanda, pack your things at once."

Gunter moved between Amanda and her father. Mr. Ashford stepped forward. "Move aside, or we will have that so-called deputy arrest you. He has been most helpful to us, including informing us of your false marriage. He also claims you were the one who defiled my daughter in the barn."

Everything Gunter loved was in danger. If the three men said anything to Jasper about her story, his mother and daughter could suffer as well. His mind raced; there must be some way to fix this.

Amanda clutched the back of Gunter's shirt in a vain attempt to move him sideways. "Don't fight him."

Gunter unclenched his fist and stepped to the side.

"Father, take your money and go home. I won't bother you ever again."

"I didn't leave your brother and mother to enjoy Europe only to return empty-handed. Besides, I can still arrange a marriage that will be most beneficial."

Amanda closed her eyes and let out a long breath, her shoulders slumped. "May I have a moment alone with my husband?"

"Mr. Braunig is not your husband. I will not permit you to be alone with him."

"Please, just a few minutes, in the kitchen. You can watch us the entire time."

The attorney nudged Mr. Ashford. "Let her say goodbye, and she will be more compliant."

"Stand where we can see you."

Amanda led Gunter into the kitchen.

"Stop holding his hand."

Reluctantly, Gunter dropped her hand.

She turned to face the window, putting her back to the men. "I don't see a way out of this. I thought I could trust them. If they tell Jasper, you, Greta, and your mother…"

"I know."

"I will come back. I don't know how, but I will."

"What if they put you in an asylum?" He would be powerless to get her out.

"Father has plans to marry me to someone. He won't endanger those plans. Putting me in an institution would do more harm to my reputation than anything else."

"I can't let you go."

"You must. If Jasper puts you in jail..." Amanda shuddered.

"I don't like this."

"Neither do I."

"I must find a way to warn GW."

"Promise me you'll tell him they are wrong about the boss?"

"I will." Even if he didn't agree, he'd pass on the message.

"And, Gunter, always remember, *Ich liebe dich*. I hope I said it right. Greta taught me."

The three men in the other room glared at them. Kissing Amanda would only anger them. "I love you too."

"Stay here. It will be easier."

Under her father's direction, she packed only her valise.

Then she was gone.

⬥

They crossed the bridge on foot. "Aren't we going to Austin?"

"No. I want my money back from the bank. We arrived after closing yesterday."

"Can't they wire it to you?"

"No. I sent it in gold."

Amanda tried not to gasp at the news. Gold!

"So where are we staying?"

"The only hotel this town has to offer."

"We could stay in Austin and come back Monday morning." If they were in Austin, Father couldn't let anything slip to Jasper.

"Another ride over these bumpy roads? I think not."

They passed the bank. If the gold was in the vault, why didn't the men steal it? It would be so much easier than trying to marry her.

The hotel lobby was adorned in reds and golds. A tall, thin man in a brown suit sat in a chair next to the window. GW. He didn't look at her, but she was sure he'd seen her enter. How could she warn him? Her father's grip on her arm tightened as they neared the staircase. A clear warning for her not to draw attention to them. As if three men escorting a woman through a hotel lobby was normal—though she didn't have much experience in hotels. Maybe it was usual. No one seemed to be looking at them. Once she was in her father's room, she was sure to be locked in. It was now or never. Amanda deliberately missed the second step.

Her father's reaction was swift and predictable. "Get up, Amanda."

Amanda clutched her ankle and moaned. "I can't, Father."

"Can I be of assistance? I have some medical knowledge." GW spoke to her father.

Amanda bit her lip to keep from smiling.

"Pay my daughter no mind. I am sure she is not hurt." Father tugged on her arm, eliciting a real groan.

Although Amanda had taken part in some of the school plays and readings, she had never been particularly good at acting. She prayed she could be believable now.

The attorney reached down to help her up. Having two men trying to lift her by the elbows kept her off balance.

"Sir. You risk hurting your daughter further that way."

Amanda groaned.

"What is your name sir?"

"George Morgan. At your service."

"You're a doctor?"

"I have medical training. Army and all that."

"Help me get her to my room, and you can look at the ankle."

"If you let go of her arm, we can help Miss—?" Amanda took the hint that she was not to recognize GW in any way.

"Ashford."

"—Miss Ashford to stand."

The immediate relief of having the use of her arms back was drowned by her father's voice. "Hurry up, girl!"

From her crawling position, it would be nearly impossible to stand in the bustled traveling suit without putting pressure on her supposedly injured ankle, so she pivoted on the good ankle into a sitting position. Her father's frown grew. Amanda extended her hand to her father. "If you would give me a hand, I think I could stand now."

Her father's grip was not as strong as Gunter's. She pulled herself up, careful to balance on one foot.

"Now, can you stand on that foot?" asked GW.

Amanda set her injured foot down, surprised to find it did feel a bit bruised. She made a face. "Only a little."

"Can you navigate the stairs leaning on your father's arm?"

"I am not sure."

"Sir, can you carry your daughter up the stairs?"

Father looked properly affronted. "Is that necessary?"

"Unless you wish her to injure herself further—" GW raised a brow.

"She is far too heavy for me to lift." Her father looked at Mr. Dewey and the attorney. They were both smaller than her father. He looked back to the supposed doctor. "Can you carry her, sir?"

"It would be my honor. Begging your pardon, Miss Ashford." GW lifted her as easily as Gunter had. "Lead the way, men."

Amanda stayed silent while being carried. Her father opened the room at the end of the hall. In the two-room suite, Father pointed to a fainting couch. "Put her down there, and you can examine her."

GW did as her father asked while Mr. Dewey and the attorney went to their rooms on the other side of the hallway.

Father hovered over her. "And, Amanda, not a word. The man will not believe your tales of rangers and opium. I am sorry to say my daughter is suffering from losing her fiancé and has even tried to create a sham marriage. I am taking her home to Boston so she may recover."

If GW couldn't figure out everything from her father's warning, the Rangers should be rid of him.

"May I remove your daughter's boot?"

"Of course."

GW unbuttoned her boot, occasionally pushing harder on her foot than necessary, Amanda moaning each time.

He did the same as he examined her stocking-covered foot.

"Not broken. Perhaps twisted. It would be best if Miss Ashford stayed off it for a day. Have you any ice?"

"I will send my man to get some." Father stepped into the hall and banged loudly on Mr. Dewey's door.

Amanda took the opportunity to say a few words. "Father didn't believe me. He already spoke to Jasper. He wanted to arrest Gunter. We leave Monday with the money. It's gold."

GW didn't look up from his position on the floor. "Fast thinking."

"Also, I don't think Jasper is the boss. Eb didn't know who the real boss was."

Father returned to the room. "If there is ice to be had in this place, my man will find it."

"I need something to wrap it with. Do you have a scarf or necktie or some other length of cloth?"

"I don't. Aren't you doctors supposed to carry things like that with you?"

"I am not a doctor. I don't carry a medical kit when I am visiting a town. But I thought you might have something of use."

"Of course not."

"If you could inquire at the front desk, they may have an old sheet that can be cut up."

"And leave you alone with my daughter?" Father stomped over to them.

GW stood. "I'll inquire. If your man returns with the ice, have her hold it on her ankle."

Father strode across the room to stand in front of her. "I don't know what you thought you would accomplish with that stunt."

Amanda rubbed her ankle to avoid looking at her father. "I was trying to walk up the stairs in a narrow skirt while you were bruising my arm."

"On the bright side, I don't need to worry about you trying to leave on an injured foot."

"I won't try to run." *Yet*.

"You'll thank me in time, dear."

Mr. Dewey and GW returned at the same time.

GW wrapped her ankle in a professional manner. "I suspect her ankle will be well enough to walk on in a couple of days. If you need me, I am upstairs in the first room on the right."

"What do I owe you?"

"Nothing."

Father smiled for the first time since they arrived. He liked nothing more than saving money—except earning it. Father closed the door.

"May I have my book so I can read?"

"Novels? No. Dangerous thing to give to a woman."

"How about my crochet?"

"You don't need to earn money anymore."

Father had heard part of her story. "I enjoy crochet, and if I am to be your prisoner for the next couple of days, I should do something useful."

"You are not my prisoner, you are my daughter."

Holding in the words she wanted to say hurt more than a real turned ankle.

36

Having heard the bang of the outhouse door, Gunter sat up in bed. Greta knew to use the chamber pot at night. Amanda wouldn't…Gunter wiped his hand down his face. The door banged again.

Gunter pulled on his pants, then went to check on Greta. She slept curled up, clutching a handkerchief doll Amanda had made as she packed.

The door banged again. There was hardly a breeze. Gunter grabbed a broom in case it was some sort of animal. The door to the outhouse opened, then slammed shut as if someone had kicked it. Gunter wished he'd thought of grabbing his gun rather than a broom. He crept up to the side and waited for the door to open again. As soon as it did, he pushed the broom through the opening. Someone grabbed it.

"Gunter?"

"GW?"

"First time I've ever had to fight off a broom in an outhouse." The ranger grinned. "We need to talk."

"Yes, we do." Gunter led the way inside.

GW didn't wait to be asked to sit at the kitchen table. "I saw your wife and her father. How much does he know?"

"Too much. Amanda thought if she told him everything, he'd listen. I gather he's been here since Friday and already believes Jasper's story. Threatened to have me arrested. Amanda agreed to leave after that."

"She is one smart woman. Pretended to twist her ankle so I would know something was wrong. I guessed there was when the three men brought her into the hotel like they were marching a prisoner to the gallows."

"Her father's attorney suggested putting her in an asylum. She doesn't believe her father will ..."

"Hard to tell. But we plan to move before they leave town. We found three poppy fields—the one on your land and two others. I hope you can help me figure out who the others belong to."

"Oh, I am supposed to tell you that Amanda says Jasper isn't the leader."

"She said something about that. Do you know why?"

"She said Reverend Coolidge would have had his guard up around anyone he suspected. Since they said he died in his sleep, he must have been poisoned. So he must have trusted the person with his food. Jasper doesn't cook for himself, so Eb would have been wary of a meal from him."

"She has a point. But the man was a preacher; he may have been trying to redeem a wayward soul. But I can't think of anyone ..."

"Neither could she," said Gunter. "Now, about the land ..."

GW took a paper from his pocket and spread it on the table where the moonlight coming through the window was brightest. "Hope you can see this. Don't want you to light a candle."

The lines were faint, but Gunter could see them.

GW traced one of the rectangles. "This plot is registered to Herman and Mildred Braunig. Your parents?"

"Yes."

"This one above it is yours, correct?"

"Yes."

"And your old house was here." GW tapped on the map.

"Close enough."

"You already know about the field here in the dell that crosses both yours and your parents' land."

"Did you ever till your land?"

"No. I was going to run cattle."

"This section here, at the far north, got turned over more than a year ago, maybe as far back as two. But the soil isn't as good as it is in the hollow. It is small enough we assumed it had been a kitchen garden, except it would have been hard to see from the house."

"Then, over here on the west in this little square of land is the third farm. In another hollow is the biggest field. The only problem is we can't find out who owns it. It was part of the Alamo grants to the heirs of M. Grayson. Mrs. Grayson Dodge died about five years back. Both Grayson boys died in the Civil War. Mr. Dodge, her second husband, made no claim on the land before his death. The property tax has been paid, but the records are a mess."

"My former brother-in-law has tried to buy that land because he owns this section. If he could get that piece, he would purchase my land too."

"Does he know the owner?"

"Nope."

"Your barn was used to process opium. Good thing you didn't go out to check the land in the late spring. We talked with a doctor who grows poppies near San Antonio for medical use. Until November, there shouldn't be much to do on the farms; we can't catch them harvesting until next April at the earliest, but likely into June."

"Which coincides with Reverend Coolidge's death. So what are you looking for now?" asked Gunter.

"They must be storing the opium someplace. They need to keep selling it at a consistent rate throughout the year to make money."

"There are hundreds of caves in the hills. I found two of them on my spread, and I haven't even been looking."

"Caves would be good. Where are the ones on your spread?"

Gunter marked them as best he could. "These are only general areas. I didn't explore any of them."

"It's a start."

"What happens to the plan? I can't go claim the money in a week. You thought that would draw them out."

"Amanda's father is withdrawing it Monday, isn't he?"

"He didn't say anything while they were here."

"Amanda said it's in gold. Did they say anything about that?"

"Gold?"

"We are keeping a close eye on the Ashfords and the bank. Robbery is the most logical move. If nothing else holding them up on the way to the train is a possibility." GW slapped Gunter on the shoulder. "Don't worry. We will watch out for Amanda."

"How do I get ahold of you if I need to?"

"Visit Reverend Coolidge's grave. I'll come find you." GW got up to leave. "Out of curiosity, who is the person you would least expect to be the boss?"

"Mrs. Roberts."

"Why?"

"She hates her stepson, Jasper. She is from the north, and she helped Amanda. Although she was also the reason Amanda married me."

"What do you mean?"

"She told Amanda about the rumors that she had been ruined. Amanda was so upset that she agreed to marry me. If you could hurry up and solve this, I would appreciate it. I want my wife back."

"I'll do my best, though I can't promise you'll get her back. As far as I can tell, Mr. Ashford isn't breaking any laws."

GW slipped out the door and into the night.

Gunter sat at the table. He needed Amanda. How could he convince her father?

Birds began to chirp as the dawn broke.

37

Amanda spent most of the night trying to figure out anything that might change her father's plans. Asking to go to church required walking. She could pass a message to Gunter through Mrs. Roberts. But what message? That she loved him desperately? She couldn't let him know GW was here. She didn't trust Mrs. Roberts not to read the note, if only for more gossip.

"How is your ankle?" Father brought in two slices of bread, a hard-boiled egg, and a cup of tepid coffee. He didn't remember she didn't like coffee.

"It feels better. Mr. Morgan was right. I just twisted it."

"Mr. Lewis thinks you should be seen at church with me. Says it strengthens our claim that you are still under my guardianship if all your friends see you sitting happily with me."

"Hardly anyone in this congregation knows me."

"What? My sanctimonious daughter, who can't miss a single service during her vacations, hasn't been to church?"

"I go to the German church." She broke off a corner of the dry, butter-less toast.

"Why?"

"Because I had no desire to go to Eb's church." She wouldn't elaborate. He would not believe her if she did.

"So you're telling me that no parishioners would see you happily at my side and remember you?"

"I am sure they would remember. I'm the woman they tried to marry off to another man."

"One of your tales, I assume."

"I'm not lying."

"You expect me to believe they were trying to marry you off when you arrived here? I have it on good authority that it was the second part of the funeral. Here in Texas, where it gets so hot, they sometimes have to bury the body first."

"I've never heard of such a thing." The idea was preposterous. There had been a funeral since she'd arrived—a mother who'd died in childbirth. Though Amanda hadn't attended, she was sure they'd buried the woman after the funeral.

"Have you attended any other funerals since you've been in town?"

"Nobody I know has died."

"See, you just failed to understand local custom."

"Since when is it custom to play Mendelssohn's wedding March at a funeral?"

"The deputy sheriff assures me it was a funeral. Perhaps you imagined the march since you were expecting a wedding."

It figured Jasper would say anything to make her look bad. "Were there any other witnesses who told you this tale?"

"I thought I taught you better than to question your superiors."

"So certainly you're going to trust the Boston police?" Father spent more dinners than she could count raging about graft in government and how the Boston police were part of the problem.

"We are not discussing the corruption in the Boston Police Department. We are discussing your failure to respect the deputy sheriff here."

There were at least two dozen witnesses that day; surely not all of them would lie for the sheriff. Amanda asked her question again. "Did you find anybody else who said it was just a funeral and not a wedding?"

"Matter of fact, that Mrs. Roberts you seem so fond of said you were quite overwrought and ran out of the church before you knew what was going on."

Amanda stared at her father. Why would Mrs. Roberts lie? None of this made sense. She ate her toast. Fighting with her father wasn't helping things.

"You should drink your coffee."

"I do not like coffee. I never have." How many mornings had she sat at breakfast with him and requested the maid bring her tea instead? Had Father never noticed a single thing she did?

"The cook told me she put something in it to help heal your foot faster."

She wasn't going to drink anything that supposedly had something supposed to heal her when they sat in the middle of the biggest opium ring Texas had ever seen. "Thank her for me, then. If my foot starts to throb, I will drink it."

Father grunted and went into the other room. Perhaps he would go to church. If she could get upstairs, she could leave a note for GW. He needed to know that somebody was trying to rewrite the last six weeks of her life.

Father came out of his bedroom, his tie straightened. "Well, at least I should go to church. I'm taking Dewey and the attorney with me. So you don't get any ideas, I'm locking the door. Deputy Roberts said he would have somebody sitting in the lobby. Don't even try to leave. The attorney believes he could get a judge to commit you to an asylum.

I am beginning to think he is correct. I prefer you return to Boston first. Your mother would never forgive me if you were locked away down here. Hopefully we won't need to resort to such measures. No one would have you then."

"I would be the fool to try to walk anywhere." She could avoid the lobby to get to GW's room. He needed to know that Mrs. Roberts might not be the sweet widow she pretended to be.

⟞⟐⟝

Greta fussed and fretted so much that Gunter was forced to leave her hair down for church. There wasn't an effective way to explain Amanda's disappearance to an almost five-year-old. It seemed Greta was taking it harder than the death of her mother.

With Greta in tow, Gunter crossed the street to the boardinghouse. He didn't bother knocking on the back door before walking in. The kitchen was empty. Gunter opened the pie safe, hoping there might be a bit of strudel from yesterday. It was empty. "I'm sorry, Liebling, Oma doesn't have any leftover strudel for you this morning. Would you like me to see if she has any of her bread?"

"I don't want bread. I want baked beans." Greta crossed both arms over her chest and sat on the stool she used in the kitchen. Someday, when Amanda was back, they could laugh over Greta's insistence that she liked baked beans. His mother entered the kitchen. "What is all the fuss? I thought a *Panzerschwein* was loose in here."

"Miss Amanda is gone. She was going to be my mother."

Mutter picked Greta up. "I know it is difficult, child, but Miss Amanda's father came and said she must go. She chose to honor her parents and leave with her father."

"But she should've honored Papa. They were getting married. And I heard the minister say that it was more important to love your mouse and leave your parents to be married."

"Spouse, not mouse." Mutter looked at Gunter and shrugged. "I cannot help logic like that."

"Neither can I." His mother had only heard a condensed version of last night's happenings but enough to know that Amanda had not made an easy choice. "We should get to church so we are not late."

Greta fidgeted all through the opening hymn. Gunter pulled her into his lap to try to keep her quiet. "Hush, little one."

"It isn't right. Someone should sing in English, but I only know the first words, 'A mighty fortress.'"

If Gunter had known all the English words, he would have sung them. He needed a fortress of protection.

38

The key twisted in the lock with a loud click. True to his word, Father had locked her in. Amanda waited several minutes before tiptoeing across the room and checking the knob. It wouldn't budge. She crouched down to peer through the keyhole. The hall appeared to be empty. Still, she must be quiet. Amanda pulled out a hairpin, straightened it, and fed it into the lock until there was resistance. But try as she might, she couldn't find the magic spot that released the lock. She should have paid more attention when Catherine had picked the lock to the dorm to let them in when someone had locked the door early.

Amanda again tried the straightened hairpin, rotating it slowly. Suddenly, the end of the pin caught on something and there was a soft plinking noise. Amanda tried the doorknob.

Still locked.

A rustling in the hall alerted her to somebody's presence. Amanda squinted through the keyhole. Mrs. Roberts?

Amanda hurried back to the couch. It was possible her father had given Mrs. Roberts a key. If not, she needed to be across the room when she called out that she couldn't let anybody in.

A moment later, Mrs. Roberts knocked at the door. "Amanda, are you in there?"

"Mrs. Roberts? Yes, I'm here."

"Be a darling and let me in."

"I can't. My father locked the door." Amanda didn't comment on the locking of the door; it could've been for her own safety. And keeping Mrs. Roberts out was a good use of her father's protection.

A key turned in the lock, and Mrs. Roberts opened the door. "It is fortunate that I have a master key." The widow closed the door and locked it behind her.

Amanda sat up carefully, keeping her "injured" foot on the couch. "Why are you here?"

"Because, dear, you've put me through an awful lot of trouble. I see you didn't drink your coffee. Tsk. Tsk. This would've gone so much easier if you had."

"What would be easier?"

"I need the $10,000. Your father will give it to me to have you back alive and unharmed. In fact, he will probably offer up the entire $15,000." Mrs. Roberts didn't know her father very well if she thought he would pay to get her back.

"You're the boss. You are the one who ordered that man to—to ruin me." Amanda could hardly get the words out.

"Yes. I am. You left me so little choice." Mrs. Roberts sat in the chair nearest the fainting couch.

"I don't understand. Why would you do that?"

"Because I need $10,000. And you were being so stubborn about getting married. I figured the shame would force you into a hasty match."

"Why do you need the money?"

"Like any business, I have creditors, those who must be paid. The good reverend ruined my last opium shipment.

Fortunately for him, he had the necessary funds coming on a train. Ebenezer was going to give the $10,000 to me in exchange for his life. But, so like a minister, he had that conscience. Of course, he didn't realize he was giving it to me, didn't know I was involved. Not until the end as he lay dying. Do you know that the last thing he tried to say was your name?" Mrs. Roberts paused.

Amanda felt ill. This woman had murdered Eb and then befriended her.

"I need you to drink your coffee. All of it. Don't worry. I'm not going to kill you today. It is quite possible your father will demand proof you are still alive, and I'll need proof. It doesn't work to cut a finger off a corpse. It won't bleed. Neither will an ear. But I will make it easy on you. You will be dreaming the sweetest of dreams, perhaps of your beloved Gunter or even Ebenezer. I don't care which. Now, drink your coffee, dear."

"Why me?"

"It is a shame, really. You are quite sweet. But the money comes with you. That document of your father's was such a convoluted thing. If you had married Mr. Fife that first day, you would be home in Boston by now, quite possibly untouched. Mr. Fife doesn't enjoy women. It is highly likely he would've never been able to consummate the marriage. Which is why I chose him to be your spouse. I didn't want to hurt you more than I had to. Drink up."

"I don't like coffee."

Mrs. Roberts took a vial from her purse. "We can do this the hard way—I force a few drops of this through your lips. But I might use too much. It is difficult to measure when one's victim is struggling. Just ask my late husband. You're much better off drinking the coffee. There's enough in there to make you sleepy and dream for the next several hours. If you are very good next time, I'll put it in lemonade. I'll even add a bit of ice since it is such a hot day."

"What are you going to do with me?"

Mrs. Roberts laughed much as Amanda pictured the devil might laugh—a sound without mirth. "I told you. I will keep you alive and unharmed until your father gives me the money tomorrow. Or, rather, gives Gunter the money. Then Jasper will swoop in and arrest Gunter. Then, in your distress, you will poison yourself with strychnine, the same way your dear Eb died. Don't worry. Although painful, it is fast. If you're very good, I may let you die by laudanum overdose and you won't feel a thing. It's immensely popular among women who wish to commit suicide. Your poor father will suffer from a heart attack. The doctor will certify it. He is one of my best customers."

"Why would I kill myself?"

"Have you never read *Romeo and Juliet*? Gunter will be facing the gallows. Murder, kidnapping, rape. He will hang for all my deeds."

Never had Amanda sensed a bit of evil in the widow. Maybe if she kept on talking to her, she could form a plan. Maybe GW would use the opportunity to come try to talk to her during church. "Why opium?"

"As I said, I'm a war widow. My first husband died in the opium wars. I was angry because he died so England could become richer. I learned everything I could about the drug. Oh, the money."

"I thought you said he was buried at Gettysburg."

"No, that was husband number two. He isn't part of this story. Opium, you see, is like gold, only better. Men get gold fever and waste their lives away. But once somebody is hooked on opium, they will give anything to get more. And laudanum is perfectly legal. Drink your coffee and you will see."

Amanda picked up her cup but didn't drink.

"It was Mr. Roberts who gave me the idea to grow it rather than import it. He read about that doctor near San Antonio and thought it would be possible to grow the opium poppy in this part of Texas. My mother needed laudanum for months before she passed; she was in such pain. And it cost so much. However, if we could grow it here, it would not have to be shipped from overseas. Mr. Roberts helped me at first but realized that not all of what we grew was going to go to help poor people obtain pain relief." Mrs. Roberts sighed and pointed to Amanda's cup.

"I didn't mean to kill him so quickly. But no one realized, not even his stupid son. The rest is, as they say, history. Ebenezer found out about the trade quite by accident. He simply drank the wrong lemonade. I tried to convince him he'd only been sick, but eventually he realized he'd been drugged. I pointed him to all the wrong places, but he didn't give up, so I led him to my idiot stepson. I'll leave him behind, too, as soon as he is no longer useful. Just like Mr. Fife. Don't look so shocked, dear. Mr. Fife was only supposed to spy on the reverend, but he bungled that. After he couldn't marry you, I had no use for him, and he tells all his secrets when he is drunk." She gestured to the coffee. "This is your last chance. Drink up or take a sip from the vial. As I've said, my vial isn't measured, and you may never wake up."

Any way Amanda looked at her options, she would be dead by tomorrow. The longer she could live, the better chance she'd have that someone would figure everything out. She could attempt to overpower the widow. Amanda was smaller but more agile. Then she could run for the door and freedom. But if one of Jasper's henchmen was in the lobby, she wouldn't make it far. Chances were that GW was not upstairs in his room. Even if she got there, she would be cornered on the third floor. It was ridiculous to believe Mrs. Roberts didn't have a backup plan, upon a backup plan, upon a backup plan. Amanda had never suspected. Perhaps if she drank most of the coffee and spilled some, she wouldn't get a full dose and, in a few hours, would have a second chance. Amanda turned the coffee cup in her palm and lifted it to her lips.

"Smart girl. Drink it all." Mrs. Roberts pressed her finger to the back of the cup, forcing Amanda to finish it. "Now, we will sit here and wait for it to take effect, then I will move you and leave the ransom note. When those Rangers arrive in town, they will have enough clues to look in the wrong direction.

Amanda didn't feel anything at all. Perhaps it was not working. She turned and put both feet on the floor. There may be time to put on her boots. It would be better to go in her boots.

"What are you doin'?"

"Mother raised me to be a lady. If I am to be kidnapped, I will go fully dressed."

Mrs. Roberts laughed again but didn't interfere. Amanda pulled on her boots and used the buttonhook to close them, but instead of her putting the hook away, she slid it into the back of her boot. It could come in handy later.

"Take the hook out of your boot or I will have one of my men search you later. Remember, not getting harmed is only good until your father pays me. Then I might let them do anything they wish to you."

Amanda's stomach turned. She was sure she would throw up. If she did, Mrs. Roberts would pour the drug straight into her throat. Amanda swallowed the bile down and put on her gloves and hat.

"Tsk. Tsk. No hat and no hatpin. We have all heard about your famous hatpin."

Amanda set the buttonhook and hatpin next to her bag with her hat on top. Maybe someone would be smart enough to know that she would not have willingly left the hatpin. The room began to turn and weave, and Amanda wobbled as she crossed back to the couch.

"It's starting to take effect. Just a few more minutes and I will have you moved to a much safer place."

The dizziness increased, and Amanda shut her eyes, still trying to fight the nausea. How could this trusted woman betray her? The lock clicked. Mrs. Roberts spoke quietly to someone.

A man threw Amanda over his shoulder. Her stomach rebelled again. Amanda clenched her teeth and stayed limp, knowing if she fought, things could get worse. The man carried her across the room and into the hallway. Instead of going to the stairs, he opened another door and stepped up, not down—up was where GW was. Maybe when she awoke, there would be a chance.

39

A pounding on the door interrupted Gunter's supper. He hurried to the door, hoping they wouldn't wake Greta.

He opened it wide to find GW in a brown suit. "My name is George Morgan, and I've been deputized to help search for Miss Amanda Ashford. I've been told to search your house."

Gunter stepped back to let the man in, his mind refusing to form the questions he needed to ask.

"May I search upstairs first?"

"Ja." Gunter closed the door and lead GW upstairs. He pointed to Greta's room and whispered, "She's sleeping."

They stopped in Gunter's bedroom. "She isn't here."

"I know. Listen fast. Amanda disappeared while her father was at church. I had inquired about her ankle and returned to the hotel with him. Her boots were gone, but she left her hat. There was nothing to indicate she was forcibly removed."

"What of her hatpin?"

"It was sitting under her hat."

"She uses it as a weapon. Why not take it?"

"Does Amanda like coffee?"

"Detests the stuff. Can't make a decent pot of it either. Why?"

"Mr. Ashford was surprised she drank the cup he left her. She'd refused it earlier, even though he told her the cook put something in it to help ease the pain in her foot."

"She wouldn't have."

"My thoughts exactly."

Someone pounded on the door below.

"Open up!" Jasper's voice boomed through the windows.

Gunter and GW rushed downstairs. The door flew open as they reached the parlor. The deputy and another man rushed in, grabbing Gunter by the arms.

"Gunter Braunig, you are under arrest for the kidnapping of Miss Ashford. Where is she?"

"I searched the house. She isn't here." GW stood between the men and the door.

"Well, the ransom note says otherwise."

"Vhat ransom note?" Mutter stood in the doorway.

"Leave, lady. Ain't none of your business." Jasper attached a handcuff to Gunter's left wrist.

"Where is Greta?"

"I said leave!"

"Not without my granddaughter." Mrs. Braunig stood firm.

GW hadn't moved from his spot. "Let her get the little girl or everyone in town will be talking about the deputy who left the child."

"You heard the man. Get the girl."

Mrs. Braunig gave the men as wide a berth as possible as she skirted the room to the stairs.

Leaving peaceably or allowing Greta to see him in shackles—neither of Gunter's choices was palatable. "I didn't kidnap my wife, but I will come with you. We must find her."

"Didn't expect you to confess yet. But you were stupid enough to use paper with German on the back." Jasper wrenched Gunter's other wrist behind him and into the handcuffs. "Morgan, you join the other men in the search. The boardinghouse is next. Move, Braunig."

Gunter stumbled from the shove Jasper gave him. Half the residents of the street stood on their porches or in their yards. Gunter hoped they were praying for him as Jasper and his minion frog-marched him down the street.

He had no idea where GW had gone but hoped the rangers would hurry.

⊰⊱

Oppressive heat pushed at Amanda from every side, her foundation garments sticking to her skin. Someone needed to douse the fire in the stove. She pushed back her hair and sat up to call the upstairs maid. This wasn't her room. She stood on unsteady stockinged feet, puzzled. She'd put her boots on today. The memories came back: Mrs. Roberts, the coffee. Amanda stood and explored the tiny room. The window was nailed shut. A corner of the graveyard was visible, cast in the long shadows of the church. She must still be in the hotel, though higher up than her father's room. She swallowed, her mouth feeling like she'd eaten a pillow. A pitcher of water stood on a table. Amanda poured herself a glass, but as she brought it to her lips, she thought of the coffee and set it back down.

Not surprisingly, the door was locked. A hairpin. Mrs. Roberts had thought of that. Amanda's hair cascaded down her back. No hairpins. She ran her fingers through her tresses, hoping one had been missed. Nothing.

There had to be something. She wore the good corset, but even if she worked some of the boning out, she couldn't pick the lock. The only metal she wore was Gunter's silver ring. They hadn't taken her jewelry. The cameo. Amanda's fingers fumbled with the silver-and-ivory broach at her throat. The pin wasn't nearly as long as the hairpin.

Amanda looked through the keyhole before inserting the pin side of the broach. Only the papered wall of the hotel met her gaze. She tried and fumbled, but it was no use; the pin was too short to catch on the mechanism. Amanda sat on the floor and closed her eyes, trying to remember everything Catherine had done when she'd picked the dorm lock. Wait—she hadn't used one hairpin but two! No wonder the lock in her father's room hadn't opened this morning. Brilliant. Now instead of one pin, she needed two.

Her bustle poked her backside, protesting against the position. This bustle had wires in it that allowed it to collapse when sitting. Amanda lifted her skirt and untied the bustle. Not caring if she ever wore it again, she ripped into the fabric, freeing the wire. Soon she had two wires the length of her hand.

She tried to copy the moves of her friend, feeding both wires into the lock but only moving one, attempt after attempt failing, the wire scratching the palm of her hand and causing it to bleed. Frustrated, Amanda jammed the wires in as hard as she could. If she broke the lock, her assailants couldn't get in without breaking the door, which should bring someone.

The lock clicked.

Amanda tried the knob again. The door opened.

The hallway was empty. Why hadn't Mrs. Roberts left a guard? There must be someone. Probably on the staircase. They'd used the servants' stairs to bring her up. Amanda stepped into the hall and tested the doorknob to the left of her room. Locked. There was a number on the door, higher than her father's room number. She must be on the third floor. Which one was GW's room? First room on the right. So close to the stairs. As quietly as she could, she moved down the hall, listening for any movement below.

As she neared the room, she heard voices and laughter. She turned the knob. It opened. A gun cocked, and someone grabbed her wrist, pulling her into the room. A hand clamped over her mouth, cutting off her scream. Amanda kicked.

Another man came into view. GW. "Amanda?"

She stopped fighting.

The hand over her mouth loosened.

"Sorry, miss," said the man behind her as he let go.

GW turned the key to the door and pointed to a single chair in the corner.

Amanda sat down with only one thing on her mind. "Water?"

The other man handed her a glass.

GW sat on the bed. "Where have you been?"

Amanda gulped down a mouthful. "Down the hall. A small room."

The other man moved to the door. "Must be the one where the kid kept cleaning the doorframe."

"Mrs. Roberts drugged me. She's the boss."

GW nodded. "Came to the same conclusion."

"Someone is coming," the man near the door said in a hushed voice.

Amanda set the glass down. Every part of her felt limp. "I'm so tired."

"Probably still the opium."

She yawned and tried to keep her eyes open.

Footsteps pounded in the hall.

"He found the empty room."

GW shook her shoulder. "Amanda?"

"Tired."

"How do we hide her?" asked GW.

The other man answered, which was good because Amanda couldn't find her words.

"Amanda?" GW helped her stand. "I need you to lie down on the bed and pretend to sleep. Whatever you do, don't move until I tell you it is safe, no matter what you hear. Can you do that?"

"Sleep." Had she been drugged again?

"Mrs. Roberts must have given her enough for a man twice her size." The other man was closer now.

Amanda tried to open her eyes. They fluttered, and she saw that the man had turned down the bed. "Nice."

"Amanda, I need you to take off your stockings and pull your skirt up to your knees," said GW.

Sitting on the side of the bed, Amanda tried to pull off her stockings, but they wouldn't come.

"Look at me, Mrs. Braunig."

Amanda smiled and opened her eyes as wide as she could.

"Tell your husband he can hit me later. I am taking your stockings off for you." GW tugged them off so fast that one ripped.

"Lie on your stomach and turn your face to the right. Don't look at the door."

Amanda lay down and was immediately covered with a sheet, except for her feet. The men muttered something and put a blanket across her back.

"Don't move, Amanda. Your life depends on it."

Other than the blanket making her warm, she had no desire to move.

⟹◆⟸

"See the proof." Jasper shoved a paper at Gunter's face before punching him in the stomach again. "Confess, you German dog."

Chained to the wall, Gunter felt the ache in his face and body. One eye was too swollen to see much of the paper Jasper waved at him. The other eye caught enough of the

German scrawled across the back to give him hope. The writer had used the discarded notes of Reverend Ellerbrock's sermon to write the ransom note on. Only a fool or someone who couldn't read German would have written a demand for $15,000 in gold on the back of a sermon based on Matthew 20:20–28. Of course, Jasper probably wouldn't recognize the verses in an English Bible, which ended with Christ declaring His life a ransom.

Someone entered the jail, but it was not GW, Gunter's only hope of rescue.

"The room is empty. She's gone."

Jasper spun around. "Weren't you watching?"

"Been standing there for hours without a bite to eat. I was only gone for ten minutes. Joe was in the lobby."

"Idiot." Jasper took the paper and keys. "I'll be back. You can sit and think about how you are going to beg the boss for your life."

The "she" had to be Amanda. "*Lauf schnell, Schatz*—run as fast as you can, darling." If only saying his wish in both languages would make it true.

40

GW threw his shirt on the floor as Hawke hung the ripped stocking on the bedpost. People ran up the stairs next to his room. Their time was up. It would have been better if they had been able to explain to Amanda and have her remove her skirt and blouse. Hopefully, someone standing in the doorway would only see what he wanted them to. GW sat on the bed and removed his boots. Removing his gun left GW feeling naked, so he slid it under the pillow.

Hawke took up his post behind the door, gun drawn, and GW used both hands to mess up his hair.

A moment later, someone pounded on the door. GW put his hand on Amanda's back, and she let out a soft snore. If there was a God, He'd keep the woman from waking.

A second knock came.

"Hold your horses." GW stood. "Coming."

He opened the door only a few inches and leaned his bare shoulder against the frame. "Deputy, what is wrong?"

"Morgan. Thought you were searching."

"Didn't find anything other than that distraction." GW jerked his head toward the bed, opening the door a fraction wider.

"Who is she?"

"Don't rightly know, but I don't want her Pa—"

"Well, as soon as you're finished, get over to the jail."

"Will do."

GW waited for the men to turn away from the door before closing it and locking it with a click he hoped they heard.

He scooped his shirt off the floor and put it back on. "Ready to make our move?"

Hawke stepped away from the wall. "If she can stay awake long enough. The others have the stash from the cave and the guard they found. They're waiting for my signal."

With his gun in his holster and his circle star badge in place, GW was ready to put an end to the opium ring. "And Mrs. Roberts?"

"Jax is watching her house."

"Well, then, I'd better wake my star witness." GW nodded toward the bed.

41

"Wake up, Amanda." Someone waved something sharp-smelling under her nose.

GW knelt at the side of the bed.

She blinked and rolled away.

"It is important. You need to save Gunter."

Again with the smell. Sleep slipped away. "Save Gunter?" Amanda pushed herself up. "Water?"

The other man handed her a glass.

Amanda drank. "Is it safe?"

"Yes, you slept through the entire thing."

Amanda pushed her hair out of her face. "Do you have something I can tie my hair back with?"

The other man fumbled through a bag and handed her a strip of leather. "Thank you, Mr.—"

"Hawke. Also a ranger."

Out of habit, Amanda smoothed her skirt. She had been sleeping in a hotel room with two men in it. How would she ever explain this? "What happened?"

GW stepped back. "I'll explain later. What is important is what is going to happen now. Hawke is going to leave. At his signal, I am going to carry you down to the lobby, where your father and his two friends are trying to get the bank president to open the bank early."

"I can walk."

"If you can, you may. Meantime, six other Rangers and the sheriff and his other deputy are going to swoop into town and things will be a little crazy. If any shooting starts, I want you to get on the floor and hide behind anything."

"Shooting?"

"It's possible. People don't like to be arrested," Hawke said. "I'll leave now."

GW went to the window. Amanda stood, the braided carpet feeling firm beneath her bare feet. Why had GW taken her stockings? Before she could ask, the ranger turned from the window. "Let's go."

Amanda gripped the banister, GW by her side.

When they reached the landing, someone shouted from behind them. "There she is!"

"Run to your father." GW drew his gun and turned.

Amanda hurried down the remaining flight of stairs. "Father!"

Everyone looked up as she ran through the lobby.

A gunshot came from upstairs and another in the street.

Amanda dropped to the floor and crawled behind an over-stuffed chair. A moment later, her father joined her. "Where have you been?"

"Later. You wouldn't believe me anyway."

⬦

Gunter sat on the couch in the boardinghouse parlor with Greta curled up on one side of him and Amanda on the other. Every few minutes, Mutter checked the ice pack on his eye. Mr. Ashford sat on the other side of the room with his attorney and Mr. Dewey. GW stood near the door, where he explained the events of the day.

Herr Schellenberger and the Kerksiek sisters shared the couch, and Reverend Ellerbrock sat in a chair he'd brought in from the dining room. People stood on the veranda around the windows and filled the hallway.

The ranger continued with the story. "We'd been investigating the new influx of opium for some time with no solid leads until Miss Ashford brought us Reverend Coolidge's Bible."

Gunter ignored this part of the story; he knew it well.

"I met with the Braunigs in Hiramsville, and we made a plan that gave us a week to find more evidence while we waited for Mr. Braunig to get the promised dowry money. It nearly fell apart when Mr. Ashford showed up and insisted his daughter leave. As much as the situation surprised us, it surprised the opium ring more; they needed the gold."

Gunter leaned his head back.

"In a moment of alertness, despite being drugged, Mrs. Braunig managed to escape and find her way to another ranger and me, and we hid her while everyone got in place for the arrests."

Amanda stiffened beside him. There was more to the story than GW was telling.

"Mrs. Roberts is being charged with two murders—that of Reverend Coolidge and Mr. Fife, who did not leave town as reported. Her stepson, Jasper, is being charged as an accomplice and with starting the fire that killed the former Mrs. Braunig and her son and a host of other crimes. Among their accomplices are the vice president of the bank and a half-dozen men they employed in their operation. The county sheriff is expected to step down for his failure to recognize what was going on and his deputy's involvement. Because some of you will be called to testify at the trial, I can't answer any questions about particulars or say more." GW stopped to take a drink. "Although it is not within my authority, I suggest that Grünlauf put forth its own candidate for sheriff, perhaps from the German community."

Cheers erupted from the hallway and outside. Gunter heard his name mentioned. He wasn't the man for that job. Eventually, his neighbors left for their homes. The new boarders left too, leaving only a few people.

When Gunter rose, Amanda stood too, supporting his side while Greta held his hand. "Now, if you don't mind, it is late. I would like to go home."

Reverend Ellerbrock stood. "There is one problem. Is Miss Amanda your wife or not?"

"We do have the marriage certificate." She looked at her father.

Mr. Ashford huffed. "This should be discussed in private."

The reverend turned to the attorney. "Is there any legal reason why these two are not married?"

"Since the marriage can still be annulled after more than three weeks…if the father objects to the union, paperwork would have to be filed, but technically, they are still married."

The reverend looked into Gunter's eyes. "What did you intend to do, son?"

"We were going to ask you to perform the marriage again at your earliest convenience. Greta wanted us to have a wedding in a church and serve pies and cakes."

Greta clapped her hands. "Then Miss Amanda will be my mutter!"

The reverend looked around the room. "Mrs. Braunig, could you put your granddaughter to bed? And may I use your private parlor to speak with Gunter, Miss Amanda, and her father?"

"Of course. Come, Greta." Mutter took Greta by the hand and left the room.

Gunter tried not to lean on Amanda as they walked down the hallway.

Reverend Ellerbrock held the door to the sitting room for Amanda to help Gunter through.

When her father tried to enter with his entourage, the reverend stopped him. "Sorry. Not your friends, Mr. Ashford. You won't need a lawyer here."

Amanda helped Gunter sit before taking the seat beside him.

Her father sat in the chair opposite, while the reverend remained standing. The reverend studied Gunter for a long minute. "You were very injured today, ja?"

"Ja." Gunter bit back a groan.

Amanda was helpless to relieve his pain. After today, she would never suggest laudanum to anyone.

The reverend turned to Mr. Ashford. "It is good for a father to be concerned for his daughter. However, it is not good for any man to force others to his will. Your money has done much harm in this community. I have witnessed many things the ranger didn't talk about but perhaps you have been told."

"I have been told conflicting stories."

"What has your daughter told you?"

"She has been very distraught."

"Has she lied to you?"

Mr. Ashford looked at Amanda, then at the floor. "I thought she had, but I was wrong."

"I have five children grown and gone from my care. There was a point where I had to let them make their own choices. If, after all that has happened, your daughter wants to marry Gunter, will you allow it?"

Amanda scooted forward. "Please, Father. You can even keep my dowry."

Mr. Ashford raised a brow. "You'll be poor."

"We won't be destitute. I'll have a house, a daughter, and a husband who cares for me."

"What about the mortgage?" asked her father.

Gunter did his best to meet his father-in-law's stare. "I will sell the land."

Mr. Ashford didn't speak. Mrs. Braunig's cuckoo clock ticked the minutes away. A whirring sound preceded the bird exiting its door ten times to sound the hour.

"I will not object to your marriage, and I will leave you your dowry so that you can all come for Christmas. Your mother will want to see you from time to time."

Amanda squeezed Gunter's hand.

The reverend bobbed his head. "Good. Vill you stay for the second wedding?"

"Would you like me to?" Mr. Ashford addressed Amanda.

The answer surprised her. "I would like it very much."

"We should give Gunter some time to heal," said the reverend.

"I can be ready tomorrow." Gunter winced as he spoke.

The reverend tapped his chin. "That is not enough time to make Greta her cakes and pies. Perhaps Saturday?"

"Wednesday?" asked Amanda.

The reverend shook his head. "Once, when I was a young man, I was beaten very badly because of the *Burgermeister*...but that does not matter. Gunter needs a few days to heal. It will be better to wait a week."

"Ja. You may be right." Gunter slumped a little more on the couch.

"Miss Amanda, perhaps it would be better if you stayed with Mrs. Braunig this week?"

"I will do that."

"Come, then, Mr. Ashford. We will leave them to say good night."

Amanda waited until the men left. "Do you mind waiting?"

"No, darling. The reverend is right. I can hardly kiss you right now."

"Then I will need to kiss you."

Gunter chuckled and grabbed his side. "There is one spot on my forehead that doesn't hurt."

Amanda kissed him at his hairline. "You winced. Even that hurt."

"I'm sorry, Schatz."

"Here, let me help you to your house. I want you to recover quickly." Amanda helped him to the door.

GW waited in the hallway. "No offense, Mrs. Braunig, but your husband could use my help more."

Amanda stepped back. "It is just as well. We are getting married again on Saturday. And the reverend doesn't want me—" She felt her cheeks flush.

"Saturday sounds like a lovely day for a wedding."

"You're invited." Amanda relinquished her place at Gunter's side.

GW smiled. "Come on, old man, let's get you home."

Amanda watched them cross the street. She turned to find her father still there.

"Father?"

"I wanted to tell you I am sorry. You have never lied to me before. If I had believed you, today would have gone much differently."

"Will you stay for the wedding?"

"Yes. Mr. Dewey will return home tomorrow. And I'll wire your mother and Charles. I don't know my daughter as well as I should. Do you really carry a hatpin?"

"Quite often."

<hr>

GW helped Gunter up the stairs, each riser more painful than the last. "I don't think I can make it down again."

"Then it is fortunate I am staying in town for a few days to tie up loose ends."

Gunter sat on the edge of the bed, then reached for his boots, but the pain that tore through his body stopped him. "I can't take off my boots."

GW removed his boots. "Before I help you with your socks, I should confess I took your wife's stockings off today as well."

"What?" Asking the question hurt. The ranger had good timing; Gunter was helpless to defend his wife's honor.

"Hawke and I hid Amanda in my bed. She was still affected by the drugs she'd been given and extremely tired. I don't know that she remembers much of it. She tried to get her stockings off but couldn't. We covered her with a blanket and the sheets so only her hair and feet showed. Otherwise, she was completely dressed. When Jasper pounded on my door, I answered dressed only in my trousers. I made sure he saw her bare feet."

"Did he know it was her?"

"Not at the time, but he probably figured it out."

"She wasn't awake?"

"Not really. She was sleepy enough that she didn't understand what happened. I told her I'd let you punch me for taking off her stockings."

"I couldn't if I wanted to right now."

"You are welcome to later."

"I'll think about it." He wouldn't have to think for long. The ranger had been honest about the ruse that had likely saved Amanda's life. If GW had neglected to tell him…Well, that would have been worth defending his wife's honor.

"You'll want to explain things to her before Jasper says anything."

"Maybe I should save my punch for him."

"I would."

The laugh hurt too much. When GW helped him to bed and promised to remain close, Gunter closed his eyes and was met by the sweet, dreamy face of his wife, or wife-to-be. The reverend may not know it, but it was a very good thing he was incapacitated because second wedding or not, Gunter had a signed marriage certificate.

Epilogue

I know what people say about mothers-in-law. I vill try to be a good one. But you must tell me if I am overstepping," Mrs. Braunig said as she helped Amanda with the veil.

"I will try to be a good daughter-in-law too. But I don't promise to like sauerkraut."

"Fair enough. I will not feed it to you." Mrs. Braunig stepped back. "You are a vision. Almost too pretty for my Gunter. No one will notice his bruises with you to look at."

"Is he well enough?" Amanda bit her lip.

"He is. He even ate two servings of sauerkraut last night, just in case it would help him be stronger. I will tell you a secret. Sauerkraut doesn't work on everything. Don't eat it when you are in the family way, or you will be sick. Also, it doesn't heal broken bones faster."

Amanda laughed and hugged Mrs. Braunig. "Would you mind very much if I called you Mutter?"

Mrs. Braunig dabbed at her eyes. "It will make me enormously proud. Come, your father is waiting."

Father helped her into the open carriage he'd rented in Austin. Their week together had been as enjoyable as possible under the circumstances. His grudging respect for Gunter had earned them his blessing on the wedding and an invitation to come to Boston for Christmas. Greta was especially enamored with the idea of "Flirting on the Ice." Her enthusiasm had her new grandfather laughing for the first time Amanda could remember in years.

There had been no apology beyond that said last Sunday night after her rescue. If money was how Father showed his love, then he was trying to make amends. Father encouraged her to go to Austin and purchase anything she needed. Amanda replaced the torn stockings and bustle and purchased a few foundation garments Mrs. Maple said a new bride should own, as well as a new dress for Greta to make her day special. While she found these items to be more than adequate, Father insisted she buy more, so she purchased an English-to-German dictionary and a lace-trimmed nightgown.

The German church overflowed with people. Herr Unger waited for her father to help her out of the carriage, then bowed to her. "You made a better choice. Gunter is a good man."

A violin played softly as they entered the door. Amanda didn't recognize the tune that swirled around her and hushed the audience. She walked next to her father until they stopped near Gunter. Her father kissed her cheek.

Gunter smiled down at her, drawing all her focus. His eyes widened when Reverend Ellerbrock spoke in English. "The bride has asked that I conduct this wedding in German. She spent some time with me, learning the German words and their pronunciation. For the few guests who don't speak German, if she kisses him at the end, she agreed."

Most of their friends laughed.

"Gunter und Amanda, sind Sie freiwillig und bereiten Herzens gekommen, um miteinander die Ehe einzugehen?"

She stumbled on her words only once.

Finally, Gunter lowered his head to kiss her, whispering, "I love you."

Amanda pressed her lips to his and held on to his shoulders, not wanting the kiss to end.

Gunter pulled back. "You are full of wonderful surprises today."

"That was only the first kiss."

"I can't wait for more," he whispered in her ear before they turned to face their friends.

Greta jumped out of her seat and came to hug their legs. "Are you my Mutter now?"

Gunter lifted his daughter up between them.

Amanda kissed her new daughter's cheek. "Ja, Liebling."

"Papa, Mutter can speak German!"

Gunter laughed along with everyone else.

"Now we can have pie!" Greta wiggled down and ran out the door. Knowing her new daughter was safe under so many watchful eyes, Amanda wrapped her arms around her husband's neck and kissed him again. Some things were better than pie.

Historical Notes

ike many stories, this one started with a "what if" question. "What if there were drug cartels in Texas in 1880?" An article from *The Weekly Democratic Statesman* published in Austin, Texas, February 19, 1880, gave me the answer I needed for a foundation to my story. According to the paper, a Dr. Wheatley started an opium poppy farm east of San Antonio. Today, growing the opium poppy in the United States is highly regulated. So it is only my supposition that it could be grown in the area where I placed the imaginary town of Grünlauf.

Opium addiction has a long and sad history that continues today. During the nineteenth century, its use was only partially controlled. Laudanum, a tincture of opium and alcohol, was legal and readily available. Mothers used it to soothe babies to sleep, not knowing or understanding the dangers. Doctors prescribed it for relief from pain. Addicts drank it as it was often cheaper than alcohol. These addicts were known as opium eaters. And while legal, many of the dangers of Laudanum were known. Several newspapers of the time lamented the spread of opium usage. If you or someone you love is addicted to opioids, please seek help.

Several towns in Texas were settled by German immigrants in the mid-1800s, immigrants hoping to start a new Germany. Among the most famous are Fredericksburg and New Braunfels. In some of these towns, German was spoken widely by residents as late as the 1970s. Grünlauf is entirely fictional. I chose the name because I wanted a play on words and as a nod to Benjamin Greenleaf, one of Bradford Academy's former principals.

As I mentioned in *Rescuing the Sheriff's Heart*, Bradford College, or Bradford Academy, existed during this time, although my heroines are completely fictional. One legacy of Bradford is the distinction that the first American female Christian missionaries to serve abroad graduated from the college. Ann Hasseltine Judson and Harriet Atwood Newell both traveled to India with their husbands, only to be turned away by the British East India Company because proselytizing was bad for business. They went on to serve elsewhere. Lucy Goodale Thurston is perhaps one of the most famous of the Bradford missionaries. After answering a newspaper advertisement to become a missionary in the Hawaiian Islands, she married a stranger in order to go. She spent most of the rest of her life on the islands.

While combing newspapers, I found the oddest article in the *San Marcos* [Texas] *Free Press*, January 4, 1879, at the bottom of the page. I am not sure if it was filler by the typesetter or not: "It is estimated that every American boy would eat 350 pounds of candy a year if given the chance." And, like Amanda, I could eat a pound of chocolate a day too.

One of my favorite finds was the popular 1877 song, "Flirting on the Ice," written by Arthur W. French and set to music by W. S. Mullaly. The song is dedicated to a Mrs. Charles Backus, whom I assume was a great pairs ice skater in her day. The music for this piece can be found at: https://levy-sheetmusic.mse.jhu.edu/collection/028/048

Acknowledgments

I've had this story rumbling around in my head for more than a year. Like many of you 2020 and 2021 created new challenges for me and writing lost much of its joy. Huge thanks to my assistant, who has become a dear friend, for pushing me to write. Without Mara this book wouldn't exist.

Grandma, Mildred Kerksiek, was the daughter of German immigrants. She dedicated thousands of hours to doing genealogical research and writing down family stories, none of which appeared in this book. Although I learned her father was a baker and in my mind I picture him making strudel in a bakery in a building which is now a Mexican restaurant. The Kerksiek sisters are lightly based in a memory I have of Grandma laughing with her sister. Also a little shout out to a reader whose last name I stole!

As always, thanks to Tammy, Nanette, Julie, Jori, and Cami who are so willing to help make all my projects better. I would never make it through a day without Maria, Nichole and Cindy whose texts and messages keep me writing.

Big thanks to Michele for the excellent edits. And to my excellent proofreaders who are not to be blamed for any remaining errors. Thank you all!

My family, for sharing their home with the fictional characters who often get fed better than they did. Seriously I haven't cooked in a year. And my husband who encourages me every crazy step of the way.

And to my Father in Heaven for putting these wonderful people, and any I may have forgotten to mention, in my life. I am grateful for every experience and blessing I have been granted.

About the Author

orin Grace was born in Colorado and has been moving around the country ever since, living in eight states and several imaginary worlds. She holds a degree in graphic design which comes in handy with creating book covers. Currently, she lives with her husband, and a dog who is insanely jealous of her laptop.

When not writing, Lorin enjoys creating graphics, visiting historical sites, museums, painting furniture, texting emojies to her children, and reading. Three of her books, her debut novel, *Waking Lucy* (2017), *Mending Fences* (2018), and *Not the Bodyguard's Baby* (2020) have won Recommend Read awards in the League of Utah Writers Published book contest.